An Illusion
Shattered

To everyone who picked up book one after solely hearing
"it's sapphic Great Gatbsy",
I found my people and this story's for you.

And to Zelda ~ you would've loved divorce.

"Those men think I'm purely decorative, and they're fools for not knowing better."

~ Zelda Fitzgerald

A Love Letter to my Readers

Thank you for coming on this journey with me and with Daisy and Jordan.

When I started this, I thought I was alone in my annoyance about being told the Great Gatsby was a straight book. It's very clearly Nick's diary about how much he loves Gatsby, but sure, no homo I guess? I've been saying for a while now that Tom is the token straight person in the Great Gatsby, and that is very much still the hill I will die on.
The book received so much more support than I was expecting, and I love and appreciate every one of you that when you heard "sapphic great gatsby" were immediately on board. I really feel like writing this has helped me find my people. That's why this book is dedicated to you.

Of course, not everyone agrees. Some people say I twisted the story to fit my gay agenda, and I'll be honest I wish I had. It would've been a hell of a lot easier to write if I had, but I painstakingly stuck to canon, dialogue and all. It was important to me to give you Daisy's side of the story in the same way Nick's version of the story was told. To anyone who's saying I made the book gay and there's nothing gay in the original - I challenge you to prove my version of events wrong. Also, I defy you to explain how the elevator scene at the end of Chapter Two is straight.

To everyone else, thank you so much for your patience in waiting for the sequel. I've written more versions and endings than I could count, but this one finally felt right. It took longer than planned for everything to click into place, but once it did, finishing their story was the easiest thing I've ever written. I loved getting to really show how much Daisy has grown through the books. She's flawed of course, but I'm so proud of her growth.

In Beautiful Little Fool, things happen to Daisy. She doesn't have agency over her life or her choices.

As you'll find in An Illusion Shattered, Daisy's had enough of that. An Illusion Shattered shows why Daisy is no one's beautiful little fool and I loved every second of writing her growth.

Lastly, in this house we stan Zelda Fitzgerald. I'm sure some of you are thinking, what about Francis? Well...F. Scott Fitzgerald. If Francis has one hater, it's me.

xoxo

Sarah Zane

Trigger Warnings

Please be aware that this book contains difficult topics that may be triggering to some, and I would rather potentially spoil the plot than potentially spoil someone's day.

This book includes:

Domestic Violence

Depression

Alcohol Abuse - not by the main characters

Mentions of Racism - not beliefs of the main characters

CHAPTER ONE
Daisy

The beautiful baby boy we wanted was born with a horrible affliction; the baby was a girl, and even worse, she looked like she would be a mirror image of me. I couldn't have imagined a worse fate for my child. I was inconsolable.

For the whole first week, all I could do was cry. I hoped my sadness would fade, but each time I looked at my beautiful daughter, I could only think of how she would grow up. She would become a beautiful young woman in the same society I had. The same society that breaks young women, that forces them to ignore the passions of their hearts in favor of security. The society that would tell her she was only valuable as long as she was beautiful, and only if her beauty was valued by men. I grieved for her as I had grieved for myself. How I wished she had been a boy.

I saw her future laid out before her with no care for her wishes like my own had been. I saw myself powerless to protect her from society and from the will of men. I felt helpless. It pained me to know she might experience a fraction of the grief I was now, a fraction of the hopelessness. I hoped she might stay ignorant of the ways of the world for as long as possible. I hoped she might stay the beautiful little fool I once was. I vowed to do all I could to shelter her and protect her from seeing the cruelties of life.

I spent every day and night caring for her and catering to her every need. I tried to get her father to spend time with her, but he wasn't interested. He kept telling me we could afford a nanny to take care of her. He didn't understand that it wasn't about the money; I wanted to care for her myself.

He continued to press me to hire a nanny, saying he didn't feel close to me anymore and was feeling like she was more important to me than he was. I wasn't sure what to say to that. How was I supposed to respond to that level of crazy? Of course, I was giving her more attention. She was our child, and she was a baby. She needed the attention. He didn't need me.

I felt him drifting again, only this time I knew it wasn't my fault. I knew he didn't feel connected to me. I didn't feel connected to him either. I had felt real love now and knew what I had with him wasn't it. I hadn't been able to get Jordan out of my heart. It had been almost a year since the last time I had last seen her, and the separation hadn't gotten any easier. I thought maybe I should write but couldn't bring myself to. We had made it clear things had ended, and I didn't know how to go back to just being her friend.

I wanted to be a good wife, but my heart wasn't in it. I had left my heart back in the States with Jordan. For a while, I had thought I was happy. Tom and I had both been excited about our baby. We had talked endlessly about what we would name our son and of the things we would teach him. We were planning to name him after Tom's father. When she was a girl, we were both disappointed, but he withdrew from both her and me. He couldn't care less about her name, so I named her Pamela. It was the name of what I pictured to be a sweet, hopeful, bright-eyed little girl. A hopeful name was the best I could give to the daughter we hadn't wanted.

While he became disconnected in his disappointment, I channeled my feelings into being overprotective. I took care of her every need.

It didn't bother me anymore that he didn't feel connected to me, but he didn't seem to feel connected to her, either. He would continually bring up that she looked nothing like him and looked just like me. He would say it as if it were a bad thing or as if that had been under my control. She did have my dark hair and pale complexion. Truthfully, she looked quite a bit like me, but she was my daughter, too. Why was it a bad thing that she looked like her mother?

Finally, after another of our arguments about hiring a nanny, the truth came out that he didn't think she was his daughter. I couldn't believe him. I hadn't even dreamed of cheating on him before he became a jealous monster. When Tom stopped being the man I married, I had stopped feeling loyalty to him. I would like to think even still I wouldn't have cheated unless he had first, but I'm not sure if that's true.

In truth, I can't believe I had been blind to my attraction to and love for Jordan for as long as I had. I'm not sure I would have been able to resist her, or that I would have wanted to, even if I had been in a happier marriage. I loved her with my whole being. I loved her then and never stopped. But I wasn't the first one to break our wedding vows. He was. Why was it my integrity and fidelity being questioned and not his?

I was sick of staying silent. I finally brought up the hotel maid. I knew she couldn't have been the only woman, but he couldn't deny her existence. That made him angry, but he didn't bother to deny it. His only response was that he didn't get her pregnant, unlike my boyfriend.

I couldn't believe him. I had broken our wedding vows, too, but I knew without a doubt our daughter was his. I was so shocked at his cruelty that I hadn't known what to say. I had hoped his kindness had been here to stay, but it appeared I was wrong yet again.

When he was home, he showed no interest in Pammy. I loved spending time with her, but I wished he would have made an effort. He was her father, and I knew how important it was for a girl to have a relationship with both of her parents. I didn't want my daughter ever feeling the way I did toward my parents. I told him time and time again that he needed to make more of an effort with her, but he would just scowl at me and tell me to tell that to her real father. It was hopeless, so I gave up and just tried as much as I could to shelter her from his anger.

When he was around, I made sure to be busy with her and to stay out of his way. I was worried she was starting to understand parts of what was going on. She was still an infant, but she seemed to get anxious whenever he was around. I wondered if she was sensing my anxiety. I stopped trying to persuade him to be in her life and poured myself into caring for her. If he didn't want to be the father he should, I would work twice as hard and be twice the parent to her. She deserved nothing less. My beautiful, innocent, sweet Pammy deserved better than I had to offer, but I would try my best to be the best for her.

His absences increased and, when he did come back, he smelled of perfume and alcohol. I could no longer turn a blind eye to the fact that my marriage had fallen apart again. At least I knew it wasn't my fault this time. I had flung myself into our relationship and our family, doing everything I could to make him feel loved, to be enough for him. Maybe he knew deep down that he didn't have my heart, but I gave him all that was left to give.

I still wasn't enough for him. I knew now, without a doubt, that I never would be. I had tried hard for our daughter, but I couldn't single-handedly fix our marriage. My heart wasn't in it and neither was his.

While the betrayal stung, it didn't hurt nearly as bad as it had before. If I was being honest, I had suspected for a while that he might stray again. I understood now he didn't love me. I doubted very much whether he ever had. I know he had cared about me, but he had rushed head first into our marriage, intent on rescuing me. When he heard of my supposed engagement to Marcos, he came running back as quick as he could with a hero complex and a proposal.

When he found out after his proposal had been made that I hadn't needed rescuing, he had had too much chivalry to back out. I hadn't seen that at the time, but I understood now. I should have questioned his intentions more, but his proposal seemed a godsend. Yes, I didn't need saving from Marcos, but I needed saving from the life my parents had planned for me. It was evident he cared for me and I cared for him. I thought that caring could turn into a tender love. I wanted the safety, the security, and the comfort that he could provide. I dismissed my doubts as normal pre-wedding jitters. I refused to see them for what they were; premonitions. I should have listened.

Tom's latest betrayal had been inevitable. My heart was still hurting, but not for him. I was heartbroken that I hadn't fought harder for Jordan. I had told myself I was letting her go for the sake of my child and for my marriage, but I knew now it was an excuse. My child would have been better off as a Buchanan, but it was clear now that Tom wouldn't accept her as his own. I had known the extent of his jealousy, but I had chosen to look past that and believe him that we could start anew and raise our child as a happy family. I had been a fool to believe him.

I had been an even bigger fool to let Jordan go for the sake of my marriage. I had done what I always did in life. The moment things had gotten tough, I had backed away. I didn't feel I deserved her, so I stepped back and let her go. She had let me, but I was the first to back away. Who knows what might have happened if I hadn't. Who knows what my future could have held if I hadn't been a coward.

I hadn't even written to her. I had tried to give her the space she might need to move on. If I couldn't do anything else right by her, at least I could do that. I told myself I shouldn't force my friendship on her, but again I was shielding myself. I was scared she would reject me, so I stayed silent, but she always found her way back into my thoughts.

The sky always seemed to be the same shade as her eyes, cloudy and grey. I hated the sun for shining when I was miserable, but cursed the grey skies for making me miss her even more. In a moment of weakness, I wrote to her. The next day, I thought better of it, but it was too late.

CHAPTER TWO
Jordan

Walking away from Daisy was the hardest thing I had ever had to do in my life, but it was the right thing to do. My own feelings didn't matter. All that mattered was Daisy's happiness and the happiness of the perfect little baby she was going to bring into the world.

What kind of monster would I be if I let myself be selfish, if I had told Daisy how I really felt and begged her to stay with me? I knew I had to be strong for her. If I had loved her less, I might have let myself be selfish, but I couldn't be selfish with her. She deserved so much better than me. She deserved to be happy.

She had always wanted a child and a family. It pained me more than anything that I knew that was something I could never give her. She would have been my whole world, but I could have never given her the child she wanted. I could have never made her happy. She would have always been looking for more, wanting that life I couldn't give her, and I wasn't selfish enough to condemn her to that. My own happiness be damned, I wouldn't do that to her.

I hoped over time, my feelings would ease and that the pain would let up. But no matter what I did, no matter where I went, I couldn't escape her memory. She chased me everywhere.

I tried staying in California. I thought that would be safe for me, since I knew she was leaving, but everything reminded me of her. I moved across town and avoided everywhere I had been with her, but I couldn't escape my own thoughts. I longed to ease my troubles. I would have left town much earlier if it hadn't been for Dorothy.

I had been drowning my sorrows at the bar, ignorant of everything around me. Daisy hadn't said the words yet, but the writing was on the wall. She had chosen to hear Tom out and hadn't given me a second thought. She let me leave, and I knew the next time I saw her, she would end things. I was trying to come to terms with that. It was inevitable; I knew that, but knowing the inevitability of something and coming to terms with it are quite different affairs. I was wallowing in self pity when I heard a voice from the seat next to me that I could have sworn was empty just a moment ago.

"What brings a girl like you to a place like this?" a husky but unmistakably feminine voice asked.

Surprised more so by the voice than the words themselves, I turned around.

The first thing I noticed wasn't the color of her eyes, the curves of her figure, or even the dark tone of her complexion. Though these details were all striking once I noticed them, what I noticed first was the hunger in her eyes.

Watching in surprise, I waited for her to blush at my noticing her stare, waited for her to turn her eyes away or to giggle. Instead, she cocked an eyebrow challengingly, and stared a moment longer before slowly moving her eyes up and down my body. I felt her eyes on me in a way that surprised and confused me. Never had a woman been so aggressive toward me. I was always the aggressor, the chaser. I wasn't sure how I felt about being chased. I was almost positive that was what this woman was doing, but it would be a first, so I couldn't be sure.

I had never felt as challenged as I did by her, but I wasn't one to back down or be intimidated. "Like what you see?"

She took her time roaming the rest of my body before meeting my eye again. "Very much. If you're free for the evening, I could help take your mind off your troubles."

I was too shocked at her forwardness to respond to the first part, so I latched onto the second. "How do you know I'm having troubles?"

She laughed and threw an exaggerated look around the room. I followed suit, really taking in my surroundings for the first time. The place was dark and dingy. The patrons were less than respectable. In short, it was the last place a woman with any concern for herself should be. It was a last resort for people to drink away their problems, not that I was intending to do that. I always limited myself to only one or two drinks, never enough to truly get drunk. After seeing how badly the drink affected others, I could never bring myself to like the stuff, but on nights like tonight I cursed myself for my self-restraint. I wonder what it would have been like to let loose and drown my sorrows, but I knew better.

Her eyes came back to mine and saw my glass was nearing empty. "Can I buy you a drink...?" She paused, looking at me curiously, and I somehow knew the pause was for my name.

"Jordan."

"Dorothy. Can I buy you another, Jordan...?" She drew out my name and I couldn't help but notice how nice it sounded on her lips. I looked at her, really looked, and let myself appreciate the beauty in front of me. Let myself imagine what might happen if I let myself give in to desire and temptation, into the pleasure her eyes were promising. If I were another person, I might have. If I had loved Daisy less, I might have. But I couldn't stomach the thought of touching anyone that wasn't her. Even knowing that I was going to lose her, I couldn't make that choice.

Dorothy was surprised when I turned her down as politely as I could and when I left her at the bar and made my way to my hotel; I didn't look back once. I knew I did the right thing.

But the next night felt different. I had waited all day for Daisy, but our normal meeting time had come and gone and she hadn't shown. I had waited all day for her, pacing back and forth in my room, not daring to leave in case that was when she came, but by the time nightfall came, I knew she wasn't coming and I was starving.

I found my way to the same bar and was two drinks in when I heard the same husky voice from the night before. This time, I didn't resist.

I almost felt guilty and embarrassed when Daisy saw Dorothy leaving the next morning, but after Daisy explained she was leaving not only me, but the country, I couldn't bring myself to regret it. I had half a mind to do it again, but whatever my plans, I never found myself in that same bar again.

Dorothy was beautiful, but she was a poor substitute for Daisy. Anyone would have been so it wasn't worth trying.

CHAPTER THREE
Jordan

The nights were the worst. I kept busy during the day, playing in tournament after tournament. It was the only thing that kept my mind off her. I couldn't let myself stop. If I kept going and pushed my body to its limits, my brain was too tired to relive my past.

Some nights I was lucky and passed out quickly, other nights I tossed and turned, thinking of her. I hoped she was doing well, but I worried about her. I hoped for some sort of news. Any news was better than nothing. The doctors had come a long way with childbirth, but it was still far from easy. It was dangerous, and I was worried about her. I hoped she would write and tell me she was okay, but there had been no word.

I tried to reason with my more irrational thoughts that if something had happened to her, her parents would have told someone. Word would have gotten around. I would have heard now that I had moved back to town. Nothing spreads faster than bad news, so she had to be okay.

I got into the habit of picking up the paper daily just in case her parents had something published about her. I wasn't desperate enough to ask them for news, though. They never liked me and I couldn't imagine that had changed. The feeling was mutual. It was their faults she was in this mess in the first place, that she was shackled to an ass of a husband who didn't deserve her. Even if they were civil to me, I couldn't stand to look at them. I didn't trust my tongue.

When her due date passed with no word, I resolved to go see her parents by the end of the week if I didn't hear anything before then. Thankfully, the paper saved me the trouble.

That morning when I picked up the paper, I read:

Mr. and Mrs. Thomas Buchanan welcomed their darling daughter Pamela J. Buchanan into the world last Friday. Their beautiful baby girl is happy and healthy and so are her parents. The Buchanans are continuing their stay in France, spending time together as a family, but the Fays are sure they will come visit before long. Congratulations to what we are sure is a beautiful family.

The relief that she was okay was immediate. She survived and was healthy. She had a daughter. The thought stopped me in my tracks, immediately transporting me back to the day she found out she was pregnant. The last time I held her. She had hoped for a boy. I knew she must have been devastated, and my heart ached for her.

After Daisy's daughter was born, I hoped she might write, even just to tell me the news herself, but she didn't. I reasoned she was a new mother, and that she was too busy with her daughter and with her husband. She had her own family now. Even if she hadn't outgrown me, she would certainly be too busy to write. It wasn't personal, or at least that was what I kept telling myself.

She wasn't avoiding me, she just hadn't found time to write. As the days went on, the lie became less and less believable. I considered writing to congratulate her, but I dismissed the idea almost immediately. It wasn't my place, and I didn't want to intrude on their family.

I continued to push my body to its limits with my athletic training, but the nights became more and more difficult. I went out more at night. When I didn't, I was up tossing and turning, thinking of her. I wasn't sleeping anyway, so what did it matter if I stayed in bed? There was always some sort of party going on. The city didn't sleep, and neither did I.

I quickly fell into bed with a new girl, but it didn't feel the same. She had beautiful red hair and a cute smattering of freckles dusting her nose and cheeks. She grinned at everything I said and her eyes sparkled when she looked at me, but it didn't matter. She wasn't Daisy. Neither was the next girl... or the next. Try as I might, nothing could replace her or erase her from my mind. The dalliances were nice distractions until, inevitably, I would think of her. There would be something about the way the girl smiled, or laughed, or kissed that would make me think of Daisy. Once the comparison crossed my mind, I knew my night would be ruined. The comparison was never favorable. No one could ever measure up to Daisy.

The only thing any of them had over Daisy was that they were here. They weren't off gallivanting around France with their two-timing husband and new daughter. They weren't ignoring me and pretending I didn't exist. They didn't forget about me the second I left. I knew that wasn't fair for me to think, but it was hard to not feel bitter about it.

I had held back with Daisy for so long because I was worried about ruining our friendship. I hadn't wanted to lose her, and even though she had wanted me too, it hadn't mattered in the end; I had still lost her.

It was hard not to be bitter about my worst fear coming true. We weren't lovers anymore; I understood that, but it seemed now we weren't even friends and that broke the rest of my already shattered heart.

On one of my seldom days off, I grabbed the post and almost dropped the envelope when I saw a letter addressed to me from France.

I dropped everything I was holding onto the counter and ripped the envelope open.

My Dearest Jordan,

It is with a heavy heart full of regret that I pen this. I should have written to you far sooner, but I convinced myself I would be bothering you. I held off for so long, but my dear, you must allow me to indulge my selfishness this once.

I miss you terribly. A part of me hopes you have moved on and are happy without me, but a bigger, more selfish part of me hopes you're happy to hear from me. I was stupid, the worst kind of stupid, letting you get away. I know what I felt for you, what I still feel for you, is stronger than anything I could ever hope to feel for anyone else. I would have run away with you, you know. Before little Pammy, I would have done anything to stay with you.

Pammy's my daughter. She's absolutely beautiful, and certainly the most perfect baby in all the world. I don't know how I got so lucky. I worry about her of course, but I hope the world is kinder to her than it was to me. Her full name is Pamela Jordan Buchanan. If she grows into even half the woman you are, I would consider myself lucky. I hoped if I gave her something of yours that she might get some of your bravery that I lacked.

I'm borrowing a little of your courage now to say this. Little Pammy came along and changed everything, but she didn't change my heart. My heart never left you.

I know I have no right to be asking this, but is there any chance I still hold your heart as you do mine? My feelings haven't changed. If yours are still the same, consider writing me back with haste. I will be harassing the postmaster daily, so take pity on him and write swiftly.

If you no longer feel the same, know that I understand. I deserve and require no explanation, but know that I miss you in more ways than one. I know no one here in France and miss your friendship more than I can express. We will be returning at some point, and I hope that when we do, no matter how you feel, that you'll take the time to meet my darling Pammy. She's beautiful, healthy, and as happy as I can make her.

Most days, I'm able to shield her from her father's scorn, but he doesn't look kindly on her and what little caring I had for him died with seeing how little he cares for her. I know how important it is for a young girl to have strong role models around and since her father clearly isn't stepping up, I hope you'll spend time with her so she might learn from her dear Auntie Jordan what it looks like to be strong and still kind. The Fay girls could both really use you back in our lives.

I love you with all that's left of my heart and miss you with every fiber of my being.

With all my love,

Daisy

CHAPTER FIVE
Daisy

All winter, I waited anxiously for a response. I knew it was too much to hope for after the way I had left things, but still I hoped to hear from her. As winter passed into spring, I gave up hope. I had tried to make peace with Jordan being forever lost to me, but lately it had been harder to fight off the tears at night after putting Pammy to sleep. When I was trying to drift off to sleep, I couldn't help my thoughts from drifting to her. I wondered what she might be doing and who she might be doing it with. My answer came one day that spring.

I was getting Pammy ready for the day when I heard a noise. It was a loud knock. I thought that was odd. We seldom had visitors, or rather, I seldom had visitors and Tom was God only knows where. My heart dropped at what sounded like two more hesitant knocks. It couldn't be, but I would know that knock anywhere.

I ran over and flung open the door and almost couldn't believe my eyes; it was her. I couldn't believe she came. Never in my wildest dreams had I imagined she would actually come visit, especially after our painful separation. But here she was on my doorstep, as if nothing had changed.

She was holding my letter and a suitcase. I threw my arms around her with such vigor she had to drop her suitcase to catch me and stop us from toppling over. She laughed and said it was good to see me, too. I was crying again. I cried a lot these days, but I was glad to have a happier reason. I ushered her inside and immediately brought her over to meet my pride and joy, my dear Pammy.

Jordan bent down to be closer to Pammy and took her little hand in her own. "Wow. You're going to have your hands full, my dear."

"I'm not sure what you mean?"

"Well, it seems she has your looks and God knows she'll probably have your pension for finding trouble."

We both laughed at that. Pammy was fascinated by Jordan, looking at her with wide eyes. Jordan seemed surprised by Pammy, too. "It really is uncanny how much she looks like you. She's growing to be quite the beautiful little girl. How old is she now?"

"Next week will be a year."

"Wow. I can't believe it's been that long since I've seen you."

"Longer. But you're just in time for her birthday."

"Of course, I should hope our little Pammy here has heard all about Aunt Jordan and knew enough to know that even with an ocean between us, I wouldn't dream of missing her birthday."

Pammy couldn't take her eyes off her 'Aunt Jordan'. It was like I wasn't in the room. I had never seen her like that before. Usually I was the only one who mattered to Pammy and when I did leave her with anyone else, she would be upset until I took her back. I indicated Pammy's adoring look and said, "You've already made quite the impression."

She grinned, her eyes full of mischief. "I can't say I'm surprised." I raised an eyebrow at her in question. "It seems I have quite an effect on the Fay girls."

A blush spread across my cheeks. I didn't know what to say, so I playfully said, "And here I thought you might have come for me?" She was clearly in a teasing mood, but the suspense was too much for me. I needed to know what she meant in coming.

My hopes were increasing by the second, and I needed to shut them down quickly if I had misread her intentions. There was a chance she had come as my best friend to meet my daughter, or because I was upset and grieving the failure that was my marriage. I hoped against hope that there was some small chance she hadn't lost the feelings she had, though. I hoped she might have come here for me to see if we could rekindle what we had started.

I hadn't expected her to come all the way across the ocean to see me, especially when she had never left the country before, but I really shouldn't have been surprised. I should have known the moment I so much as expressed to Jordan that I needed her; she would be here the moment she could.

She dropped her playful tone and looked at me. "I can't believe you still don't understand the effect you have on me. Of course I came for you. I haven't stopped thinking about you since the moment you had left. I drove myself mad with worry. I went back and forth between hoping to hear from you and hoping not to. I wanted you to be happy, I really did, but it would have been hard to hear about. I hoped for your sake and for hers," she looked at Pammy lovingly, "that you and Tom might work things out. I didn't want to come between your family, but don't think for a minute I didn't want you. Don't think for a minute that I didn't get on the first ship I could find to France. The moment I read your letter, I came running. All you had to do was ask. I would have swam here for you."

I was speechless, but thankfully she didn't wait for a response before pulling me in for a kiss. I had dreamt of her lips and her kisses often enough, but even the best dreams had paled in comparison to how amazing it felt to be in her arms again, to have her lips on mine. I got lost in the moment, never wanting it to end.

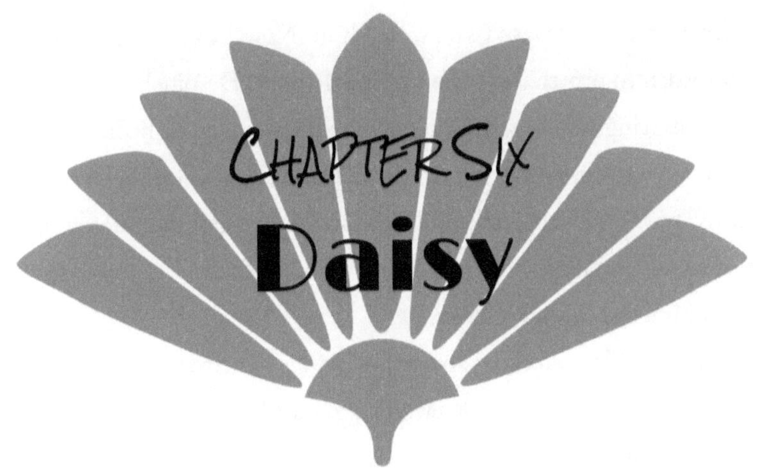

CHAPTER SIX
Daisy

The next couple of weeks passed faster than I imagined possible. Jordan, Pammy, and I did everything together. Seeing the way Pammy looked at Jordan strengthened my own feelings for her. If Tom was surprised or displeased to see Jordan, he didn't let on. He told us it was nice for me to have another woman to spend my time with. I knew without him saying it, he meant he was glad I was distracted from his affairs. He had stopped being at all discreet, but I had stopped caring. I was with the love of my life and my daughter loved her too. Nothing could sour that for me, except Jordan's rapidly approaching departure.

I couldn't bear the thought of being separated from her by an entire ocean again. Tom and I had talked of moving back after a year or two, but that might mean another year. I wanted to ask what the plan was, but he had long since stopped including me in his plans and decisions. I worried if I asked to leave that he might become suspicious.

Jordan and I hadn't quite been sneaking around or hiding our affection, but he was never around. When he was, I doubted whether he understood there was more than our already strong friendship. I felt guilty, but knew it wasn't safe to tell him. Now I had not only myself and Jordan to protect, but also my dear Pammy. Despite her being very much his daughter, he still didn't believe she was, and he hadn't formed any sort of attachment to her. In truth, I think he resented both me and her for how much she looked like me and how much she adored me. I tried to tell him if he spent more time with her, she would feel the same about him, but he didn't listen.

I tried to hide my feelings about how things were from Jordan, but she was too observant. She was determined to start saving money to help me, and now Pammy, leave Tom.

I hoped it would be easy to get divorced since Tom didn't want to be married either, but I was still worried. My biggest fear was that he would try to take Pammy from me, whether because he actually wanted his daughter or out of spite. I held on to the fact that he continually claimed she wasn't his daughter. If he truly believed that, he wouldn't bother to fight me for her. Jordan hoped I was right, but explained that unless her aunt agreed to lend her money, it would take a few years for her to save enough for the divorce and to be able to support herself, me, and Pammy. I couldn't express how grateful I was or how blessed I felt that she cared as deeply for my daughter as I did, and that she cared as deeply for me as I did for her.

However, a few years of continued marriage was less than ideal. Even worse, our plan couldn't afford for her to come back to France to visit. This would be the last time I saw her until we moved back to the States.

She said the moment we moved back, things would be different. She said it might take a little longer for her to save the money, but that she would follow me wherever I moved. While I wanted the divorce as soon as possible, I couldn't imagine living without her for very long.

She was usually so practical that I was surprised she was open to spending some of her savings to move wherever Tom decided to settle, though. It was a true testament to how much she cared about me that the idea of not following me was also abhorrent to her. We were lucky that she relied on sport for her income. She could golf from pretty much anywhere.

Our only problem was not knowing when Tom would want to move. I worried he might have grown attached to whomever he was seeing and it might prolong our stay. When I told Jordan about my concerns, she told me she would take care of it. I asked what she meant, but she didn't know herself yet, just that she would find a way.

I didn't find out what she meant until years later, when she sheepishly admitted that later that same afternoon, she had followed Tom to his mistress's home. After Tom left, she had knocked and introduced herself as Tom's wife. Jordan says the woman nearly fainted of fright. Apparently, she was married, too. Her husband was returning home shortly, and she begged Jordan to leave. Jordan agreed if she agreed to stop seeing Tom. Jordan had said she watched the woman's eyes widen, and it seemed she would protest, but then her gaze fell on a man approaching the house and she hastily agreed. It turns out the man was her husband returning from work. Jordan told me she introduced herself as one of the women from the town church. I had burst out laughing at how confused they must have been. Jordan being a representative of the church was about as believable as me being the pro golfer.

However, I didn't find any of this out until much later so at the time I thanked God for what I considered to be a miracle of divine intervention when the very next day Tom told me we were leaving as soon as it could be arranged. He said his parents had been pestering him to return and that he had decided to appease them, if only to stop their begging. I kept my responses neutral, but inside I was celebrating. I know now there was little to no truth in his reason for wanting to leave. The real reason, that his mistress had abandoned their affair, wasn't known to me. At the time, I was grateful for his parents' invention and overjoyed to be heading back to the States.

Jordan wasn't able to delay her own return any longer than she already had, but only a few weeks after she left, Tom and I set out for Chicago.

The moment the plans were set, I sent word to Jordan. I hesitated whether to tell her to arrange to move to Chicago, though. I knew Tom hadn't wanted to settle down in Chicago before, but I didn't know if anything had changed. I told her I wasn't sure what his plans were, so she shouldn't make any arrangements until we were more settled. I didn't want to pressure her, so I didn't say anything about a visit, but I secretly hoped she might visit shortly after our return.

Upon our arrival to Chicago, we were whisked away to a reception at the McCormicks. It was the last thing I wanted. We had been travelling tirelessly, and all I wanted was some sleep, but I wasn't in a position to be seen as ungracious toward his parents. Who knows what they might have heard about me from Tom? The last thing I wanted was to give them more reasons to think poorly of me or of my daughter.

When we arrived and I saw their home for the first time, my jaw dropped. I had never seen so large or extravagant a home. It made my parents' home look like a humble shack in comparison. I wondered what they did with as much space as they had. It turns out just about every room was occupied with guests waiting to celebrate our arrival. We were given the curtesy of the second best room in the house, second only to the room permanently occupied by his parents. We rushed to make ourselves presentable as quickly as possible.

They had laid out a dress for me and for Pammy. I was touched that they had thought of it. Pammy wasn't fond of hers, though, and I hesitated about making her wear it. I hated to see her upset and wanted to let her change, but I knew we couldn't afford to insult his family, so I soothed her as much as I could but kept the dress on her. The lace was a little scratchy, but I hoped she would get used to the feel after a few minutes.

Tom snapped at me to hurry, which was beyond frustrating. He hadn't lifted a finger to help me get our daughter ready, and now he had the audacity to tell me to hurry. I was indignant, but it wasn't worth the fight. We were ready anyway. I told him as much. He turned and stalked out of the room, not bothering to make sure we were behind him. I scooped Pammy up in my arms and quickly rushed after him.

When we arrived at what appeared to be the entrance to the ballroom, he snapped at me to put her down. When I hesitated, he insisted saying, "If she were a true McCormick, she would walk into the ballroom."

I didn't know how to respond to that. I had thought the comments about her parentage would sting less with time, but the hurt hadn't changed. I wasn't hurting for myself, but for Pammy. I hoped she was still too young to understand what was being said, but I didn't know how much longer I could shelter her from him. My heart broke for my beautiful little girl whose father had no interest in getting to know her.

It was clear he knew little to nothing about babies or about her. She was still a baby. Yes, she could technically walk, but not confidently. She had practically just started walking. There was no real need to make her walk by herself. He didn't need to show her off in that manner, and no one would be impressed enough to make the feat worth attempting.

"I really don't think that's a good idea. She hasn't been walking quite long enough on her own."

He glared at me with an intensity that chilled my bones. "And whose fault is that? It wasn't a request. She'll walk in, or I'll tell everyone the truth. She's no daughter of mine."

Feeling I had no other option, I relented and put her gently on the ground. She made a face, and I knew tears might closely follow. I bent down to be level with her.

"Baby, Mama knows what a big girl you are. You look so pretty in your dress!" She started to smile again. I saw Tom continue to glare at me. I barely stopped my eyes from rolling. If he wanted the facade of the perfect family and didn't want his daughter screaming and crying, he would have to wait a minute. "Why don't we play a fun game, baby, okay? I'm going to hold your hand and let's see how far you can walk, okay baby?" We would try it his way, but the second she faltered I would pick her back up, consequences be damned. I looked at Tom. I hoped he was satisfied. I held her little hand, and he reached for my other. He had a tight grip that told me he still wasn't pleased, but I had done what I could. It was a miracle she wasn't already crying.

When the doors opened and I saw the ballroom with all those people, I was whisked back to my debut three years ago. The night Tom and I met. I could remember how excited and anxious I was, how hopeful. I could almost laugh at my young self's dreams of being swept off my feet by a handsome stranger. I had been full of hope that that night would be the start of my happily ever after. If I could have gone back, I would have told young Daisy to run. I would have told her to stop being so blind and foolish and notice the perfect person had been right in front of her that whole time. I would have told her to not agree to marry just any handsome boy who asks. I was pulled back to the present when I felt a little hand squeeze my own.

Pammy. My beautiful, perfect daughter. I would do anything for that little girl. I sighed. I knew in my heart even if I could have changed the past, I wouldn't have. I wouldn't have given her up for anything.

I had grown so much since that night three years ago. I was no longer as naïve about the world. I was older and wiser and for once I could say definitely that I knew what I wanted. I wanted Jordan.

Jordan, my love, my other half. I had missed her terribly since the moment she left France. I hoped I would see her again soon. My mind again flashed back to my debut and how beautiful she had looked that night. I had been such a fool to not see what was right in front of me.

Tom pulled me forward, and I stepped carefully, helping Pammy to move forward. I was ecstatically proud that she was walking as well as she was. She hadn't faltered yet. I took my eye off her for a moment and looked to the crowd. I wasn't sure who I was looking for, but I had the feeling I was looking for someone. When I saw her, my jaw dropped.

Jordan.

She was full of surprises. I couldn't believe she was here. The moment we met the crowd, she moved forward and whisked Pammy up into her arms. She spun her around while Pammy giggled, delighted. After a few moments, she held Pammy tighter and extended her arm to me. I wrapped my arms around her and my daughter. I was home.

Jordan arranged to stay with us in Chicago for a couple weeks. She and I hoped to find out what Tom's plan was in order to make arrangements, but it seemed he wasn't sure either. But from what I saw of his interactions with his family, he wasn't happy to be here.

To my dismay and relief, his family didn't want much to do with me or Pammy. They had gushed over meeting her that first night and given her gifts, but the following day, they had left us to ourselves. I had overheard a few comments from his family about the inappropriateness of my fawning over my child. They said I would spoil her without a good nanny. They said maybe my family hadn't raised me as well as they had assumed. I ignored the comments and was content to keep to myself. I was happy to not spend time with them. That meant more time to be spent with Pammy and Jordan. I knew it couldn't last, but I was grateful for our little piece of paradise.

When Jordan left a week later, I had known things would get worse in her absence. I thought I was prepared, but I was sorely mistaken. I busied myself with Pammy, trying to keep my mind off missing Jordan. Pammy was the only thing that could take my mind off missing her.

Pammy missed her, too, though. She hadn't learned Jordan's name yet but, much to mine and Jordan's amusement, had taken to calling her 'Jo'. The next day, she asked for Jo quite a few times. I tried to explain to her we would see Jo again, but she didn't understand. She was too young.

She kept looking at the door, waiting for 'Jo' to walk through. I couldn't help the bit of hope I felt in my heart that she might be right, but I knew better. I knew Jordan had left. The next day, Pammy seemed to understand 'Jo' wasn't here. She was inconsolable. She cried the entire day. The only words she uttered that day were "Mama" and "Jo". I struggled to hold in my own emotions and console her.

Thankfully, the following day passed without as many tears. I felt lucky for her short attention span. I doubted I could have handled many more days of her crying for 'Jo' without breaking down myself. I was glad I at least had Pammy to distract me.

I should have known it was too good to be true. A couple of days later, Pammy and I were approached by Tom and an older woman I didn't recognize. I knew two things immediately from the look on his face. The first was that I wasn't going to like what he had to say, and the second was that it wasn't up for debate. I steeled myself for the worst. I imagined he had found out about Jordan. I imagined we were moving back to France. I imagined we were going to live with his family indefinitely. I worried until he opened his mouth, but I couldn't have possibly imagined what he was going to say. He introduced the older woman as Pam's new nanny.

I was livid. I didn't ask for much and didn't question his choices. I let him do whatever he wanted with whoever without complaint, and he couldn't grant me this? He clearly knew how I felt about hiring help for our daughter. He knew without a doubt that I wanted to be the one to care for her. No one else would pay the same attention to her that I did. I didn't want her to bond with some strange woman. I didn't want some stranger seeing all her firsts. I wanted to be there for everything.

I didn't want to miss a minute of her growing up. I greeted her, but stammered over my words. With Pammy in my arms, I didn't want to make a scene. I didn't want to scare her.

The look on Tom's face told me this wasn't up for debate, but I couldn't help myself. I couldn't stay silent. This was too important. I started to say something, but he grabbed my arm tightly. I grimaced at the pain he was causing, but didn't pull back. I didn't want Pammy to notice anything was wrong.

She was still smiling, but when he took her from my arms, her smile wavered. When he handed her to the nanny without so much as a word to her, she started crying in earnest. I pulled away from Tom as much as I could to pat her head soothingly. I was just barely able to reach her and his grip had tightened, but I ignored the pain as much as I could. It was too important to me to comfort her, even though I felt the same panic she did, maybe worse.

"Mama has to talk with your father right now, baby, but you're going to go with this nice lady..." I shot the woman a warning look. She better be the nicest lady possible, or I would be sure she was dismissed immediately. I planned to dismiss her immediately regardless, but she still had better be as kind as possible to my daughter. "She's going to take care of you for a bit, but Mama will be back soon. I promise." Her tears kept flowing. "Mama will be back, okay, baby?"

She looked at me, considering, "Like Jo?"

I had to laugh at that. I felt his grip tighten more than I thought was possible. I winced before telling Pammy, "You're so smart, baby! Yes, like Jo, but much, much sooner."

She smiled at that and let the nanny take her away. The second they were out of sight, he pulled me by my arm around a corner and threw open a door. I saw it was a sitting room before he roughly pushed me inside. He shut the door and turned on me, his eyes blazing.

"How dare you! I have let you conduct yourself in whatever manner you choose for too long! I must have been too lenient, too kind. How dare you question me!"

Too lenient? I was speechless. Did he really think he had been showing me kindness? I was mad, but had never seen him this angry. I could sense that this might be dangerous. A gentle approach was probably best. I took a deep breath and tried to look as contrite and confused as possible. "Darling, I don't-"

WHAM!

The first thing I registered was shock. I hadn't even seen him move, but he had struck me across the face with enough force that the sound bounced off the walls back at me. I couldn't believe him. So much for the gentle approach. The contrite expression had been wiped off my face by the force of his hand, replaced with shock. He had never laid a hand on me before and I hadn't thought he would ever stoop so low.

"Don't darling me. I'm not your darling any more than that brat of a child you call Pammy is my daughter." I saw his mood darken when he added, "Whoever Jo is, he's damn lucky to not be married to you and raising his brat of a daughter." I couldn't believe he thought Jo was her father. It was incredibly ironic. Had I not been so angry, I might have been amused. I would have corrected him, but didn't trust myself to speak. "Why I subject myself to it, I don't know. You were difficult enough to deal with, but now that your daughter is getting older, she's becoming more and more like you every day. Crying at the littlest of things, just like her mother."

He smirked as the shock on my face was replaced with hurt. He knew I couldn't care less about his insults toward me, but he knew that would hurt me. Even with my face still stinging from his hand, I hadn't thought he would stoop low enough to insult our daughter.

I felt the tears threatening to come, but held them back. I wouldn't give him that satisfaction. I opened my mouth again to tell him I didn't want a nanny, but he cut me off. "And not one more word about the nanny. I've let you do whatever you wanted for far too long, parading around with our daughter on your hip. Making a show of us and our family. 'The Buchanan's', they say, 'they must not have as much money as we thought if they can't even afford a nanny.' I'm done letting you make a fool of me! I won't stand for it any longer."

He must have seen from the look on my face, that I still had hope, because he added, "If I hear one more word about getting rid of the nanny, I will see to it that Pammy stays here with her grandparents to get the proper attention and raising she needs."

I couldn't have heard that right. He must have meant for us all to stay with his parents. He wouldn't think I would let go of my daughter. He grinned at the look on my face and added, "After all, if her mother keeps protesting the nanny, no one would blame her husband for saying she must be unwell. Pammy would need somewhere to be cared for while her mother got the mental help she needed."

I went cold with fear. The thinly veiled threat had found its mark. I had heard enough of the "mental health institutions" to know that no one that went in ever came back out. No one ever got better. And I knew enough of my husband's influence to know that it wouldn't matter that I was competent. At his word, they would lock me in an asylum and throw away the key.

The man I agreed to marry would never have threatened his wife or insulted his own daughter. That was the moment I stopped mourning for him. I stopped feeling guilty for cheating on him. I stopped caring. Tom was gone and all that remained now was the monster who masqueraded himself as my husband.

Daisy

Against my wishes, the nanny stayed, but I resolved to not let it interfere with me spending my time how I liked; with my daughter. I thought I could still spend time with her and would get used to the nanny. I thought it might even be helpful to have an extra set of hands to help with Pammy. She was quite energetic and was a lot more mobile now. It wouldn't be unwelcome to have someone to help me care for her and keep her out of trouble. I had wanted that someone to be her father, but I resigned myself to having to be okay with the addition of the nanny to the time I spent with Pammy. I should have known it wouldn't be that simple.

The nanny and I got along well enough until Tom took notice. He had started paying more attention to me while we were under his family's roof. Apparently, his sole mission lately was to ensure my misery. I had been trying to make the best of the situation, but Tom wouldn't be satisfied with anything less than my misery.

A few times, I saw him speaking to the nanny in hushed tones. After, I quickly noticed the nanny looking at me differently. She started inserting herself between me and Pammy. She became more assertive toward me and even tried to dismiss me from Pammy's presence a few times. I would have fired her on the spot if I hadn't feared what Tom might do.

I wondered more than once if I should write to Jordan. I knew she would want to know what had been happening, but I couldn't bring myself to tell her. I didn't think his violence was likely to happen again, and I didn't want to worry her. I was worried about his threats but knew if I just submitted and did whatever it was he wanted, that he wouldn't go through with them. I didn't want her to have to share my fears. I knew now that I had to be more careful. I wouldn't let him hurt me again.

I knew Jordan would have told me, Tom be damned, that I should fire the nanny, anyway. She would have told me to stand up for myself and not cow to his demands, but I couldn't risk angering him. I was too scared he might make good on his threat, so I just watched day after day as Tom poisoned the nanny against me. I suspected he told her I was unwell since some of her actions seemed out of concern for me, but I hated it regardless.

The combination of Jordan's absence and my forced distance from Pammy pulled me back into depression. I didn't know how I would survive without Jordan. Pammy was the only thing that could make me happy and take my mind off Jordan. Now I wasn't even allowed that. Despite my struggles to hold back my tears, I cried myself to sleep most nights.

I spent my nights alone on the couch of our sitting room. I was afraid to share a bed with Tom now that Pammy wasn't sleeping with us. She used to sleep in between us, but now she was confined to the nursery with her nanny. I had tried in vain the first few nights to sleep with my daughter, but wasn't admitted into the nursery. I had tried to keep her with me at night, but inevitably the nanny would force me to release her charge for the night. I couldn't bear being without Pammy, but I feared what Tom might do if I pressed too hard. I fed myself scraps of hope that he might soon change his mind. Even I knew how unlikely that was.

His mother sought my company more often now. I had tried as well as I could to put on a brave face and pretend to be happy. I hadn't much else to do, so I agreed to spend time with her. She and I were getting along well until she told me how happy she was that we had finally taken her suggestion and hired a nanny. She told me how improper it was that I hadn't hired one before. After that, I kept to myself. The amount I was allowed to see my daughter decreased by the day. The nanny and Tom conspired to keep her from me, and I fell even deeper into depression. The only thing that kept me going was the hope that I would see Jordan again soon, but it was a minor consolation, since I had no way of knowing how soon.

I still wasn't sure what Tom's plan was. I prayed he might want to leave soon since I knew he must be growing tired of staying with his family. Heaven knows I was. But I didn't know what he planned for us next. I worried about what the future might hold, holding close to Jordan's promise that whatever the future held that she would be there with me.

The longer we stayed in Chicago, the worse Tom's mood became. I had hoped he would leave me alone when he saw I wasn't fighting the nanny anymore, but even that didn't satisfy him. He insisted I go out with him. Apparently, his friends had been asking about his charming wife and it seemed he still cared about keeping up appearances. It was the last thing I wanted to do, but I understood it wasn't a request. I went along and tried to stay out of his way as much as possible.

His friends were hardly charming. Like Tom, they all drank way too much. I was the only one who didn't indulge. I could tell that annoyed Tom to no end, but he could bully me into a number of things, but not into drinking. I hadn't touched alcohol since before the wedding and didn't plan to. His friends were all loud and rambunctious, although I suspected they would have been like that without drinking, too. I couldn't think of a worse way to spend my time, but they liked me enough that Tom kept insisting I come.

When I was lucky, he let me stay home. I was grateful for those nights, until one of his drunk friends let slip that he was only doing that so he could bring his latest mistress around his friends. As if it wasn't humiliating enough to be paraded around as his trophy wife in front of his friends, now it was even more well known how much of a sham our marriage was. I was humiliated and made it my personal mission to make him feel a fraction of the humiliation I did.

When I was required to go out with his friends again, I was the picture of class. I was as charming as could be and his friends sung my praises. They told him how lucky he was to have me. When they drank more, they told me I was far superior to the classless women he paraded around them and they didn't know why he bothered with anyone else when he had me. Of course, they couldn't have known he didn't have me. I saw how frustrated that made him. That brought me some joy. I don't know what he expected. He told me to make a good impression with his friends, so I did. Now he was angry they were charmed? Now he thought I was going too far to impress his friends? Now he was annoyed they liked me more than his mistress? I hoped he felt a fraction of the humiliation I did.

After a couple nights, I realized I only had to be charming until after the first couple of drinks they had. After that, I could stop trying and anything I said or did was still charming. It was some relief to not have to try as hard, but it was a small relief. I didn't know how much more I could take. I needed some change.

Unfortunately, the change that came wasn't a positive one. A few days later, Tom let me know that a couple of his friends were visiting for the weekend and that he expected me to make a good impression. It went without saying that it wasn't optional. I wondered what was so special about these friends, but figured it wouldn't be much more difficult than spending time with the friends I had been.

I should have known it wouldn't be that easy. That night I got dolled up like usual. He was more impatient than usual, but his cruel smile worried me. Lately, he was scowling in my presence. I couldn't imagine what he was smiling about, but I knew I wouldn't like it.

When we met up with his friends like usual, there was only one new addition. Tom left me immediately to go get a drink, so I introduced myself to the newcomer. His name was Nick. He had gone to Yale with Tom. He seemed pleasant enough and was far less drunk than the rest of Tom's friends, so we fell into conversation. I asked about his family and was surprised to find out there was a familial connection between us. He was a cousin of mine, well, a second cousin once removed, but he knew my family. It turns out he, too, was a bit of an outcast with his part of the family, something we had in common.

I was actually enjoying myself for once when I heard a familiar voice call out, "Well, if it isn't the floozy of Louisville, or do you just go by Mrs. Buchanan now?"

I would know that voice anywhere. What was James doing here?

I tried to school my expression to neutrality. I didn't want to give Tom or James the satisfaction of knowing James had rattled me, but this was the last thing I had expected. I hadn't thought about James in ages, but Tom knew exactly how I felt about him. I couldn't believe he had the audacity to force me around him. That explained Tom's mood.

I slowly turned around, praying I could keep my cool. When I saw how satisfied James was with himself, my emotions threatened to spill over, but I wouldn't give him the satisfaction of seeing me shaken. I met his eye and adopted a look of confusion. "Mrs. Buchanan will do. I don't believe I've had the pleasure?"

His smirk fell for a moment and he joined myself and Nick. He turned to Nick and said, "She's just embarrassed she still thinks of me."

How dare he! I narrowed my eyes before noticing Nick watching us curiously. "Do you know each other?"

At the same time as James said, "Yes," I said, "I don't believe so."

To Nick, James said, "I dated her best friend. Poor Daisy here has never gotten over the slight of me not choosing her." He moved closer to me with a devilish smile and reached forward and caressed my cheek with his hand. I fought the urge to flinch away. "Don't worry, love, if you play your cards right, maybe you could have a second chance." He traced my bottom lip with his thumb, saying, "I'm sure Tom wouldn't mind sharing you. With how often he finds other ways to entertain himself, I'm sure he'd be thrilled to get you off his hands."

I slapped his hand from my face. "How dare you! You have no right to put your hands on me!"

His eyes lit up as he laughed in earnest. "Oh, I see how it is. I must not be rich enough for your taste."

I rolled my eyes at him. "More like not civilized enough."

I had forgotten Nick was there until I heard him laugh. I turned to him quickly. "I'm so sorry. That was incredibly rude of us." I glared in James's direction. "Nick, this is-"

James interrupted me before I could finish. "No need to worry, my dear, he's a Yale boy too, no introduction needed."

I looked back at Nick, who shrugged. "You get used to him."

James laughed. "Don't praise me too highly. No need to fan my ego."

They both laughed. So much for the pleasant night I was having.

I tried to excuse myself, but James grabbed my arm. I couldn't help the shiver that ran up my spine, or the spike of fear I felt at being manhandled. In my momentary panic, I looked for Tom. When I found him, I saw a smirk on his face. I couldn't believe it. Here was James with his hands on me, and my husband was doing nothing. He didn't bat an eye at his friend's behavior. He didn't move an inch to protect his wife. The man I married had once fought to defend my honor. Even after he had changed, he was still a jealous man. I couldn't believe he was allowing this! Apparently, this monster who called himself my husband was only jealous when he thought I liked the attention. I would have pushed James away, but Tom noticed my intent and shot me a warning look. I was on dangerous ground.

I took a calming breath and turned to James. He pulled me closer to him. "I'm not sure what kind of ideas you have about me, but I can assure you my husband wouldn't like another man's hands all over his wife."

He pulled me even closer and whispered in my ear, "We both know that hasn't stopped you before." I couldn't believe him. Seeing the shocked look on my face, he smiled. "You can drop the innocent act. Now that Jordan's out of the way, you don't have to keep resisting."

I just barely managed to keep my voice low. "How dare you? I'll never understand how Jordan put up with you for so long. She was always too good for you."

His smile faltered. I had hit a nerve. A moment later, the smile was back, and I thought I might have imagined the lapse. "She certainly never complained when she was sharing my bed."

I'm sure the shock showed on my face. I knew he and Jordan had been serious, but I hadn't imagined she might have slept with him. There was no way. "You can't be serious. She would have told me."

His smile widened at my reaction. There was no way he understood just how much his words affected me. He couldn't have suspected. "I'm sure there's a lot she never told you, but I can assure you with me she was always quite open, in more than one way. I doubt she ever told you, but we even talked about bringing you into our bed, but she said you were too prude for that."

"What?" was all I could ask through my shock.

He laughed. "It started as a joke. I told her since you never left her side, we might as well make good use of you. You can imagine my surprise when she actually entertained the idea." He laughed again. "I knew you were close, but never imagined you might be that close."

I couldn't believe it. I knew Jordan had feelings for me for a while before she told me, but I never imagined she had known that long ago. My mind was reeling. She had feelings for me when she was with James.

Things started to click into place. No wonder she was so quick to break up with him for how he was treating me. No wonder she had wanted to murder Marcos. I hadn't questioned her reactions because I knew how much she cared about me. I couldn't help but think about everything I unwittingly put her through. She had told me herself that she had to watch me date man after man and overlook her day after day. I couldn't imagine how she dealt with that. Especially after my jealousy when I saw her with another woman at her hotel in Santa Barbara. Thinking back, I could even admit I had been jealous of her with James. I didn't understand it then and thought I was just jealous of losing her time. Now it was clear as day that I was jealous of him being with her. The sight of him touching her was revolting, and I couldn't stand to see it. I still didn't understand what she ever saw in him.

I couldn't believe she had known that long and had never said any-thing, that she watched me fall for Tom and stayed silent. She even talked me through my doubts about the wedding, and stood up with me at the wedding. I knew she was selfless and strong, but I never knew just how strong she was. I doubted I would've been strong enough to have been there for her in that way if our situations had been reversed.

I was brought back to reality by James's laugh. "So she never men-tioned that to you. Well, make sure to give her my regards when you talk to her." There was an amused glint in his eye. "I'm sure that will be quite the conversation. But, like I was saying, she knew you were too much of a prude. I can't say I was surprised. I knew you were wild about me and would've jumped in my bed in a heartbeat, but Jordan didn't want to share. There was more than enough of me to go around. I'm sure I would have been more than enough to satisfy you both." He grinned, looking me up and down. "But her loss could be your gain."

I couldn't believe him! I pulled my arm away from him. This time, he let me go. "You're disgusting. I'm a happily married woman!"

He smirked. "That's not what I heard."

I rolled my eyes and went to storm off, but noticed Nick out of the corner of my eye. I couldn't believe I had forgotten we had an audience. I turned to him. He had been looking down at his drink, clearly embarrassed. He had enough class to act like he hadn't heard, but I had the good sense to be embarrassed, even if James didn't. I turned my back to James and took up conversation with Nick, asking about his plans and where he was living. He looked grateful for the change of conversation, and I did my best to ignore James for the rest of the evening.

I had half a mind to give Tom a piece of my mind about James being here, but knew it wasn't worth it. James would be gone before I knew it, and it wasn't worth the fight that I knew I wouldn't win.

The entirety of the next morning and most of the afternoon was spent processing my feelings about the night and avoiding my husband. I couldn't believe that I had stupidly turned to him in a moment of need. I hated that a part of me had still expected him to help me, and that he had stood back and enjoyed my misery. As much as I couldn't believe James's audacity, I was more mad at myself for thinking for even a moment that my husband might have helped me.

Now I was facing another night of James's unwanted attention, and I had no idea how I was going to get through another night like that. I was wallowing in my misery when an idea struck that was so crazy it just might work.

I spent the rest of my afternoon getting ready for the evening. I wanted to look my best. When Tom came storming in to find me, I was rewarded by his surprised, resentful look of appreciation. I smiled at him and asked where we were headed for the night. He didn't answer, just roughly took my arm and dragged me along beside him. He kept stealing glimpses of my body. When I made eye contact with him after one of his many stolen glances, he scowled at me. It seemed he was distracted. *Good.* My plan was already off to a better start than I imagined it would be.

When we got to our destination, I was surprised James wasn't there yet. As the minutes swept by, I was filled with hope. Maybe it would be a peaceful evening after all.

"Well, well, well, looks like someone can't stay away from me."

I restrained myself from rolling my eyes and took a deep breath. I wouldn't let him rattle me. I turned around and smiled at him like he was the answer to my prayers. His eyes were too busy roaming my body to notice. I had picked a particularly form fitting dress for the night. I was both disgusted and pleased that things were going to plan. When he finally tore his eyes from my body and looked at my face, I was treated to his shock at my smile. I sidled closer to him.

"And someone can't tear his eyes from me."

His jaw hit the floor, but after a moment, he noticed he was still staring and tried to regain his composure. "How anyone could miss you in that dress is beyond me. You certainly aren't leaving much to the imagination."

I smiled coyly, batting my eyelashes. It was nauseating, but I was done being toyed with. I was done with being pushed around by the likes of him and done pretending to be the perfect wife for my husband's reputation. I was done being made a fool. Being forced to be in the company of his friends whenever he demanded it. I was sick and tired of being the laughingstock of the city when he paraded me around one night and his latest mistress the next. I was done being his puppet, and I was sick of James thinking he could push me around, too. I was sick of men in general. The whole lot of them.

I ran my hands over my dress, hugging my curves. "Oh, this old thing?" I met his eye and batted my eyelashes more, giving him my best doe-eyed, innocent look. "Do you like it?"

He looked nervous. *Perfect.*

I took a step closer and ran my hand along his arm. "I wore it special for you." I couldn't believe the words coming out of my mouth, and from the look on his face, neither could he.

He took a step back, out of my reach, and shifted uncomfortably. His eyes darted around the room. I wasn't sure what he was looking for until I saw him find Tom. Predictably, Tom was getting himself a drink. His back was turned to us.

I cocked an eyebrow at James and took another step closer. In a low voice, I said, "Don't mind him. You were right yesterday. He doesn't care in the slightest what..." I maintained eye contact with him and ran my tongue across my upper lip. Predictably, I had all his attention. *Typical.* "...or *who* I do." I couldn't stop myself from winking at him.

I was holding back both laughter and nausea at my actions, but I had him right where I wanted him. I would make sure he knew better than to cross me again. He had always pushed me too far, especially when he was with Jordan. Thinking about Jordan gave me slight pause. Was *I* taking things too far? But I shook the thought away. I wouldn't actually do anything besides rattle him. She knows how he can be. She couldn't possibly blame me. I knew her better than that. She would be fighting laughter at how I was acting and how rattled James was.

He stumbled back, and I smirked. That was a mistake. I saw his confusion and then saw the truth dawn on him. My blood ran cold at the slow smile that spread across his lips. He straightened himself up and looked at me appraisingly. Nausea crept back in.

He moved closer to me and it took all my strength to not move away. I tried to hide my discomfort, but don't know how well I succeeded. He shot one more look in Tom's direction before grabbing my arm and pulling me closer. I knew I was trapped, but I was too committed to stop now.

I ran my fingers through his hair. He started to flinch, but held his ground. He slid his arms around my waist and pulled me closer. I fought the revulsion and leaned into him. I stroked his arm, feeling his muscles. As loud as I dared, I said, "It's been a long time since I've felt such strong arms wrapped around me."

I felt eyes turn our way, and I felt his hesitation. He looked in Tom's direction again, but I didn't look away from him to see what Tom was doing. James chuckled and ran his hand down my back, but I could sense the unease in his words. "You better be careful there, sweetheart. I don't think you could handle me."

"You'd be surprised what I can handle. I've never met a challenge too big."

His eyes widened, and he gulped. The power I felt was indescribable. It didn't matter that I didn't want him. What mattered was I was the one in charge. I could get used to that. He took a moment to regain his composure and, from the look in his eye, I knew he hadn't given up yet. He had to know I was toying with him, but like I expected, he was too stubborn to walk away and let me win.

He leaned over and whispered in my ear. "I don't know what you think you're doing, but I promise you, you won't win."

In a low voice, I answered him. "I thought I was being quite obvious. Tom isn't enough for me. He was never my first choice. My first choice was taken."

His shock was laughable. My statement was technically true, Jordan had been taken. But to him, I could only mean him. I wondered not for the first time that night how far he would let me push him. "You said so yourself. I'm not satisfied. Tom doesn't really know how to please a woman. Why do you think he goes through mistresses so quickly? Why do you think he couldn't keep my attention?"

I leaned closer to him. He started to move away, but I held him in place. He looked again in Tom's direction. I didn't turn, but from the thinly veiled panic on James's face, I knew we had my husband's attention.

After a moment, he relaxed. That worried me. I couldn't imagine what he would have seen from Tom that would have relaxed him. *How far would the two of them let this go?* I just wanted Tom to feel some of the humiliation I did at being paraded around as the perfect wife in front of his friends. I wanted him to feel a fraction of the humiliation I felt at the knowledge that he paraded his mistresses around as well. If he was going to put his infidelity on display to humiliate me, the least I could do was give him a taste of what that felt like.

I had expected him to come barging over and separate us the moment I showed interest in James. I expected him to send me back home and not continue to force me to play the good wife. I expected Tom's jealousy and ego to demand he step in when he saw his friend making moves on his wife. In truth, I hadn't expected to get this far. It worried me that I had. *Maybe I should stop.* But no, I was in too far now. I wouldn't give Tom or James the satisfaction of backing down.

I steeled my nerves. I had cowered far too long to the whims of my husband. I had let his desires rule me for far too long; I was done. If Jordan had taught me anything, it was that I was stronger than I knew. I would hold my ground. I had to. The alternative, bowing again to the whims of men, would break me. I had bent as far as I could, bent until I was sure I could bend no longer, and then had bent some more. I knew with everything in me that if I bent any further, I would break. It wasn't my own happiness and safety that I thought about; I drew strength from thinking of my girls, Pammy and Jordan. They were my salvation and I would do any number of terrible things to keep them safe and happy. I would do what it took; I had to.

James leaned forward again with a devilish smile, but I stood my ground. He would break before I did; I knew it. Or else, Tom would. I had always backed down first with the both of them, but this time, just this once, I wouldn't be the weak one. "You know, I'm sure he wouldn't mind me... " He looked me up and down, letting his stare linger on my curves before coming back up to my eye. He licked his lips and my eyes were instantly drawn to them. While I watched, his lips formed a smile. "...satisfying you."

I fought to regain my composure. I was the one in charge, not him. I looked back into his eyes. "If you're sure you're up to the challenge." I exaggerated looking him up and down before adding, "I suppose you'll do."

I leaned a little closer, watching the alarm grow in his eyes as he looked toward where I knew Tom to be, but all the same, he leaned closer. He would pull away any second, I knew he would. I could tell from the fear in his eyes. Knowing that I was the cause, that I had put that fear there and for once wasn't the one being toyed with, was intoxicating.

I felt his wavering resolve and the slight shift in his muscles warned me he was going to pull away. Maybe I had grown too bold, maybe it was a step too far, but the power had gone to my head. Before he could move an inch further, I closed the small distance between us and kissed him. I channeled every ounce of passion I had for Jordan into that kiss.

I needed to be sure it looked real. I waited for his reaction, for his lips to move against my own, or him to push me away, anything. I felt him pull back. It took another moment for my eyes to make sense of what I saw. Tom had a tight grip on James's arm and was pulling him to the bar. Tom didn't spare me a glance, but James glared daggers over his shoulder, before reluctantly allowing Tom to pull him away.

I had done it.

A part of me couldn't believe it, but there was a bigger part of me that seemed to have known the power was in me all along. I had spent what felt like so long thinking of my beauty as a curse. Ever since I married Tom, I had felt nothing but disdain for the beauty that caused him to have been attracted to me in the first place, the same beauty that caused him not to trust me any longer. My beauty that he turned against me, used as evidence I was not to be trusted. He had known it for what it was before even I had, had wielded it against me before I had even understood. My beauty was a weapon, and I would wield it. I would wield it against him and any other man who sought to control me, to own me. I would bring them to their knees. I would make them beg. In that moment, I knew with a freeing clarity that I would do whatever it took to protect my girls. I couldn't afford mercy in a world without any. They were mine to protect, and I would do any number of terrible things to ensure their safety and happiness.

The thought strengthened my resolve and removed any remaining guilt I might have still had. I buried the smug grin that threatened to surface. I hadn't forgotten my surroundings, or my audience. I adopted the expression of anxiety that I knew would be expected of me. It wasn't hard when I noticed the anger in Tom's expression and the tension in his muscles. I had made him angry, and while that worried me, I couldn't bring myself to regret what I had done. Even the possibility of his anger didn't dull the victory I felt.

With both Tom and James occupied, I wasn't sure what to do next. Knowing most eyes were still on me. I took a couple of exaggerated deep breaths for my audience. I looked around the room, and my eyes fell on Nick. He stood halfway between me and the boys, looking torn. Talking with him hadn't been unpleasant, so I went to make my way over to him, but before I could move, he turned and followed them.

I glanced past him to where James and Tom stood arguing. I knew they would be awhile and didn't care to stick around. I normally wouldn't have dared to leave, would have been too worried about the consequences of defying his wishes, but since I had essentially already spit in his face tonight and I was tired, I figured another small defiance wouldn't matter. Ignoring the consequences, I made my way home alone.

As the intoxication of power dulled, I started to worry. I tossed and turned most of the night, sure he would violently shake me awake at any moment. All night I waited for the inevitable confrontation, but much to my relief and surprise, it didn't come.

I quickly realized Tom hadn't bothered to come home at all last night. I wondered idly if James or Tom's latest mistress had had the misfortune of his company last night, but I couldn't bring myself to really care. I was just relieved he hadn't come home to me.

I waited for most of the day to be met by his anger, but mercifully, he stayed absent. I held my breath for most of the afternoon, waiting to be summoned to go out with him as punishment, but he never came.

I was happy to be left to my own devices, but the longer he stayed away, the more I worried about what I might be dealing with when he returned.

The next morning, I ran into him at breakfast. He nodded curtly to me. My curiosity and anxiety got the better of me, so I asked him, "How have you been? I haven't seen you in a while."

He glared and snidely replied, "Just fine. More than satisfied with where I've been laying my head. Unfortunately, your latest attempted conquest couldn't stick around, but James sends his regards."

Inwardly, I smiled, pleased I had bothered him, but I was too smart to show that. "Good riddance. I never liked him anyway. I couldn't believe he would be sleazy enough to make a move on his friend's wife."

Tom just rolled his eyes and left. Of course, he wouldn't believe or acknowledge that James was the problem, but it didn't matter what he thought, it only mattered that James was gone.

The days slowly crept by as I waited for an end to the misery of being in Chicago with his parents. I knew we wouldn't stay here forever, but not being in my husband's confidence, I had no clue when we would leave or what to expect. Not that it mattered to me where we went, I just needed a change. Any change would be welcome; I just needed out of Chicago. I needed Jordan.

It turns out I didn't have to wait long. I started hearing rumors about his latest mistresses. Apparently, he wasn't satisfied with one mistress anymore. From what I heard, one of his mistresses was attempting to push him into divorcing me and marrying her. I had laughed at that. If only I could get so lucky.

Supposedly another one of his mistresses was threatening to tell me if he didn't spend more money on her. He must have liked her well enough to give in, because I hadn't heard from her. It was disappointing really. I would have loved to see the look on her face when she found out I already knew and didn't care.

I had also heard that one of the women he was already bored with was threatening to go to his family or to the press. After that, he started fighting more with his family.

Shortly after, he told me to pack up. I tried to keep the grin from my face, but inside I was ecstatic. This was what I had been waiting for. I needed a fresh start. I couldn't wait to leave the nanny behind and get away from his family. I asked if I should pack up Pammy, too. His answer instantly killed any happiness I had felt. He said there was no need. My blood ran cold.

He couldn't mean that. I had done virtually everything he wanted. I hadn't said another word against the nanny. I had let the two of them keep me away from Pammy most of the time. I had kept my distance to keep her safe and now he was taking her from me, anyway. It occurred to me then that maybe we weren't leaving, maybe just I was. He might've been making good on his threat to institutionalize me.

I should have felt afraid, but all I felt was numb. In the back of my mind, the thought registered that maybe Jordan could help me out of this, but I knew it was hopeless. I tried to muster an ounce of the daring, powerful woman I had been a mere few weeks ago with James, but she was nowhere to be found.

I knew in my heart there was no way out of this. I had damned us. In my determination to stick my neck out for Pammy and Jordan, I had assured their misery. I felt worse than powerless; I was devastated.

I knew I should feel panicked, should fight, but it wouldn't change a thing. I had brought this on myself and I knew nothing I could say or do would change a thing. I should have known he wouldn't let my little stunt with James slid as easily as he had. I couldn't bring myself to feel much of anything through the numbness. The voice in my head was a whisper of its usual strength. The voice was telling me to fight, but I couldn't. It wouldn't change a thing. I knew Jordan would want me to fight, but it wouldn't change anything. I could only hope she would forgive me.

I thought I would burst into tears when I saw Pammy. I was so overwhelmed with relief to see her and the nanny outside with their luggage. Pammy was coming with us! I wasn't going to be institutionalized and my daughter wasn't being left behind!

I wasn't overjoyed the nanny was coming with us, but I could live with it, considering the alternative. Anything was preferable to Pammy having to grow up without me.

We traveled east. The trip was the most fun I had had since Jordan had left. I spent every moment with Pammy. Since we were all sharing close quarters, she wasn't kept from me. I hoped the nanny might see how untrue whatever he had told her was, but she still regarded me with caution and distrust.

At least Tom's mood was improving the more distance we put between us and Chicago. I couldn't help wondering if it was his family or his mistresses that we were running from, but the result was the same. I was thrilled to be getting away. I was even more thrilled when I learned our destination; New York City. I was excited to see the city. I had heard so much about the glitz and glam and was looking forward to seeing it for myself. More importantly, Jordan's aunt has an apartment in the city.

I wondered where we might be going. I wasn't sure if he meant for us to stay in or out of the city, but for the first time in a while, I was feeling optimistic. It had to be better than Chicago.

CHAPTER TWELVE
Daisy

It didn't take long after we moved for Jordan to settle in the city with her aunt. Although she saw more of me than her aunt. She had her own room in the house Tom bought. Tom seemed happy that I was out of his hair, so she was allowed to stay as often as she liked. I doubt he would have been as happy if he knew how she kept me entertained.

I stayed out of his way, though. I had grown more cautious of him. His moods came out of nowhere and I always seemed to set off his temper. I felt I was perpetually walking on eggshells. He hadn't renewed his threats of institutionalizing me, but still I worried, enough to never mention getting rid of the nanny again. I told myself it was nice to have the help, but I knew that wasn't true; I missed my daughter terribly.

Technically, she was living with us and supposedly, I was allowed to see her when I pleased, but things had changed. She didn't seem as happy to see me anymore, and she had grown rather attached to the nanny. I had worried that would happen. I had wanted to be around for everything with her, but Tom took that away from me. I could have forgiven his poor treatment of me, but pushing me away from my daughter was unforgiveable.

I still tried to see her, despite how much it hurt, though. When Jordan was around, she would often suggest it. She loved Pammy just as much as I did. I hoped Jordan didn't notice the difference as starkly as I did.

It was worse when she wasn't there. When I went to see Pammy without Jordan, Tom would make sure to be around. He would let me play with her a few minutes before finding something to scold me for or thinking of some argument to start. Every time without fail, when I was alone with her, he would start a fight. Sometimes he put his hands on me, sometimes he just yelled, but it didn't matter, every time he would fight with me in front of her. She was getting older now, and I worried she would understand.

I told myself that it wasn't my fault and that I couldn't let him control me, but I visited her less and less. As much as I wanted to see her every moment of every day, I knew it wasn't healthy for her to be seeing us fight. I didn't want her to be scared or worried. I wanted her to have as much of a happy, carefree life as possible, even if it had to come at my expense.

After a while, I stopped visiting her altogether when Jordan wasn't around. I hadn't told Jordan about how bad things were getting with Tom. I worried she would say something to him. I knew she would try to defend me from him, but I thought that would only make things worse. I was scared she would only increase his aggression, or that, heaven forbid, he might hurt her. That was unthinkable, so I continued to keep my mouth shut.

Thankfully, now that I didn't visit Pammy on my own and stayed out of Tom's way, I didn't seem to have anything to fear from him. As long as I didn't seem too happy, he was content to leave me alone.

As more time passed, I noticed Tom was absent more and more often. I wondered what her name was this time. Whoever she was, I was grateful she was taking him off my hands.

Things were okay until the spring crept up on us and Jordan started having to focus on her golfing again. The days grew bleak for me. In her absence, I was truly isolated. Jordan was running around playing in tournament after tournament. She was doing everything she could to save up for our future, but I couldn't help but feel left behind. I loved her so much for how hard she was trying to take care of me and Pammy, but without her around, I felt lost. I worried she would change her mind and grow tired of me. I worried she already had. It felt like it had been ages since the last time I spent more than a few minutes alone with her.

Now that Jordan wasn't around, I didn't see Pammy either. With Tom gone more, I might have been able to, but I worried I had been away from her too long and wouldn't know how to interact with her. I worried she would look at me like a stranger. I felt like an intruder when I did occasionally visit her. She and her nanny had developed their own routines. She was growing up so fast; I felt like I had missed it all. Right before my eyes, she was now walking and talking on her own. I wondered if she had any memory of all the time we used to spend together, but I doubted it. I felt like I hardly knew her anymore.

Eventually Jordan confronted me about the distance I was putting between me and Pammy. She knew I was lonely and kept telling me it would help to visit her. She told me that even though Pammy had a nanny, it didn't mean she didn't need or want her mother. She told me if I wanted to, I could still get rid of the nanny. She told me that Pammy was young enough that she hadn't formed too strong of an attachment to the woman. Jordan told me I could dismiss the nanny and take back control over caring for my daughter.

I didn't know what to tell her. I could feel the tears starting again. "It's not that. I mean, you're wrong. She doesn't need me, but that's not it. I would love to take care of her myself... I just can't."

I could tell she was getting frustrated. I was a little frustrated, too, but I knew it was my fault that she didn't understand. I felt powerless in my own home and didn't want her to know how bad things were.

She sighed. "Then what is it? You're a wonderful mother, but you're holding yourself back from getting to know your daughter. I don't understand why. Before you know it, she'll be all grown up. This isn't time you can get back. You can't let yourself keep missing out on her growing up."

The tears broke all at once, and I was sobbing. I struggled to draw in breath and calm myself. Jordan held me and rubbed my back. "I know, my love, I know. You can let it out. I'm here. I'll always be here."

She held me until the tears slowed. I couldn't keep hiding things from her, even if it was for her own good. Maybe it was selfish, but I was too tired to carry the burden myself.

I was at a loss about how to explain everything I had been holding back for the last year since Chicago. I didn't know how I would explain why I hadn't told her. I knew she would be angry. The last thing I wanted was for her to be mad at me, but it seemed unavoidable.

When I caught my breath, I explained, "It's not me. I mean, I do have reservations about seeing her and I worry she doesn't care for me like she used to, but that's not important right now. I meant, it wasn't my choice, it was Tom's."

"I know he hired the nanny, and I know things are rough between you two, and I know I probably haven't been helping that, but why don't you tell him how you felt about the nanny? Or just dismiss her yourself? He doesn't control you."

"I mean, he doesn't, but I'm not as strong as you are. I can't stand up to him like you would." I hesitated before adding, "I'm scared of him. I know how weak that makes me sound and I should be braver and more like you, but I just can't. I'm terrified."

It felt good to finally voice the truth, but looking at Jordan, I doubted whether my relief was worth it. She looked alarmed and confused. She took my hand and held my gaze. "Wait, wait, wait. I don't think you're weak. Far from it. You're incredibly brave, much braver than I am. But what do you mean you're afraid of him? Has he done something to you?"

I watched her go through the emotional turmoil I had over the past year. I felt guilty at both being the cause of her emotions and at having held back from her at all. I told her about his threats about locking me away, and about taking Pammy away. I told her about his aggression toward me and him putting his hands on me, and how he harassed me in front of our daughter whenever I would visit Pammy without her.

I told her how I had tried to be strong and not let him win, but I wasn't able to. I knew it wasn't good for Pammy to see us fighting and the only way to stop her from seeing it was to stop giving him a reason to pick fights with me in the first place, so I started doing what he wanted and stopped visiting her. Little by little, I gave in to his demands and let him dictate what I did and didn't do. I told her how I let my fear guide me and that I continued to let it.

When I finally finished, she immediately burst out, "I had no idea... why didn't you tell me? I could have helped you. You didn't have to go through this alone. I can't even imagine how much you've been suffering. I'm so sorry."

"I'm sorry I didn't tell you. I just didn't want to make you feel the way I was feeling. Things feel so hopeless. You're the only good thing in my life right now. I didn't want to burden you with this."

"Daisy Fay, I will say this as many times as you need to hear it; I love you with all my heart. There is nothing you can say or do to change that. You will never be a burden to me. I want all of you. I want to be there for you through everything. You are truly the bravest, kindest, most selfless women I know. You are not in this, or in anything else, alone. I will always be with you to support you."

"That's what I was worried about. I worried you might do or say something to him and that he would hurt you."

"He wouldn't dare."

"He isn't the same man I married. I used to blame myself for that, but I've long since given up asking why. I've just had to accept the fact that the man I married isn't there anymore. It doesn't matter whether it was my fault or not-"

"It wasn't."

"Well, regardless, it doesn't matter. What matters is that he isn't the Tom we knew. I don't know what this man is capable of, and that scares me. I've had enough on my plate with worrying about Pammy. I didn't want to have to worry about you, too. I mean, I worry about you all the time, but I didn't want to have to worry about him hurting you."

"That's absurd. You don't need to worry about me. I can handle myself."

"I know you can, but I still worry. You don't know what he's really been like lately, how scary he's gotten."

I could see the disbelief on her face. "Is he really that bad that you worry about Pammy?" She shook her head to herself. "He wouldn't. He couldn't hurt his own daughter."

"He's still convinced she's not his daughter."

She looked at me in disbelief. "And who does he think her father is? You haven't been with anyone else!"

I just looked at her pointedly.

She laughed at that. "Okay, okay. Point taken. But really, who does he imagine the father is?"

"Well, you know how Pammy used to call you Jo?"

She nodded. I waited a moment for her to understand. After a moment, I watched the realization dawn on her face. "...no..."

I giggled. "Yes. I couldn't make that up if I tried."

"And you didn't correct him?"

"He didn't give me the chance and then I lost the desire to."

She laughed at that. "And you thought I was the brave one."

"I kept trying to correct him in the beginning, but he wouldn't be corrected. If he wants to think you're Pammy's father, then I say let him. You've been a much better parent to her than he has, anyway. I used to want him to know his daughter, but she doesn't deserve to be treated the way he treats others. He doesn't deserve to know her, and she doesn't deserve that pain."

She looked a little awed at that, which confused me. I added, "You can't think any part of that is wrong. I've tried so hard with him, but I know when something is a lost cause and that man is not the man I married."

"No, of course I support you. I just haven't ever seen you this strongly dislike anyone before. You usually give everyone too many chances. It's so refreshing to see you standing up for yourself. I'm so proud of you."

CHAPTER THIRTEEN
Daisy

After I opened up to Jordan, I noticed she slowed her tournaments. She didn't compete as much and was around more often. I was grateful, but felt a never-ending wave of guilt at what I was putting her through. I knew she was worried for me and knew she wanted to do everything she could to help and protect me. I knew she would whisk me away the moment she could and that it was taking everything in her to not scoop up me and Pammy and run. I wished she would, but I understood why she didn't. She was committed to doing things the right way, committed to making sure she was assured of Pammy and my safety and freedom. So I knew it had to be killing her to be competing less, but I was grateful for her company.

I loved having her around, especially in the stolen moments I could get her alone. I craved her. So when, after much prodding, I had succeeded in getting her to take a day off from her relentless training and competitions, I had certain ideas about how we would spend the day.

I had spent the night dreaming of all the places her hands would roam, all the things I would do to her. So when I found out that Tom's friend

Nick was in town and was coming for dinner and I was expected to help entertain him, I was livid. Somehow, Tom knew. He couldn't have known how badly I craved her, but this couldn't be a coincidence. He must have realized I hadn't seen her in a while and went out of his way to find a reason to spoil my plans and my happiness.

Not that Nick's company was that horrible. Quite the contrary, actually. I quite liked him. He was by far the least objectionable of all of Tom's friends and had been quite kind to me when we had met in Chicago. Under normal circumstances, I would have been happier to see him. He was family, after all, if a second cousin once removed can still be considered family. However, as it was, I hadn't had the pleasure of Jordan's attentions in a couple weeks and my body was screaming for her. The frustration I felt at knowing I wouldn't get the satisfaction I was craving, knowing I wouldn't get to spend my day reminding Jordan just how much I loved her, was nearly intolerable.

Thankfully, as luck would have it, Tom and Nick took their time joining us. I can only assume they were talking about "the good old days". There was nothing Tom liked to talk of more than "the good old days". I couldn't believe I had ever found that interesting or endearing. What a fool I had been.

At least their leisurely catching up gave me and Jordan some time alone. The tension in the room was stifling, but we were too exposed to really do anything. The room was lined with windows and the boys would be here any moment. It wasn't safe, but I still couldn't help the direction my thoughts were turning, and I knew I wasn't the only one.

I snuck a glance at her, knowing even before I did, what I would see. It was impossible to miss the mischievous glint in her eye. I was grateful she shared my thoughts, but she had to know nothing could happen. We were too exposed here and moving anywhere else would risk angering

Tom, or worse, arousing his suspicion. We needed to be here when the boys arrived. As much as I wanted to disappear with her and live out every dream I had had last night about her, I knew we couldn't.

I needed to clear my mind. I tried to pry my eyes away from her, but saw a smirk play across her lips.

I couldn't help squirming under her gaze.

I saw her look of triumph flash across her face before she quickly replaced it with a feigned look of concern. When she spoke, it was low enough that I had to lean closer to her. She asked, "Is everything quite all right, darling? You look positively heated. Is it too warm in here?" She gently fanned herself with her long fingers to accentuate her point.

After taking a deep breath, I stuttered out, "I-I'm quite all right." That only served to widen her smirk.

Her head slowly tilted to the side as she continued in a lower, somewhat huskier voice, "Are you sure, darling, that there's nothing we can do to make you more comfortable...?"

I had reached my limit and leaned forward, when I heard the heavy footsteps coming toward us. I lurched backward away from her and had just seconds to assume a relaxed lounging posture before my husband and cousin entered through the door.

Tom strode in and made his way around the room, slamming the windows shut as he went. Jordan glanced at the newcomer before looking away, unimpressed. I had hoped she might say something and give me more time to recover, but I should have known better. She wasn't one to start up a conversation with strangers. Besides, I was sure she wanted to watch me squirm; she was looking quite smug about it.

The silence carried on. Apparently, I was going to have to break it. I swayed over to Nick, laughing at the awkwardness of the silence. I hoped the laughter would veil my discomfort. I managed to squeak out a flustered, "I'm p-paralyzed with happiness."

Nick must have noticed my stutter and how flushed I was, but I hoped he would mis-attribute it to any other cause than the truth. We had been foolish. It had been far too close. We would have to be more careful.

Mercifully, if he noticed anything was amiss, he had the good grace to keep it to himself. He smiled at me and chuckled along with my anxious laughter. I quickly introduced Jordan, avoiding meeting her gaze in a hopeless attempt to keep what I had managed to regain of my composure.

My willpower was weak, though, and the moment Nick looked at her, I couldn't help but look, too. I was curious and a little worried what she would think of him. I knew better than to feel like I had to worry, but I couldn't help it. Jordan was my other half. I knew from experience how miserable my life was without her in it, and I would do anything to avoid having to ever feel like that again.

I knew how much she loved me, but I couldn't stop my racing thoughts sometimes. After all, I was married and her being with me made things unnecessarily complicated for her. She had to sneak around with me and she was going to have to support me and Pammy and finance my divorce. I wondered what she saw in me that she felt I was worth all that effort, and on my darker days, I worried she would come to her senses and leave.

However, apparently, today wouldn't be that day. I expected her to look at Nick, but she only spared him a fleeting glance before looking back at me. Her eyes sparkled with mischief and, before I could stop myself, my eyes dropped to her lips in time to see them move ever so slightly to form her trademark smirk. She nodded at Nick, but didn't take her eyes off me. That girl would be my undoing.

I rushed to grab Nick's attention, hoping he didn't notice the power she held over me, and asked some questions about his life. To be truthful, I was still distracted and could only venture a guess at what I asked and what was said in return. However, when he mentioned Chicago, he snapped me out of my daze. He said when he was just there that at least a dozen people had sent their love.

I didn't particularly care, but as I was sure it would bug Tom to hear about, so I feigned excitement and asked, "Do they miss me?"

"The whole town is desolate. All the cars have the left rear wheel painted black as a mourning wreath, and there's a persistent wail all night along the north shore."

Now I remembered why I had liked Nick's company so much. He seemed to always be willing to play along. Just to twist the knife a little, since Tom had been the reason we had fled Chicago as quickly as we had, I said, "How gorgeous!" With a glance in Tom's direction, I added, like it had been an afterthought, "Let's go back, Tom."

He ventured no reply, but kept his features schooled into an expression of indifference. I don't know why, but that irked me enough to add, "Tomorrow!"

One more glance in his direction was enough to know my comment had hit its mark. His ire was peaked. I can't explain why I felt so compelled to push him, except to say that Jordan's company made me bolder than usual. With her there, I felt invincible.

I knew I was being reckless, but I was upset. Again, it wasn't Nick that I minded, but the pretense that we were a happy family. I very much minded being paraded around at Tom's whim as his happy wife and having to keep up the charade of us having the perfect family. It couldn't be further from the truth, and I couldn't stand being forced to pretend.

I supposed it was more than that. It was more that I couldn't stand to see him pretend. When he was trying to impress friends, I saw glimpses of the man I thought I had married. For a few hours, he was his old self again, and I couldn't stand it. I couldn't stand how easy it was for him to pretend, how easy it was for him to slip that perfect gentleman mask back on. Every time he acted like that now it was like another dagger to my heart, another reminder of just how stupid I had been to fall for him.

It was a small consolation that no one else saw through it either. They were all as blind to it as I had been, but sometimes I wished they would see him for who he was, for the monster he was.

Those dinner parties where the man I married would reemerge had caused me to question my sanity and wonder if the man I had loved was in there somewhere. Then our guests would leave and the illusion would shatter again and again. Every time, a little more of my faith in the world would shatter.

I didn't love him.

I *knew* that.

Jordan had proved that without a doubt. Even at our best, my feelings for Tom had never been close to what I feel for Jordan, but I couldn't help but miss the man I married. He had been a gentleman, a confidante, a friend. It had taken a long time to stop missing that and even longer to realize there was no fixing him; he wasn't coming back. Now, seeing him slip back into the old Tom for a few hours felt like a slap in the face. That he could turn it off and on at will, that others couldn't see through him, drove me crazy. Sometimes I got so fed up I pushed back. Tonight was apparently one of those nights. Maybe it was that he ripped my evening alone with Jordan away from me, but I was less tolerant than usual of Tom, less willing to play his games.

Nick discreetly cleared his throat. I turned to him quickly, realizing I hadn't the faintest idea of what he had said. I struggled for something to say and said the first thing that popped into my head. "You ought to see the baby." I wasn't sure how Tom would react. I glanced in his direction. His face gave away nothing, so I chose to believe he wasn't adamantly opposed to it.

After all, he wanted to play the part of a happy family, what better way than to show off our beautiful daughter. I would have been lying to say I didn't find pleasure in showing her off at every given opportunity. She was only two years old, but already so intelligent.

I prayed she would become what I had failed to be; a strong, self-assured woman. She was already so curious about the world and so smart. I had given up any and all hope of her becoming a beautiful little fool. Now I was forced to hope she would be strong willed enough to take the world by storm, to force the world to bend to her whims instead of being broken by it like I had been.

I wanted the best for her. I hoped with everything in me that Jordan would rub off on her. If she ended up anything like Jordan, I knew she could handle whatever life threw at her.

Nick shook me out of my thoughts by replying, "I'd like to."

It took me a moment to remember what it was I had said, and thought better of it. If Tom was already in a mood, I certainly didn't need her to be around him. I quickly added, "She's asleep."

I hoped that would be enough to stop him from pressing further, but everyone stayed silent, so I felt compelled to add, "She's three years old."

She wasn't; she was just barely two. I don't know what made me say it, but I paused a moment, glancing at my husband to see if he would correct me. He didn't. I hated that it stung that I wasn't sure if he didn't correct me because he didn't know or because he didn't care. Either way, whatever point I had been trying to prove only ended up hurting me. For lack of anything else to say, I asked, "Haven't you ever seen her?"

"Never."

It shouldn't have surprised me; none of Tom's friends besides Nick had even bothered to ask to see her. I was happy he was different in that regard at least. There was something about his mannerisms that made him easy to talk to. He was unobtrusive and listened. He made you feel like he cared. I had to be careful, though; I was thinking of Nick as my friend. He wasn't, he was Tom's friend. Unfortunately, he couldn't truly be both and his allegiance was to Tom; I would do well to remember that.

"Well, you ought to see her. She's-"

That was as far as I got before Tom, who I imagine was annoyed about the lack of attention being paid to him, butted in and asked loudly, "What you doing, Nick?"

Nick, evidently easily distracted from his interest in myself and my daughter, immediately launched back into conversation with Tom. "I'm a bond man."

"With who?"

Nick mumbled his response, but apparently Tom heard since he didn't skip a beat before replying haughtily, "Never heard of them."

"You will." I was surprised by the bite in his tone, and even more surprised when he added, "You will if you stay in the East."

I didn't need to look in Tom's direction to feel the irritation radiating off him. From his comment, I couldn't help but wonder how much Nick knew. Had Tom told him something of his exploits back West?

Had I given more away than I intended to? He had called when we were travelling to New York. It had been a brief call, but he had asked how long we planned to stay, and I told him what I hoped to be the truth that we would be staying in the East. As glad as I was about leaving Chicago, it wasn't my doing and I wasn't optimistic enough to hope I would have any say in our next move if there was one. I hoped with everything in me that we wouldn't have to leave New York like we had Chicago. That my life wouldn't be uprooted in the matter of a day when his latest scandal caught up to us. Had I given all of that away to Nick from our phone call? Unlikely. It must have been something Tom told him, but I was surprised at him throwing that in Tom's face. Nick was usually mild-mannered and agreeable. This was new, but I can't say I didn't like it.

Tom on the other hand, decisively didn't like this new side to his friend. His thinly veiled ire leaked into his reply. "Oh, I'll stay in the East, don't you worry."

I didn't need to look up to know he was glaring at me. As if I were somehow to blame for the things Nick had noticed and said. He may be *my* cousin, but he was *Tom's* friend.

"I'd be a God damned fool to live anywhere else," he added.

I hoped he believed what he was saying since I quite liked the East. The city was charming in a way that small towns aren't. In the city, you had anonymity. You could be anyone, do anything. It was nowhere near as stifling and suffocating as being around the Elite of Louisville had been. My every move was studied and documented. I had no privacy and wasn't given the grace of being able to make any mistakes. In the city, there were too many people for anyone to keep track of, too many rich influential families for anyone to care about anyone in particular; I loved it.

"Absolutely!" exclaimed Jordan.

Her voice startled me, as did the force behind her words. I wasn't the only one. Everyone, including Jordan, seemed surprised by her outburst.

She yawned and stretched her arms over her head, tilting her neck back and forth. The action took everyone's attention away from her words and straight to her figure. I could look at her all day, but seeing Nick appreciate her wasn't a welcome sight. I didn't even look in Tom's direction. I didn't want to see if he was looking.

Thankfully, a moment later, Jordan jumped up. "I'm stiff. I've been lying on that sofa for as long as I can remember."

I couldn't help but roll my eyes at that. I had been trying to convince her all morning we should go to the city, anywhere really except here. But she had known as well as I had that I had to stay, so we had stayed. Of course, she would act the victim, like I had made her lounge about for the better part of the day. I saw the smirk on her face and couldn't help my reply. "Don't look at me. I've been trying to get you to New York all afternoon."

Her reply was interrupted by one of the staff who entered with a tray of drinks that they quickly deposited on a table at the end of the couch and made their escape. I didn't blame them for not wanting to be in the room any longer than possible since Tom was here.

Tom crossed the room and took his drink, and looked around expectantly. The tray had three more drinks on it. My blood boiled at the sight of the three drinks that should have been two. I hadn't touched alcohol in years. He, of all people, should know that. I knew he knew better. He was making some sort of statement, or seeing how far he could push me, how obedient I would be.

For a moment, I pictured myself taking the drink and smiling sweetly at him before raising my glass and dousing him with the liquor. I imagined how funny he would look standing there fuming, looking like a drowned rat. I imagined it would take him days to wash off the smell, not that it would differ from normal. I couldn't remember the last time Tom hadn't smelled of liquor.

I took a calming breath, trying to cool my thoughts. Tom was watching me with a smug smile. My hand, seemingly of its own volition, reached out in front of me for the glass. The picture of him drenched and soaking into the carpet solidified in my mind. I almost had my hand around the glass when Jordan gently moved my hand back to my side and stepped in between me and the drinks. She had a knack for knowing what I was thinking and when I needed her intervention, and I loved her for that and for many other things.

She met Tom's eye, matching the challenge in his own. "No, thanks, I'm absolutely in training."

He looked her up and down incredulously, a smirk on his face. "You are?"

Anger coursed through me. *How dare he!* I would take any number of his insults, but how dare he talk to Jordan like that! Again came the flashes of throwing a drink in his face. I knew it was reckless, but I didn't care. I went to move past Jordan, but she subtly shifted in front of me. She didn't move her eyes from Tom, not backing down.

He raised his glass in a mock toast before throwing his head back and draining his drink. When he finished, he licked his lips, a satisfied smile on his face, and took another. The last drink remained there, forgotten. As aggravated as I was with Tom's childish behavior, I was thankful he was easily distracted. Nothing moved him to ire quicker than feeling like someone thought they were better than him. In that way, he was sensitive about his drinking, sensitive that others might see it as a weakness. He didn't take kindly to self-restraint in others, likely because he himself did not possess it. Anyone with a sense of shame would have been embarrassed by that, but he wore his lack of restraint as a badge of honor.

While he normally tolerated my own not drinking, it seemed something had changed. Whether it was that me standing up to him was too much, or something else, I knew without a doubt that something had changed.

Jordan must have sensed it, too, since she had been going out of her way to deflect his attention from me. Since she had attracted his attention, he added, "How you ever get anything done is beyond me."

I felt my face heat and knew my cheeks were flushed. Whether from embarrassment or anger, I couldn't tell. Every once in a while, he would make little statements like that. Take little jabs at the amount of time Jordan spends with me. At first he had been grateful that she was keeping me occupied, grateful that I had stopped asking questions and concerning myself with his business. But as time went on, he became more and more upset that I was happy without his attention.

I didn't bother myself about his affairs anymore. Why would I when I had Jordan? I didn't care anymore that he didn't give me the same love and attention he used to. I stopped trying to win him back and I'm sure he noticed. I could only hope he didn't know Jordan was the reason.

His little comments let me know he thought she spent too much time with me, which was a ridiculous notion. With her practicing and playing in tournaments as often as she was, she was hardly ever around. For him to imply she was still around too much was too much for me to handle. If it were up to me, she would never leave my side.

I knew better than to meet Tom's eyes. I knew he was looking for a reaction from me. He wanted to ensure someone else besides himself was unhappy. Looking at Jordan wasn't an option, either. If she saw how much he upset me, she wouldn't stay silent. The last thing I needed was her rising to take his bait. He would never stop if he knew he was getting to either of us.

Jordan and Tom both remained silent, measuring the other up. With an internal sigh, I turned to Nick, ready to change the subject. To what it didn't matter; even talking of something drab like the weather would be preferable to this. But Tom and Jordan had caught his attention, too. As I watched, I realized with a start that his attention seemed to be fixed solely on the latter.

He seemed oblivious that he had my attention and took his time staring at her appraisingly, and clearly appreciated what he saw. That didn't surprise me in the slightest. What did surprise me was that when Jordan noticed a moment later, she didn't seem averse to it.

When she addressed him a moment later, I thought it would be to beg forgiveness for our rudeness or to laugh off the tension, but what she did say surprised me. "You live in West Egg. I know somebody there." Where she was going with that I couldn't possibly have guessed, but if I had had a million guesses, I never would have come up with what she said next.

Nick seemed caught off guard being addressed by her at all. He stumbled a little over his words, "I don't know a single-" before she cut him off.

"You must know Gatsby."

Gatsby! She couldn't mean Jay? Jay couldn't be here, and if she knew that, why didn't she tell me? Why was I finding out just now in front of my cousin and husband, of all people?

Here she was mentioning him casually to Nick as if she had no idea of his importance, as if she didn't know how much hearing his name would affect me. If I hadn't known better, I would think she was testing me to see if I would have a reaction, testing to see how much I still cared about him. I wondered for a moment if that worried her, but it couldn't possibly. She must know how deeply I love her, that it wouldn't matter who else waltzed into my life, I would always choose her. It would always be her. Her and I against the world.

But Jordan wasn't one to hide things or to feel insecure, so maybe she wasn't sure if it was him? Maybe it's another Gatsby? Was it possible there was another Gatsby who lived in West Egg? The sinking feeling in my stomach told me I already suspected that wasn't the case. Only a few seconds had passed before I asked, "Gatsby? What Gatsby?"

Everyone turned to me. I hoped they hadn't heard the emotion in my voice. From the contrite look on Jordan's face, I was reassured that she hadn't been intending to make a fool of me. It was comforting to know she hadn't intended to do so, but why bring up the name Gatsby in the first place?

Our moment of silence was broken by the announcement of dinner, which was both a blessing and a curse. I was able to escape their scrutiny, but unfortunately, no one had answered me, so I was left wondering.

Could it really be Jay? After all these years, could he really be settled right across the bay? It seemed too big of a coincidence, but yet, another man by the name of Gatsby having settled across the bay would also be a rather large coincidence. I hoped beyond hope that it was the latter. I didn't know if I could stomach seeing him after everything he had put me through, everything he had done to me. I would sooner rather never see him again. Especially after his last letter.

I had tried and succeeded for a while in forgetting it, but hearing his name again brought the words right back to my mind. "Don't say yes. If you do, you will regret it. I will make sure you regret it." I still wasn't able to imagine what he could have meant by that, but couldn't imagine it would be anything good. I shivered at the thought of him across the bay, watching me and plotting, waiting for his moment to take whatever sort of revenge he thought was his due. Never mind that I was the one who had been hurt, and that he was the one in the wrong. Never mind that he had left me first, I hadn't taken him back when he asked. I hadn't been waiting around for him despite him giving me no indication that I should, that that was what he had wanted. When he said he was going to come back, I didn't drop everything for him. I had moved on and I wasn't willing to upturn my entire life for him when he had flipped my life upside down in a single night and then left. And yet, despite all that, he thought he deserved revenge since I didn't follow his orders. I couldn't believe how arrogant he had been! Of course, that had been 3 years ago, I reasoned. A lot could have changed since then, but even so, I didn't relish the idea of seeing him again.

I had been lost in thought for a moment, but noticed a moment later that I still had everyone's attention. Tom and Nick were tense and confused respectively, but it was Jordan that I noticed most. I could plainly see the apology on her face. It wasn't necessary. I trusted her and even if I couldn't understand it yet, I trusted she had a reason to bring up Jay.

I looped my arm in hers and, without another word or a single glance back at the men, led her to the porch where the table was waiting.

Chapter Fifteen
Daisy

The table was set with all our finery, which at first surprised me. It took me a moment to recall that it was because of our company. While Nick's presence was welcome, it was easy to forget him. He faded into the background and remained a quiet observer most of the time. But regardless of that, he was here, and the staff had noticed, so the table had been made up to be fit for royalty, as it always was when we had company. After all, much better to be over prepared and formal than to underwhelm company.

I glanced at the table, taking in the amount of silverware and trying to stifle my groan. From the amount of forks, this was going to be a long meal. The cook had pulled out all the stops for this. I shouldn't have been surprised. Our staff was incredibly attentive and did a fantastic job and until now I had never had cause to regret it. I had hoped for a shorter dinner so I could try to get Jordan alone again. I audibly groaned when I saw the candles. Yes, candles give a dinner more of the appearance of formality, but in the afternoon in the summer, they were not only unnecessary and unwarranted, but very much unwanted.

"Why candles?" I groaned to myself before making my way around the table, extinguishing them one by one with my fingers. Thankfully, by the time I finished, everyone had claimed their seats, and all that was left for me to do was to take mine. I sunk into my seat with some relief, but the silence felt almost as stifling and oppressive as the stale summer air. I hoped someone, anyone, would say something else, but I was kept waiting.

Grasping for anything to say, feeling the full oppression of summer, and able to think of nothing else besides the time of the year, I burst out, "In two weeks, it'll be the longest day in the year." Everyone had startled at my voice breaking the silence, and I watched as their confusion multiplied at my statement. No one else could come up with anything better to say, so I kept going. "Do you always watch for the longest day of the year and then miss it?" No one responded. "I always watch for the longest day in the year and then miss it."

Jordan, who looked highly confused but was unwilling to leave me hanging, said, "We ought to plan something."

I grinned at her, happier than ever that she was always so supportive and so willing to go along with anything I wanted, whether or not it made sense to her. I loved her fiercely for that. "All right! What'll we plan?"

She shrugged, as if to say, it was your plan; you decide. I hadn't the faintest idea. I turned to Nick; he was our company after all and should be included. "What do people plan?"

Nick startled at being addressed and then took his time thinking. Not wanting to meet anyone's eye, I looked down at my hands. When I did, I noticed a bruise on my little finger. I inspected it for a moment before looking back up. I saw Jordan's attention was on my little finger as well.

She raised an eyebrow at me. I held up my finger toward her. "Look, I hurt it."

It was noticeably black and blue. While I couldn't remember this particular incident, the bruise itself didn't surprise me, nor did I need to wonder where it had come from. I knew. It had come from the same place all my other bruises had come from. I was already looking around for something else to say, some novel thing to talk about, when I caught Tom's eye.

I normally was more careful to hide my bruises from everyone, Jordan included. It was the only thing I held back from her. She knew that things were bad of course, but I knew if she knew how bad things were that for better or worse she wouldn't let me and Pammy continue to spend another night under the same roof with him. As things were, she was doing everything she could to save every penny to be able to afford to whisk me and Pammy away the first moment she could. The last thing I needed was her blaming herself for not being able to take me away yet, or doing something rash and putting herself at risk. So I had been taking care to hide the bruises from her whenever possible. But what I saw in Tom's face made me see red.

He was smirking.

He had the audacity to smirk at me while I was sitting here holding the finger he had bruised. He was smirking like he didn't have a care in the world, like it didn't matter what I or anyone else thought about him, he would still do what he pleased to me. Before I could think better of it, the accusation flew from my lips. "You did it, Tom!"

The shock on his face made it almost worth it. Almost. But the dangerous look in his eye that followed, that promise of retribution, worried me. I quickly added, "I know you didn't mean to, but you *did* do it."

Jordan's face reflected warring outrage and pride. Her support emboldened me to continue, "That's what I get for marrying a brute of a man, a great, big, hulking physical specimen of a-"

He cut me off with a glare that I should think would have silenced the tongues of even those with the steeliest resolve. He cut in. "I hate that word 'hulking', even in kidding."

He wasn't fooling anyone, except maybe Nick, who didn't know enough of our relationship to see through the sham. Jordan, me, and even Tom himself knew better than to think my words had been in kidding. Of course he would choose to continue to belittle my feelings. They meant nothing to him after all. They might as well have been in kidding for all he cared. I couldn't stop myself. I wouldn't continue to shirk from the challenge in his eyes. I uttered one word, but that was all it took to light the fuse.

"Hulking."

I almost flinched away from him, knowing what I would have expected had we been alone, but reminded myself that we were in company and stood my ground. He simply sat there in stunned silence, but I could guess this wouldn't be the end of it. I hoped my newfound strength wouldn't fail me later.

I took full advantage of his silence and carried on a conversation with Jordan. As focused as I was on her, I let myself forget about the boys. Tom remained in seething silence, but surprisingly Nick wasn't willing to stay silent. To be fair, though, I wasn't being a very good host. I should have taken more care to remember we had company.

He interjected on Jordan and my latest topic, saying, "You make me feel uncivilized, Daisy. Can't you talk about crops or something?"

Internally, I chided myself. I should have been paying more attention to him and making him feel more included. I liked Nick, I really did. The last thing I wanted was for him to feel unwelcome in my home.

As I tried to come up with a reply, I noticed his attention had drifted to Jordan. Not for the first time that evening, I found myself wondering if it was for my sake or Jordan's that he wished to be included.

Tom chose then to break his silence. "Civilization's going to pieces!" he insisted loudly, as if daring anyone to disagree with him. "I've gotten to be a terrible pessimist about things. Have you read *The Rise of the Coloured Empires* by this man Goddard?" Leave it to Tom to further alienate our guest by straying even further into topics that would make Nick feel uncivilized.

I knew where Tom's rant was going and was hoping to interrupt him before he got started, but was at a loss for words.

Unfortunately, I couldn't find anything to say before Nick responded with a surprised, "Why, no."

Whether Tom was ignorant or uncaring that the subject only interested himself, he plowed ahead. "Well, it's a fine book, and everybody ought to read it. The idea is if we don't look out, the white race will be - will be utterly submerged. It's all scientific stuff. It's been proved."

I couldn't help rolling my eyes. A glance at Jordan told me she was feeling the same, although she had always been better at masking her feelings than I had. Nick, understandably confused at the violence with which Tom had introduced this new topic, and likely having nothing to add to it, stayed silent.

Trying to lighten the mood and hoping Tom would take a hint for once, I turned to Nick and pseudo-whispered, "Tom's getting very profound. He reads deep books with long words in them." I turned to him and started to ask, "What was that word we-" but that was as far as I had gotten before he interrupted. Apparently, he was not going to be distracted from his rant.

He rushed to tell Nick, "Well, these books are all scientific. This fellow has worked out the whole thing. It's up to us, who are the dominant race, to watch out or these other races will have control of things."

I didn't try to hide my annoyance this time. Of course, my brute of a husband would want to beat down anyone who even hints at threatening his "superior position he rightfully earned by being born rich and white". How one can earn a position just by "virtue" of being born is beyond me.

I couldn't stop myself from adding to Nick, my voice dripping with sarcasm, "We've got to beat them down". He looked startled, even more so when, after a moment, I winked at him.

Jordan had heard me and from the look she gave me, both concern and warning, I knew I might have said too much. Fortunately, always my knight in shining armor, Jordan jumped in to change the topic. To no one in particular, she said, "You ought to live in California-" but wasn't able to finish her thought before Tom cut her off.

"The idea is that we're Nordics. I am," he then looked at Nick, "and you are," and then to Jordan "and you are, and-" after a long pause, he nodded in my direction. I wasn't able to misunderstand his meaning. He didn't doubt my race, but was reluctant to include me because his ideas of "the superior, dominant race" didn't readily include me. It wasn't just me, but that I was a woman. He never shied away from making it painfully obvious that he thinks of women as submissive, subservient creatures who are below him in every way and readily treats them as such.

He knew enough of me to consider me far beneath him in virtue and strength. However, Jordan was a different story altogether.

Jordan fueled both his ire and respect. He couldn't ignore how loud and outspoken she was, and was forced to recognize the dominant traits in her person that he often displays in his own behavior. Therefore, Jordan merited more inclusion in his "superior, dominant race" than I had. She had earned her spot, while I had just barely qualified by the merit of my skin color alone. "And we've produced all the things that go to make civilization - oh science and art, and all that. Do you see?"

After a long silence in which no one felt comfortable asking what it was we were supposed to have seen, we were saved by the ringing of the phone. The shrill sound broke the spell over the room.

Tom was silent, and I jumped on the opportunity to turn the conversation to something else, anything else. I turned to Nick and said the first thing that popped into my mind. "I'll tell you a family secret." I wasn't sure where I was going with the statement. I looked around the room for inspiration when my eyes fell on the spot the butler had been standing. He had gone to answer the phone, but seeing his spot vacant gave me an idea. "It's about the butler's nose. Do you want to hear about the butler's nose?"

My dear cousin jumped at the subject change. "That's why I came over tonight."

I couldn't find words to express my gratitude to Nick for playing along, but I'm sure he saw the relief in my face.

"Well, he wasn't always a butler; he used to be the silver polisher for some people in New York that had a silver service for two hundred people. He had to polish it from morning till night until finally it began to affect his nose-"

I paused, unsure what to say next, but knowing I didn't have long before Tom might interrupt again. I struggled to figure out where my story was going, but Jordan came to my rescue. "Things went from bad to worse." I couldn't help but think how grateful I was, for not only her, but also for my cousin. What a pleasant party we would have made if it hadn't been for my husband.

"Yes. Things went from bad to worse, until finally he had to give up his position."

Before I could add anything else, the butler reentered and approached Tom, stooping down to whisper in his ear. I assumed that Tom would wave him off and have his excuses made to whomever was rude enough to phone during dinner. Had it just been us, he would have gone to answer it, but we had company and I hoped he would behave accordingly. However, a moment later, he rose and, without a single word to anyone, exited toward the phone.

I knew without a doubt who the culprit was. I glanced at Jordan and saw her eyes were narrowed at the door Tom had left through. I hoped it wasn't as obvious to Nick as it was to me and Jordan why Tom had left. Trying to distract him from thinking too deeply about it, I turned to Nick and said cheerily, "I love to see you at my table, Nick. You remind me of a-" I faltered and looked at Jordan for help, but her attention was still on the other room. I could feel the tension radiating off her in waves. The intensity of her feelings startled me for a moment. A second too long, I recovered myself and glanced around the room for inspiration of something, anything, to say.

What had I even been saying? He reminded me of something. Heaven knows what I was going to say to that. My eyes stalled on the floral arrangement and knowing the silence had gone on too long already, I blurted out, "...of a rose, an absolute rose." I turned to Jordan and added, "Doesn't he?" She didn't respond.

I turned to her, but she hadn't even turned in my direction. "An absolute rose?" I tried again. She still didn't look my way. I could only imagine the daggers she was glaring in Tom's general direction. I've only ever seen the full force of Jordan's temper once before, but I knew that when someone made the mistake of incurring her wrath, she was a force to be reckoned with.

It was a wonder he couldn't feel her anger from through the closed door.

Jordan was an astute observer, but she didn't need to be to know who Tom was talking to. Jordan, like the rest of the world, was privy to the world's worst kept secret of my husband's latest affair.

His cheating itself didn't bother me anymore, but as I have told him often and loudly, I would prefer he have the decency to hide it from the rest of the world. He couldn't even grant me that kindness.

I used to try to be the good little wife he wanted, but I would never be the person he wanted. He wanted a beautiful little fool who loved and admired him and ignored and excused all his faults. I had been for a while, but I couldn't continue to be. His faults were too glaring and, even if Jordan hadn't been in the picture, my good sense wouldn't allow me to continue to ignore all his faults and make excuses for him and his behavior.

He hadn't even waited until the conclusion of our honeymoon to select himself a mistress and there had been a long string of mistresses since. This latest one was hardly a surprise. They came and went so quickly. What was surprising was that this latest mistress didn't even have the decency to wait until the conclusion of our meal to demand my husband's attention. I had been doing what I could to ignore Jordan's anger and Nick's confusion, to tamp down and extinguish my own anger, but there was only so much I could take.

As I wrang my napkin in my hands, I followed Jordan's eyes to the door he had gone through. I couldn't believe he hadn't returned yet. Here I was entertaining his friend while he chatted up his mistress. Yes, Nick was my cousin, but first and foremost, he was Tom's friend. Now Tom was making a fool out of me in front of his friend, my cousin. Tom was allowing his mistress to make a fool of me in our own home. It was too much for me to take. I rose abruptly, threw down my napkin, and followed him.

I barged through the doorway, fully intent on giving him not just a piece of my mind, but the entirety of it.

I was trembling with anger. "How dare you-" but all it took was one look from him to still my tongue. I knew him well enough to know the look meant 'stop speaking immediately, or I will make damn sure you wish you had.' I felt utterly defeated. All it had taken was one look from him. He hadn't even had to utter a single word to steal my courage and replace my anger with fear.

I used to have more spark, but he had extinguished my spirit to a mere whisper of the flame it once was. The fear subsided and was quickly replaced with embarrassment. I stood rooted to the spot, unable to suffer the embarrassment of turning around and returning to the table without Tom.

I stood there silently and tried my best to tune out his hushed, angry conversation with the latest woman. I couldn't help but feel a small amount of triumph and solace that it appeared I wasn't the only vexing woman in his life. Thankfully, he was brief and hung up a few short moments later. Without looking at me, he slammed down the receiver and spun on his heel, storming back to the table, leaving me to trail in his wake. So much for presenting a united front. Not that I needed to put on any pretense with Jordan, but it wasn't just us today. Nick was here and I would rather my cousin not know everything that goes on here.

I had hoped to have a nice dinner, but Tom couldn't even give me that.

I reentered a moment behind Tom, and Jordan's eyes immediately flew to me. For Nick's sake, since I knew Jordan wouldn't be fooled, I adopted a smile and said in what I intended to be a bright tone, "It couldn't be helped!" Even to my own ears, my tone sounded forced.

When I dared a glance at Jordan, the fire in her eyes told me she was using all her restraint to stay quiet. I tried to smile reassuringly at her. After all, I was okay. From the lack of change in her face and her mood, I could guess it wasn't as reassuring as I had hoped.

I tried to start the conversation again, but I wasn't able to tune out the continued shrill ringing of the phone. After every ring, I wondered if Tom would get up again. If again, he would embarrass me by leaving our table with our guests to go speak with her again. Fortunately, Tom was smart enough not to rise again before the conclusion of our dinner. However, his mistress was stubborn and refused to take a hint, since the phone continued its ceaseless ringing.

Mercifully, dinner didn't last much longer and we were able to escape the shrill ringing by venturing away from the table.

The four of us stood outside for a moment. I glanced at Jordan and could tell she was weighing her options. I knew she badly wanted to be alone with me, but she knew as well as I did that with Nick around, Tom wouldn't leave me and Jordan alone. As Tom's "perfect wife" I was expected to entertain his guest until he decided to step in. Jordan hesitated one more moment before all but herding Tom to the library.

Thankfully, it didn't take much prodding. As much as I wanted to be alone with her, I needed to be away from Tom more. I loved her more than words could say for knowing, without my saying, how she could best support me in any situation. She knew me better than I knew myself.

Nick, who must have been enjoying my company, stayed with me. How it was possible he was enjoying himself around me tonight was anyone's guess. I had been hardly a good host, as angry with Tom as I had been, I hadn't been nearly as welcoming or hospitable as I should have been.

I walked a little ways to the porch, not looking behind to see if he followed, but I suspected he would. A moment after I settled onto the settee, he joined me. No longer caring if I was in his company or not, he was family after all, and he had seen enough tonight to already know most of my secrets, I did what I felt like doing and put my head in my hands with a defeated sigh. When I looked up again, he was watching me and a moment later, asked me something about Pammy. Normally, I would be happy to talk about her, but I suspected he didn't really care. I wasn't in the mood to indulge him and wasn't in the mood to talk simply for the sake of talking. He didn't know my daughter. As a matter of fact, despite him being family, he hardly knew me at all either.

Before I could think better of it, the thought slipped out. "We don't know each very well, Nick. Even if we are cousins."

It occurred to me then how odd it was that I had only met him once before, especially with his having gone to college with my husband. I thought about it for a moment, wondering if maybe he had been in the crowd that had come down for our wedding, but I knew he wasn't. For lack of anything else to say, I told him so. "You didn't come to my wedding."

He looked confused, understandably not following my disconnected thoughts, and simply responded, "I wasn't back from the war."

"That's true." Although I couldn't help wondering if he would have made any effort to attend had he been home. But that was in the past, and the truth remained; him and I were still virtually strangers.

It might have bothered me, but at the moment, I was grateful. When you can't be blessed with solitude to deal with your feelings, the company of a stranger to confide in was the next best thing. As much as I would have rather been alone or with Jordan right now, being with Nick wasn't unpleasant, and he did seem concerned and curious.

I had hoped once Tom and Jordan had left that Nick would give me some space of my own and go for a stroll of the grounds himself. I had hoped that maybe he was craving solitude, too, but no such luck. Well, if he wouldn't grant me solitude, the least he could do is lend a sympathetic ear.

"Well, I've had a very bad time, Nick, and I'm pretty cynical about everything." He wasn't subtle about his discomfort, but I refused to feel bad. He could have given me a moment of solitude, but he hadn't. I was surprised at his lack of social grace though when instead of asking about my trouble or even just offering sympathy, he tried to turn the conversation to something he imagined I would find more pleasant, my daughter.

At any other time, that would have done wonders to endear me to him, but all he said was, "I suppose she talks, and — eats, and everything." Of all the idiotic things to say to a woman about her daughter, he managed to find a way to ask about her that made it clear he couldn't care less.

"Oh, yes." What else was I supposed to say to such a thoughtless question? Unluckily for him, bringing up Pammy made me think about my earlier thoughts. I couldn't help saying it, knowing it would make him even more uncomfortable, but not caring enough to stop. "Listen, Nick; let me tell you what I said when she was born. Would you like to hear?"

He didn't seem so sure, but responded quickly all the same. "Very much."

"It'll show you how I've gotten to feel about - things. Well, she was less than an hour old and Tom was God knows where."

With God knows who. By then I had long since abandoned hope of him caring for me, but really genuinely hoped for our child's sake that he would be a loving, attentive father. But yet again, I was let down. Yet again, I had expected Tom to do the decent thing, had thought he might do the right thing, but I should have known better.

"I woke up out of the ether with an utterly abandoned feeling and asked the nurse right away if it was a boy or a girl."

I held on to hope even then that if it were the little boy Tom wanted that he would be happy enough to be there for his son. I hoped against hope that it wasn't a girl. I knew firsthand just how difficult it was to grow up to be a woman without the power to stand up for herself and go after what she wants in life. A second-class citizen without the right to make her own decisions about her life.

The nurse's next words had since been branded into my mind.

"She told me it was a girl, and so I turned my head away and wept. 'All right,' I said. 'I'm glad it's a girl. And I hope she'll be a fool - that's the best thing a girl can be in this world, a beautiful little fool."

I vowed to do everything I could to protect her and shield her from the cruelties of the world. From the men of the world, my husband included. I had been succeeding, but at a steep cost. I had almost no relationship with my daughter thanks to Tom. If I had to suffer the distance from her to protect her from him, I could at least rest a little easier knowing she was safe.

I did everything I could to keep her shielded, but the older she got, the more she noticed. She didn't seem to hold any fondness for him and I wondered if on some level she knew he wasn't a good man.

As a father, the best I could say for him was that he provided a nice home for her to grow up in. If it couldn't be a happy home, at least it was a nice one.

A cricket sounded in the garden, startling me out of my thoughts. Wide eyed, I took in my surroundings and saw Nick sitting there staring at me. He was an unusually quiet person, and I had managed to forget his presence.

Knowing he thought me crazy and no longer caring, I said, "You see, I think everything's terrible anyhow. Everybody thinks so — the most advanced people. And I *know*. I've been everywhere and seen everything and done everything. Sophisticated - God, I'm sophisticated!"

As if all the sophistication in the world could make you happy. Looking up, I saw Nick had become worried to the point of concern for my sanity. I should have cared, but couldn't bring myself to. What was the point? He hardly knew me anyway. Seeing he had my attention, he quickly suggested we rejoin the others. I assented and he sprung up to head back to them with me. I was slower to rise and could feel his eyes on me, willing me to hurry. He seemed to think I was prone to another outburst if he stayed alone with me for much longer.

CHAPTER EIGHTEEN
Daisy

When we returned, I saw to my surprise that Jordan had been reading to Tom. My heart swelled with gratitude for her. I knew just how much effort it would have taken her to swallow her pride and anger to entertain him just to give me a few moments of peace. She looked up when I came in and didn't wait a moment before throwing down the newspaper with a, "To be continued in our very next issue."

She stood up and shot a quick, loaded look before announcing to the room, "Ten o'clock," despite not having checked the time. "Time for this good girl to go to bed." I barely stifled a laugh and had to fight to not roll my eyes. Jordan was many things, but subtle was not one of them. To try to explain her retreat, I told Nick, "Jordan's going to play in the tournament tomorrow over at Westchester."

He looked at her again as if seeing her for the first time, and said with a mix of surprise and respect, "Oh - you're *Jordan* Baker."

His eyes sank lower, which had me boiling, but she ignored him.

Paying him no extra mind, she bid everyone goodnight, and softly reminded me, "Wake me at eight, won't you?"

I couldn't help laughing. A stampede couldn't wake her. She was a notoriously heavy sleeper, and was never happy to be woken, until she was awake enough to realize it was me. "If you'll get up," I responded with a teasing smile.

She rolled her eyes. "I will."

She turned and started up the stairs. Before she disappeared into the hallway, she turned and added as an afterthought, "Good night, Mr. Carraway. See you anon."

Watching her dramatic exit, I couldn't help wanting to vex her a little. "Of course you will. In fact, I think I'll arrange a marriage. Come over often, Nick, and I'll sort of – oh..." I made the mistake of looking up and the look on Jordan's face nearly caused me to burst into laughter. I caught my breath a moment, trying to keep a straight face, "...fling you together. You know - lock you up accidentally in linen closets and push you out to sea in a boat, and all that sort of thing."

Jordan didn't let me go on. To be honest, I was surprised she let me get as far as I did. She interrupted, saying, "Good night. I haven't heard a word."

I knew she would give me a hard time for the Nick comments later, but I couldn't help myself.

After she left, Tom, seemingly oblivious to the fact that I had been joking, told Nick, "She's a nice girl." Just as I was thinking that was probably the nicest thing I'd ever heard him say about her, he continued, "They oughtn't to let her run around the country this way."

There it was.

I really should have known he would find some way to demean her. I suppose in his mind, it was unladylike for her to be traipsing around the country by herself. He must have thought she ought to have a husband or a family telling her what to do and controlling her as women ought to be controlled. How convenient that his aversion to her being here had nothing to do with her looking out for me and ensuring my happiness despite his best efforts to see me miserable.

Of course, he would find a way to paint her spending time with me as a defect in her character, or at the very least, as an issue of serious neglect on the part of those who should be "minding her". I glared at Tom, not bothering to hide my distaste about his comments. I couldn't stand his arrogance, especially when it came to Jordan.

If he thought I was going to let him talk about her that way, he was sorely mistaken. "Who oughtn't to?"

"Her family."

Ignoring the fact that I needed Jordan here more than I could express, a woman ought to be able to wander as she pleased. However, I knew he wouldn't agree, so I stuck to the facts. "Her family is one aunt, about a thousand years old."

But I knew that wouldn't be enough. I could already see he was trying to force her out of my life, force more of a separation than Jordan's golf career required. He was growing tired of her and, after all, his own happiness was the only thing that mattered in this household.

I could see he was trying to get Nick to agree with him. I couldn't let that happen, so I added an argument that I knew he couldn't refuse. One that might be agreeable even to him. "Besides, Nick's going to look after her, aren't you, Nick?"

I sent a pleading look in Nick's direction. I knew if Jordan overheard the conversation that she would hate every moment of it, but her being here was too important. So much of my life was out of control, but I needed this. I needed Jordan here. She was my light and my happiness. My sanity and my saving grace. I could not, would not, lose her company simply because it didn't please Tom. Without Jordan around, he could, and would, go back to treating me however he pleased. She stood up for me when I hadn't been able to myself. That he desired her absence was hardly a surprise, honestly I was surprised he had taken this long to voice it.

Nick didn't respond as quickly as I would have liked. He just looked in between Tom and I as we waited expectantly.

Unwilling to wait longer, I added, "She's going to spend lots of weekends out here this summer. I think the home influence will be very good for her."

I glanced in Tom's direction, daring him to say more, but apparently he was at a loss for more excuses. Nick must have finally felt the awkwardness of the silence and blurted out, "Is she from New York?"

Wondering to myself why the answer could possibly matter, I answered, "From Louisville. Our white girlhood was passed together there. Our beautiful white-" I was planning to describe Jordan and my time together in Louisville.

I was suppressing a smirk at my description of it being white. White was for purity and innocence, and my Louisville reputation was anything but. Louisville itself was hell, but Jordan made it bearable. Back then, it was hard to imagine where our futures were headed, but in our innocence, we never imagined the world would separate us.

I was naïve enough to imagine Jordan would always be by my side and that life would never conspire to separate us. That was before I discovered how cruel and uncaring this world could be. It was unclear just how much of that I would have expressed aloud, but I wasn't given a chance. Tom hadn't missed my reference to myself as innocent and didn't let me continue. He suddenly demanded, "Did you give Nick a little heart to heart talk on the veranda?"

Despite Jordan's distraction attempt, mine and Nick's lingering absence didn't escape his notice. I glanced at Nick, hoping to appear nonchalant, but pleading to him with my eyes to stay quiet. "Did I? I can't seem to remember, but I think we talked about," struggling for inspiration I quickly racked my memory and landed on the first topic acceptable to Tom I could think of, "the Nordic race. Yes, I'm sure we did. It sort of crept up on us and first thing you know-"

Luckily enough, since I hadn't yet determined where to go with the rest of thought, Tom, as he usually did, cut me off. He didn't even address me; instead he told Nick, "Don't believe everything you hear, Nick."

Nick hesitated a moment before agreeing with my statement that he had heard nothing at all. His discomfort was evident and predictably, a few minutes later he rose and bid his goodbyes. As I watched him go to leave, I was struck by inspiration and called to him, "Wait!"

He turned around and waited as I continued, "I forgot to ask you something, and it's important. We heard you were engaged to a girl out West."

The answer to this carried a lot of weight for my future plans. Tom, sensing no danger or great importance in the answer, added, "That's right. We heard you were engaged."

Nick seemed, as he often had in our short acquaintanceship, both confused and uncomfortable. He blurted out, "It's a libel. I'm too poor."

Delighted, but needing to be sure, I pressed a bit more. "But we heard it. We heard it from three people, so it must be true."

He denied it again, this time convincingly enough that I believed him, and again made his goodbyes. I extracted promises from him to visit soon.

Before he drove away, he took one last look at me. His face exuded pity. It was embarrassing that after our short acquaintanceship, he was already well acquainted enough with our marriage to know I ought to be pitied. As he drove away, I quickly turned and crossed the drive, entering the house once again.

Unsure if Tom was planning to exchange more words, I hastened to Jordan's room to deny him the opportunity.

I knew she wanted to talk since she retired early, and none too subtly. Besides, I needed to talk to her about Gatsby. With everything with Tom, I had almost forgotten. Before I could make it to her room, though, Tom intercepted me. He grabbed my arm hard and whipped me around to face him. "What was the meaning of that?" he asked in a low, dangerous voice.

I gave him my best innocent and confused look and asked, "The meaning of what? My asking about Nick? I saw how he was looking at Jordan and wanted to know if there were any grounds for my hopes of a possible match. I would love to see my dear Jordan happily settled."

He loosened his grip a little, the surprise showing plainly on his face. Pressing my luck since my distraction seemed to be working, I added, "I've been trying all night to speak to him about any attachments back home, since it seems to me he would make a lovely husband for my dear Jordan. I even led him outside, away from her, to try to determine if there was any hope for my wishes, but he still wasn't forthcoming. Why don't you give it a go and ask him the next time you see him about his impressions of her? I really do think they would make a good match."

While this was one of the boldest lies I had ever ventured to tell, he bought it. Tom was always quick to assume he was the smartest person in any room, so he readily believed he was too smart to be lied to.

Furthermore, I had hit upon the one explanation of my behavior that would be acceptable to him. He could easily believe me to be a woman who was focused on foolish things such as coupling off her friends.

Despite having been married three years, he still knew shockingly little of myself or my character. However, it made things easier for me that he was so easily fooled.

He loosened his hold on my wrist and said, "Nick could be just the thing she needs to really settle down and become a better woman." I knew better than to object or say anything, but the thought of some man making my dear Jordan into a "better woman" was almost enough to overpower my better judgement. However, I somehow managed to stay quiet, thinking the worst was over.

I was mistaken, since he kept going. "She really needs a good, strong man to put her in her place. I'm not quite sure if Nick is up for the task, but if I take him under my wing, he just might be right for the job."

I needed a moment to recover from my shock and anger at his audacity to speak to me about her that way. Lucky for me, Jordan came around the corner at that moment. I saw her look appraisingly at us, her eyes instantly moving to his hand still grasping my arm. I didn't even have time to blush or hope she hadn't heard us before she interjected, saying, "Daisy dearest, I am having trouble with my dress. Would you be a dear and come help me?"

Normally, I would have blushed enough to make my entire body crimson at the request and implications, but I was too startled to be embarrassed. She turned to Tom and with a civility I don't know how she possessed, she said, "We may be awhile; dresses are such a pain."

With that, she crossed the space between us, placed her arm under mine, knowing I needed the support, and ushered me to her room.

Once safely in her room, I collapsed into her arms. The tears came out before they could be stopped. She held me tightly and let me feel what I needed to.

When the tears stopped, she pulled back a little and asked gently, "What happened? Did he hurt you?" I shook my head and took a deep breath, knowing she needed and deserved an explanation.

"No, not this time, although that might be just because of your presence. You make me braver and him more cautious."

"You are brave, my love, and I promise I won't let him hurt you."

"I don't know what I have done to deserve you, but you and I both know that it's a promise you can't be sure you can keep."

"I am sure of it. Over my dead body will he hurt you again."

"Please don't talk like that."

She sighed. "Okay, okay, but if he didn't hurt you, what's bothering you?"

"Tom's trying to get rid of you. He wants to marry you off to Nick. He did his usual 'as a single woman she shouldn't be gallivanting about' rant.

Nothing really out of the ordinary, but when he started talking about Nick being the one to put you in your place, I damn near lost it."

She put her face in her hands and started shaking. Immediately forgetting my own feelings, I grabbed hold of her hands and squeezed. "Please don't worry." This only served to cause her to shake harder.

She kept shaking, but instead of sobs, the noise sounded suspiciously like laughter. As gently as I could, I pulled her hands apart to see my suspicions were correct. She was shaking with laughter. Feeling affronted, I demanded, "And what's so funny? I would love to be in on the joke."

Looking up, she saw the annoyance on my face and tried to still her laughter. "You really think that's the first time some man spoke of putting me in my place? He's not the first and won't be the last. If I got offended every time I heard something like that, I wouldn't know a moment of peace." I kept silent, so she continued, "Do you really believe me to be so easily in danger of being controlled?"

She did have a point. She was the most stubborn and strong-willed woman I had ever known. But I wouldn't be so easily distracted or made to feel better.

"You know as well as I do that once Tom gets an idea in his head, he makes it near impossible for others to resist. I know how strong you are, but you know how often he gets his way."

"Then maybe I won't resist."

I couldn't believe my ears. I must not have heard her right. A million thoughts and feelings rushed through my head. The most prominent of which were surprise and jealousy. Not willing to stay silent, and sure she couldn't have said what I heard, I uttered "What?"

Her trademark smirk was back. All she replied was, "You heard me."

"You can't mean that. He means for you to marry Nick, to settle down and become a 'real woman'."

Her eyes glinted with mischief. "I think a man could do me some good. I mean, did you see him? With his lanky boyish figure, I really could do worse."

I knew she had to be teasing with me. I needed her to be teasing with me. "You can't be serious? Nick? Of all people, Nick? My cousin?"

"Who better? Wouldn't it be lovely to be related, my dear?"

Now I knew she was teasing me, but I needed to hear her admit it. "You would actually consider it?"

"He wouldn't be the first man in my life."

Now I was actually getting frustrated. "But you can't want him!"

"And why can't I?" Her smirk had widened into a full grin.

"You know why." It took me until then to realize what she was doing. Even knowing what she was doing, it was nearly impossible to stop my jealousy.

Her grin broadened as she said, "I don't really see a reason."

Damn that girl.

"I'll give you a reason," was all I could get out before hastily crossing the room and pushing her more roughly than usual onto her bed. As I fell with her, I crushed her lips against mine with all the passion that had been building up from our heated moment earlier. I felt the vibrations of her soft moan against my lips. After a few more moments, I pulled away a little.

She laughed a little, saying, "And I thought I was the jealous one. Jealousy looks good on you."

At that, I couldn't help but blush.

She noticed and brushed her finger lightly against my cheek, causing my blush to deepen and her to laugh playfully. "There's my girl, although I can't say I mind you taking control."

Feeling much happier and more playful, I giggled and said, "You'll have to be careful, my love. Before you know it I'll be the one in charge."

Her response would have made a lady of the night blush. Then she grabbed tightly to me and rolled us over, positioning herself on top of me. Desperately wanting her lips on mine, I went to reach for her, but she held my arms down.

"Remind me again who's in charge."

I giggled, but didn't respond.

She leaned closer, and closer, her lips parting slightly as she leaned in. She stopped a breath away from my lips and whispered, "Who's in charge here?"

I knew all I had to do was say her name and her lips would come crashing down on mine, but I wasn't ready to give in. I stayed silent. Her surprise was evident, but she knew it wouldn't be long.

She stayed close another moment before leaning toward my ear to whisper something to me, but to my surprise, instead of whispering, she nibbled on my ear. I stiffed a moan as best I could, but still didn't cave.

She placed kisses up and down my neck and I knew I wouldn't be able to hold out much longer. As I felt her work her way back up to my neck, getting closer and closer, my need grew. I needed to feel her lips on mine again more than I had ever needed anything. "You," I whispered, and in an instant her lips were on mine. Knowing we didn't have much time, we made the most of the few more minutes we had together.

That was the sum of our relationship, the stolen moments we were able to share when I could sneak away from my husband. Luckily for me, the moments had been happening more and more lately, curtesy of my husband's new mistress. But unlike Tom, what I had with Jordan was much more than a simple fling like the countless women he had entertained since we first took our vows.

Jordan was different; she was my other half. She made me a better person and fueled a passion in me that I didn't know was possible. She was the only person I have ever felt so deeply for, and now that I had her, I was determined to keep her.

The night was quiet in a way that most nights here aren't. Normally, nights were for entertaining, filled with crowds of people, some new faces, some regulars. They always came in hoards and always demanded so much from me, always wanting more. They were more than happy to come gawk at me and my home, drink my liquor, and go wild in West Egg, but the very same people would stick up their noses at me in East Egg. I was only good enough for their company at my own house.

Even as guests in my home, they didn't spare me their respect or civility. I heard the rumors floating around. They said my money was dirty, and while I knew they said that of everyone in West Egg, I couldn't help but cringe at how close to the truth they were.

What I have never understood is why time passing, why money being passed from generation to generation is all it takes to give it legitimacy. While my money wasn't the cleanest, I knew I wasn't the only one. The only difference between myself and the East Egg-ers who stuck their noses up at me was that their grandparents or great grandparents had been the ones to do the dirty work. You don't become as wealthy as they are without greasing a few palms, without getting down in the muck. It's impossible to come out spotless and as rich as they are.

At the risk of sounding arrogant, their fortunes are small compared to mine. That's one of the reasons I threw the parties I did every night. It made me feel like one of them. They wouldn't socialize with me on their own terms, so I threw parties grand enough that everyone who was anyone was dying to come. Scoring an invitation meant you were somebody, even more so because most showed up without being invited. I used to send out invitations, but have long since stopped. I never needed to. All I needed to do was throw the party, and that was enough. They would all come.

Well everyone, except her. The other reason I had been throwing these lavish parties was my long lost love; the one that got away. She haunted my dreams and nightmares alike. Long before I built myself up from nothing, I had fallen hard for her. She was everything I wanted and everything I dreamed of for myself. Had I met her now, with everything I have now, I would have had her in a heartbeat. She would have been mine without question, but life has never been easy for me.

I had to make my own luck in the world, and I met her a while before I hit my lucky streak. I had promised to make something of myself; I had promised her the world, and I knew I could deliver. I knew, even then, that I was destined for great things, but she didn't. She couldn't wait for me, or more accurately, she wouldn't. I asked her to. I all but begged, and still she wouldn't. She married some lucky bastard named Tom Buchanan. I had heard of her engagement and begged her not to go through with it.

I had known how close I was to coming up in the world, how close I was to being considered worthy of her, but she didn't believe me. I wasn't enough for her, so she chose him.

I knew then, and still know, that she never loved him. She couldn't have. She felt too deeply for me. What we had was too real for her feelings to have gone away. She gave me her innocence. That isn't something a girl soon forgets or simply moves on from.

I haven't been able to forget it myself. Sure there had been Violet, Rose, and even Lily, who I was briefly fond of, but none of them held a candle to my Daisy, with her natural charm, beauty, and her indefinable grace. There was something about her. She exuded wealth and good breeding.

As a young man, I was instantly drawn to her; she was my ideal woman in every sense of the word. Once I had a taste of her, and a glimpse of her lifestyle, my ambitions grew to new heights. Sure, I had always been ambitious before, but she gave me a goal.

I knew now she was the only one for me, and I told myself that one day I would make something of myself and that would show her. She would grow to regret her decision; I knew she would.

When I started with these parties, I hoped one day she might wander in. I dreamed of her often. Vixen that she was, I couldn't escape her memory, not that I truly wanted to.

On nights like tonight, it would have been impossible to sleep. It would have been impossible to quiet my restless thoughts of her, so I gave in to my urges, silly as they were.

I had thought the long walk to my pier would do me some good. I reasoned the fresh air, exercise, and change of scenery would help calm my nerves and tire me out, but I knew the truth. I was only kidding myself. I did it for her.

Everything I did nowadays was with her in mind; tonight was no different, except that tonight I allowed myself the luxury of solitude.

Solitude was something I had grown unaccustomed to. I lived for the parties in the hopes that she would wander in.

What I hoped to happen, I can't quite say. I longed to see her experience one of my parties, to see her again after all these years, to see what kind of effect I would still have over her.

I even longed to meet her dolt of a husband that she chose over me. I had never met the man, but knew he would be odious. I fantasized about seeing the regret and longing on her face when she finally came face to face with me again after all those years. Longed to see the pain it would cause her to see how high I had risen, how much I had made of myself, and how much she missed out on. I dreamed she would beg to be mine again, but that was where the dreams stopped.

Even in my wildest dreams, I don't know what I would do. Even I don't know how I would respond if she truly begged. Would I take her back? Push her to leave the brute and run away with her? Make an honest woman of her and marry her myself? Let the world see how much of a vixen she truly is and lure her back into my bed and make her the laughingstock of society? Laugh in her face before shutting her out of my life forever? There was something to be said for any of these, but what I would actually do, I couldn't begin to say.

When I finally reached the pier, I knew what I had known all along, the fresh air didn't do a thing for me. The change of scenery didn't help. It might have, had I picked a better destination, but I let myself come here.

It was a clear night, and on such a clear night, there was no hiding the object I sought. I hardly even noticed the clear skies and the calm expanse of water before me. I only had eyes for the light I could just barely see in the distance, the green siren call from across the bay. Even on cloudy nights, when I couldn't see the light itself, it called to me.

On nights like tonight, when I was weak, I allowed myself ten minutes of hope. Ten minutes of unrestrained longing, of imagining what it would be like to have her in my arms again. I let myself wonder what things would be like with her by my side instead of separated from me by a bay that might as well have been an entire ocean for how far she was from me.

The green light was all that remained of her, staring across the bay into that light, the only piece left of her I had, I let myself dream of her. I let myself imagine everything I knew I could never have. I imagined how society would respect and revere me with such a well-bred beauty like her on my arm. No one would dare to disrespect me then. No one would ask, or even wonder, where my money came from. Well, they might wonder, but it wouldn't matter. As her rich husband, no one would dare ask.

No more being called dirty, no more being looked down on, no more being ignored. They would respect me; they would have to.

I gave into my thoughts for a few more moments before turning away, back toward the lonely expanse of a house I called home. With a sigh, I began the trek back to the house, but didn't restrict myself from one last glance.

The light had grown to stand for my hopes of a life with her, my dreams of her and of legitimizing myself above anyone's scorn. It was just a green light at the end of a pier, but it wasn't just any green light at the end of *any* old pier, it was a green light at the end of *her* pier, and that made all the difference. It was the only piece of her I could find, and so it became my world.

My favorite part of the day was standing at the end of my pier. Sometimes, as lost in my thoughts as I was, I wouldn't even notice until minutes later that my arm had been outstretched toward the light. The green siren never failed to call me, and as much as I liked to pretend otherwise, I knew the truth. As long as she called, I would answer.

Every part of me was ruled by that green siren, that vixen across the bay. It was pathetic, a weakness I couldn't, wouldn't, let others see, but a weakness nonetheless. Every time I made the return trip to my home, I chastised myself for my weakness. Every time I resolved it would be the last, but every time without fail on a clear night like tonight, I knew she would call and I would be there.

It wasn't until the next morning that I remembered to ask Jordan about her Gatsby comment.

"So about last night," I started.

Jordan was lounging on our favorite sofa, her head sprawled in my lap, with her eyes closed. She opened them with a little groan and turned her storm-cloud eyes to me. "What about it?"

I looked around quickly to ensure we were alone. We were, thankfully. Tom was out for the day, possibly the night, if I was lucky.

"What was that whole thing about a Gatsby?"

She cocked an eyebrow at me. "Gatsby? What Gatsby?" she asked in a high-pitched voice that I guessed was her best approximation of mine. I narrowed my eyes at her, but her grin was enough to make me smile, too.

"Is it really him? What have you heard?"

She frowned. "I'm not sure yet. I haven't heard much, just the name thrown around. Whoever he is, he's been throwing massive parties. It's all anyone's been talking about lately."

"You mean the West Egg parties people are raving about?"

She nodded. "They're being thrown by some Gatsby. There's always a ton of people and liquor. I have no idea how he does it or why. The huge mansion is more than enough to show he has money. Why throw away the huge amounts it must cost to entertain that many people and keep the liquor flowing with the prohibition? If it is your Gatsby, he's come into more money than he knows what to do with."

Jay was always dreaming big, and I used to believe he would make something of himself. "It's not impossible, but really, what are the odds?"

"I'm pretty determined to find that out for myself."

"What do you mean?"

"I'm going to crash one of his little parties and find out for myself."

I hadn't expected that. "Why?"

"Something entertaining to do." She laughed at the incredulous look on my face. "Okay, fine, I figured it'll bother you until we know if it's him, and I don't want you worrying about it a second longer than you have to."

She was right. I was anxious to know if it was him. I didn't like the idea of him being so close. "I would love to know if it's him. The thought of him just across the bay plotting, scheming, and dreaming about me makes my skin crawl."

She pushed herself up off my lap and stretched before turning back to me. "Then consider it done. I'll find out, and if it is him, I'll drive him off."

I laughed at that and pulled her into me, kissing her quickly. I pulled away a few seconds later, not daring to kiss her longer. Tom wasn't around, but the staff still were, and we weren't in a private room. It was too risky to be too close in the sitting room.

"Do be discrete, love."

She smirked. "When am I not?"

I hoped for my sake and hers that it wasn't him. Discretion wasn't her strong suit, and I knew she wasn't joking when she promised to run him off.

Maybe Daisy was right, discretion wasn't really my strong suit. The moment we got to Gatsby's mansion, I ditched my party to go snooping around.

It took me a few minutes of asking people to figure out that no one here seemed to know Gatsby. They knew of him, but even at his own parties, at his own house, he seemed to be more of a legend than an actual person. The few people I asked about where I might find him looked at me like I was crazy, so I had taken to wandering about the mansion looking for any clues I could.

I didn't know if it was Daisy's Gatsby, but I was determined to stay at the party until I found out. I wasn't sure if I would recognize him if I saw him, though. It had been so long ago that I had seen him with her, so I was looking for any sort of monogram or personalization or even a piece of mail that would give me his first name. Unfortunately, I didn't find anything.

After a frustrating search, I figured I should rejoin my party before I was missed. I had come with some people I knew from golf and their wives. I wouldn't call them friends, but it was better than turning up alone.

I exited the mansion, pausing at the top of his ridiculously ornate marble stairs and surveyed the crowd for my party. Before I spotted them, I heard, "Hello!" I looked in the voice's direction and was surprised to see Daisy's cousin Nick, all dressed up in a white flannel suit, making a beeline for me.

I had a mere moment to gain my composure and pretend he didn't look ridiculous before he was in front of me. In the sea of wild drunk partygoers, here was bondsman Nick in his pristine white flannel suit. He clearly hadn't understood the nature of these parties. No wonder he was running over to me.

Although how he hadn't heard about the parties was a mystery. You couldn't talk to anyone lately without hearing about the mysterious Gatsby and his roaring parties. People were taking to calling him the party king of New York City. I wondered for a moment what Nick was even doing here until I remembered how close he lived. "I thought you might be here. I remembered you lived next door to-"

Before I could finish, I was interrupted by two girls wearing matching bright yellow dresses. "Hello!" they cried in unison. "Sorry you didn't win."

Their synchronicity was uncanny. I knew they must be talking about one of the golf tournaments I had played lately, but I didn't recognize them and wasn't sure if I was supposed to.

"You don't know who we are," one of them said.

"But we met you here about a month ago," the other finished.

Ah, so they were drunk. It was easier to play along than correct them. That was always the way with drunk people.

"You've dyed your hair since then." I said. Apparently, I needn't have said anything though, since they were already gone.

With nothing better to do, I slung my arm around Nick and followed them. They thought they knew me, so maybe they would be helpful.

Nick and I took a seat at their garden table. It was the two of them and three men, the yellow twins introduced us to them, but in the noise of the party, I didn't hear them.

"Do you come to these parties often?" I loudly asked the yellow girl closest to me.

"The last one was the one I met you at," I internally groaned. Maybe I hadn't picked the right group to attach myself to. Clearly, they wouldn't be any help if they didn't even realize I wasn't whomever they met last month. "Wasn't it for you, Lucille?"

The other yellow girl, Lucille apparently, nodded enthusiastically. "I like to come. I never care what I do, so I always have a good time. When I was here last, I tore my gown on a chair, and he asked me my name and address - inside of a week I got a package from Croirier's with a new evening gown in it."

I couldn't stop myself from asking, "Did you keep it?" I knew she did before she responded, though. The type of people that came here didn't care a wit about using and abusing the hospitality of this mysterious Gatsby. Why would she turn down a gifted dress despite having done nothing to earn it besides being a clumsy drunk?

Sure enough, she continued, "Sure I did. I was going to wear it tonight, but it was too big in the bust and had to be altered. It was gas blue with lavender beads. Two hundred and sixty-five dollars."

I didn't know how much longer I could sit here and listen to them prattle on and brag about things they should be ashamed of. I was moving to excuse myself, when the other yellow girl chimed in, "There's something funny about a fellow that'll do a thing like that. He doesn't want any trouble with *anybody*."

"Who doesn't?" Nick asked. I almost rolled my eyes. He seemed sober enough, but clearly wasn't if he hadn't followed the conversation so far.

"Gatsby," said the other yellow girl. "Somebody told me-"

She paused, and I didn't hesitate to lean in. Maybe she would give me some helpful information about him.

In a quieter voice, she continued, "Somebody told me they thought he killed a man once."

The men, Nick included, all leaned closer at that.

"I don't think it's so much *that*," Lucille said skeptically, "It's more that he was a German spy during the war."

I saw one man nodding vigorously. "I heard that from a man who knew all about him, grew up with him in Germany."

If that was true, then it couldn't have been Daisy's Gatsby.

I felt a quick wave of relief before the first girl chimed back in, "Oh, no, it couldn't be that, because he was in the American army during the war."

Back to square one. This Gatsby was in the army and so was Daisy's Gatsby, but so were most of the men in the country. I was going to have to find someone who actually knew something about him if I had any hope of bringing news back to Daisy.

I made my excuses and went to find my party, and wasn't surprised when Nick followed. Apparently, I had a little white flannel-suited shadow for the night.

A few hours later, the party was still in full swing. The champagne was flowing, people were dancing, peals of laughter were heard every few seconds and yet the host was still nowhere to be seen.

Nick, my ever-faithful shadow, hadn't left my side, but he was a good deal more drunk than he had been when we started. He and I were sitting with a young girl with a grating laugh and a well-dressed man who seemed to find her charming. I was about to switch tables again when the man leaned over to speak to Nick.

"Your face is familiar. Weren't you in the First Division during the war?"

"Why yes. I was in the Twenty-eighth Infantry."

The man smiled at that. It was an easy smile that even I found charming. "I was in the Sixteenth until June nineteen-eighteen. I knew I'd seen you somewhere before."

I was distracted by a large group of dancers who were dancing rather clumsily and didn't catch the rest of their conversation. When I turned back, Nick was more relaxed. "Having a gay time now?" I asked.

He nodded with a champagne smile. "Much better." Then he turned back to his new friend. "This is an unusual party for me. I haven't even seen the host. I live over there," he paused and gesticulated wildly in the vague direction where his house must be, "and this man Gatsby sent over his chauffeur with an invitation."

The man looked confused for a moment before saying plainly, "I'm Gatsby."

I couldn't believe my luck. I instantly paid more attention to him, but there was nothing that remarkable about him. He was tall, blonde, and well dressed. The only thing that really set him apart was the easy smile. He was a blond army man named Gatsby with a remarkable smile. It was starting to look more possible this was Daisy's Gatsby after all.

"What!" Nick exclaimed in alarm, almost knocking his latest champagne glass off the table as he did. He recovered himself after a moment and said, "Oh, I beg your pardon."

The man's smile didn't falter. "I thought you knew, old sport." His look grew sheepish. "I'm afraid I'm not a very good host."

I was about to use this as an excuse to ask his first name when a butler came rushing over to him with an urgent call. He made his excuses and said he would try to come back later. I hoped he would, because now that I had seen him, I couldn't leave without finding out if this was Daisy's Gatsby.

Nick turned to me the moment Gatsby was gone and asked, "Who is he? Do you know?"

I suppose he thought I knew because I was here, but I hadn't a clue. After all, I had tried asking him about Gatsby the other day at Daisy's house. I shrugged, trying to act like it didn't matter to me. "He's just a man named Gatsby."

"Where is he from, I mean? And what does he do?"

The questions of the hour. If I knew any of that, I wouldn't be here searching for clues. The way Nick was looking at me, though, I could see the champagne sloshing around in his brain and knew he wanted to be entertained, so I used one of the random pieces of gossip I had heard that night about Gatsby.

"Now *you're* started on the subject. Well, he told me once he was an Oxford man." He didn't, but I had heard it tonight. "However, I don't believe it." It wasn't any more credible than the other wild rumors I had heard all night. Why would that one be likely to be true when the others certainly weren't?

"Why not?" he asked, hanging on my every word.

I shrugged. "I don't know. I just don't think he went there." The only other thing I knew about him was his parties. "Anyhow, he gives large parties. And I like large parties. They're so intimate. At small parties, there isn't any privacy."

The orchestra leader cut off Nick's response by loudly announcing they were playing a score at Gatsby's special request.

I looked in their direction and sure enough, Gatsby was standing above them, alone on his lavish marble stairs, surveying his party kingdom.

When it was over, I turned back to Nick and saw he had been watching Gatsby, too. I was about to comment when I was interrupted by a, "I beg your pardon."

I looked quickly and saw it was the same butler that had announced Gatsby had a call earlier. I wondered what he could want. I looked at Nick, but the butler was looking at me.

"Miss Baker?" he asked. I nodded. "I beg your pardon, but Mr. Gatsby would like to speak to you alone."

Of all the things I guessed he might say, that hadn't made the list. Gatsby had barely even looked at me when he was with me and Nick earlier.

"With me?" I clarified.

The butler nodded, "Yes, madame," and turned, indicating I should follow him. With a raise of my eyebrows at Nick, I hurried along after him sure this would be my one and only chance to find out if this was Daisy's Gatsby, and if it was, what he wanted.

"It was him!" I hurriedly whispered the moment I shut Daisy's door.

Daisy's smile fell from her now pale face. She looked ghastly. "Are you sure?"

I hadn't expected this strong of a reaction. I knew she didn't care about him, but I didn't really think she would be this anxious either. The plan I had been turning over in my mind since I talked to him last night might not work now.

I nodded.

"How do you know?"

I took a deep breath and dove into recounting the night. I told her what he told me, about how he was in town to find her, how he wanted to be with her.

"But he knows I'm married," she said.

"That's the part that had me rushing here to tell you. He said he didn't care, and that there wasn't anything love and money couldn't fix."

"How arrogant," she muttered.

I chuckled, and she whipped around and glared at me. I put my hands up in defense, still chuckling. "You're right, it is."

She crossed her arms and said, "I can't believe him."

I put my hands on her forearms, making her pause and look at me.

"Why do you look so happy?" she asked, but she was relaxing a little, which I took as a success.

"Don't you see how this could be a good thing for us?"

"How? And shouldn't you be jealous?"

I paused for a moment, examining her expression, but it hadn't changed. "Should I be?" I asked carefully.

She let out a sigh. "Of course not, but I don't understand why you're so happy he's here."

I took her hands in mine again and started cautiously, "Well... I had an idea."

"What kind of idea?"

"You might not like it and if you don't, I won't ever bring it up again, but there's a good chance this could be a good opportunity."

"Meaning?"

"He wants to see you, and maybe - with supervision, that wouldn't be a terrible plan."

She huffed a frustrated sigh. "I told you, I don't have anything to say to him. You know I don't care about him. He left me. I'm grateful for that now, but that doesn't change the fact that he was a jerk."

"I'm not saying it does, and I'm definitely not saying to give him a chance. Obviously, I'm not saying that. When it comes to you, I'm too selfish for that."

She smiled a little at that, and leaned into me. I held her tightly to me. I wouldn't give her up for anything and I really hoped she knew that. I hated myself a little for what I was about to suggest, though.

I wished I could swoop in and rescue her on my own, but to do that, I would need more time. If Gatsby was willing to finance her divorce, it would mean she could get away from Tom quicker, which was an opportunity I couldn't ignore. With Tom getting more and more volatile, I hated the thought of her with him for a moment longer than she had to be. Besides, Gatsby had seemed harmless enough. A little lovesick and desperate, but harmless and with more than enough money to solve her problems.

I held her a little longer until she pulled away. "So what are you suggesting?"

"He wants to meet up with you. He told me he's befriending Nick in order to get him to invite you both over to his home. He's hoping seeing him again will make you want to rekindle what you had."

Her eyebrows furrowed at that. "He can't really mean to say he thinks I'll take one look at him, forget about the past, and go running into his arms?"

I laughed. "He doesn't seem like the sharpest tool in the shed. Actually," I corrected, "it's not so much a lack of intelligence as a lack of sanity. He's delusionally hopeful. He has a terminal case of ambition mixed with incurable optimism."

"So you think if I play into it a bit, he would finance my freedom?"

"I think it's worth a shot." I might have felt bad if I hadn't already seen his lavish parties. I knew the amount it would cost him to pay her way out of her marriage would certainly be less than he spent on parties for a single week.

"Do you really think he'd go through with it? I'm not sure I'm that good of an actor. I might be able to hide my disdain for how he abandoned me, but I doubt I could make him believe I still feel anything for him."

I thought about it for a moment, before saying, "I don't think it will be too hard. He wants to believe it. All you're doing is letting him fool himself. He already pulled the wool over his own eyes. You're just not removing it."

She started to smile. "When you put it that way, I suppose it doesn't sound too bad. If he's as rich as they say, he really wouldn't miss the money."

I nodded quickly. "Richer even. You should have seen the palace he lives in. Dais, it makes this place look like a shack."

She rolled her eyes.

"I swear I'm not exaggerating, but I'm sure you'll see for yourself soon enough."

"So what's the plan?"

"He told me he's going to tell Nick your story and ask him to invite you both over. He's going to ask Nick to do him the favor of reintroducing you two."

"Why the formality? Didn't you say he lives right across the bay? Why not just come over?"

I had wondered that myself, but the way he told the story, he seemed to think he was living in a fairytale. "That wouldn't live up to his imaginings of how it should be. He wanted to come back a war hero and sweep you off your feet. Clearly that didn't happen, so now he wants to bump into you seemingly by accident and have your eyes meet from across the room and it'll be like no time has passed at all."

"He can't really believe that." Her voice was dripping with incredulity.

"He didn't say it exactly like that, but that's the impression I got."

"Okay, okay. I'll meet him. I won't promise I'm going to be convincing, though."

"If it goes badly, or he makes you uncomfortable, we'll call it off right away, I promise."

"There's just one problem. What about my cousin?"

"Nick? What about him?"

"He's friends with Tom."

"And?"

"And you really think that he'll help Jay meet me behind his friend's back?"

"Gatsby seemed to believe it, and my god apparently his optimism is catching. I hadn't even thought to question that."

"You know..." she said slowly, with a mischievous little grin on his face, "I might have an idea for that."

"You do?" I wasn't sure where this was going, but was skeptical I would like it.

She nodded. "I think there's a reason Jay asked *you* to ask him."

She was right. I didn't like where this was going.

CHAPTER TWENTY-FOUR
Jordan

I supposed it was fair what Daisy had suggested. After all, I was telling her to play nice with Gatsby, entertaining and distracting her cousin was a fair enough request. Besides, she wasn't wrong, he did seem easily distracted when I was around.

I had spent most of the last few weeks with Daisy. She continued to change her mind for and against our plan. Ultimately, I convinced her to agree to just meet him. I wouldn't push her to do anything beyond that, even if I did think it was in her best interest.

When I was convinced she was ready, I went looking for Nick to see how Gatsby's little plan was going. He was easy enough to find; I ran into him at the first party I tried. I was invited by the wife of some golfer or another and the host was in finance. Normally I would have turned it down, but since Nick was a bondsman in the city, I figured there was a chance he would be there. My hunch paid off.

I was annoyed to learn that Gatsby hadn't spoken with him, but thankfully Nick was quick to continue to call on me and invite me to things. I was sure eventually Gatsby would make his move, but I was impatient. Nick wasn't bad company; he just wasn't Daisy. This was important, though, so I kept giving Nick my free time while waiting for Gatsby to come around. If this was going to work, I knew I couldn't push Gatsby or Nick into it. I would have to continue to be patient, which wasn't my strong suit.

I suffered through some boring afternoons, but it would be unfair to say the entirety of my time with Nick was boring. There were a couple of good parties. One of which was a house-party up in Warwick. It was becoming clear to me that with how often he invited me around, he might be reading something into me spending time with him. I didn't want that, so I was determined to find a way to make him think ill of me while still making sure he was captivated enough that he would agree when I asked him to help me get Daisy and Gatsby back together.

The best plan I could come up with ended up with me borrowing a car. Although, borrowing is generous since I didn't ask first. I was careless with the borrowed car and drove more recklessly than usual. We were never in any danger. I was a good driver, but he was quick to worry and I can't say I didn't have some fun with that.

After the second seemingly close call with another car, he yelled out, "You're a rotten driver! Either you ought to be more careful, or you oughtn't to drive at all."

"I am careful," I protested while swerving back into our lane.

"No, you're not."

"Well, other people are," I said matter-of-factly.

"What's that got to do with it?"

"They'll keep out of my way." I punctuated my point with another swerve into the opposite lane before correcting my course. "It takes two to make an accident."

"Suppose you met somebody just as careless as yourself."

It wasn't carelessness; it was calculation. I didn't take risks without weighing out their worth beforehand. This wasn't a risk. I was in control of the car. I was having a good time, and I was sure this would cool his feelings for me. I felt like he was starting to fall for me, and I wanted to spare him that if possible. It was a calculated risk from a calculated person, not a careless one.

"I hope I never will. I hate careless people. That's why I like you." He was neither careless nor calculating.

To punctuate the point I had been making, I was careful to leave the borrowed car with the top down, knowing rain was coming. When the owner, who was a particularly nasty rival of mine on the golf course, saw his car, he was livid. He interrogated everyone at the party, and with Nick watching, I lied to him.

I saw the disbelief and disgust on Nick's face, and considered the day a success.

It took what felt like ages for Gatsby to get in touch with me. He sent his butler to my aunt's with a letter telling me he was taking Nick to lunch and wanted me to meet with Nick after for tea. I was grateful the plan was in motion.

Today was the day. I had been carefully cultivating a friendship with my neighbor, Daisy's cousin, Mr. Nick Carraway. That's not to say I didn't like him. I did. He was quiet, but likeable enough. However, I would be lying if I said I would have spent as much time with him as I did if he didn't have the advantage of being cousins with Daisy. Daisy was undoubtably the one that got away, the girl that haunted my every dream waking and asleep. Befriending Mr. Carraway was the first in a series of steps to winning her back.

The second step was befriending Daisy's best friend, Miss Jordan Baker. Luckily, Miss Baker was easily swayed like most women are when it comes to love. She swooned at our love story and was immediately on board to help me become reunited with my darling Daisy.

The next step was taking longer than I would have liked, but that was my fault. I had hoped Miss Baker would have informed Mr. Carraway of my plans, but picking up on subtle clues didn't appear to be Mr. Carraway's strong suit. I doubted very much that he knew anything. I had told Miss Baker I would tell him myself, but I had hoped she would grow impatient and do it herself.

I knew I should just ask him myself, but what if he said no to me? There was too much riding on this. After all, I knew he was friendly with Daisy's soon-to-be ex-husband. It was possible Mr. Carraway would disapprove of my plan. At least if it were coming from Miss Baker, who I was sure he was sweet on, he would be less likely to say no.

As I pulled up to his drive, I had already made my mind up. I couldn't just ask him today. It was a favor too grand to come from me. I would simply tell him more about myself and then send him off to tea with Miss Baker and let him know she had something to ask him for me. She would have to tell him then and he wouldn't say no to her.

I spent most of the drive telling him about my more noteworthy accomplishments and feats. I could see he didn't understand why I was doing so, but was too polite to ask, so I took pity on him.

"I'm going to make a big request of you today, so I thought you ought to know something about me. I didn't want you to think I was just some nobody."

It was imperative that he know I was good enough for Daisy. I didn't want him to think I was some low life trying to tempt her to break her marriage vows. I was a stand up gentleman and I needed him to know that.

"You see, I usually find myself among strangers because I drift here and there, trying to forget the sad things that happened to me."

I hadn't been in one place for long since I found out about Daisy's wedding. I had roamed from place to place, hoping to outrun my heartbreak, hoping to distract myself with the pleasures of other women, but no one held a candle to her. She was mine in my youth when all I had was the shirt on my back, my boyish smile, and my name. Now that I had come up in the world, she was the only one I wanted to share it with. She was the only one that would do.

Having her by my side would prove to myself that it had all been worth it and prove to everyone else that I was more than just another new money nobody. I was worth something, and winning her back would prove that. "You'll hear about it this afternoon," I finished.

"At lunch?"

"No, this afternoon. I happened to find out that you're taking Miss Baker to tea." Of course I hadn't found out so much as requested she do so, but it all amounted to the same. They were going to tea and she would tell him my story.

"Do you mean you're in love with Miss Baker?"

I choked on a laugh. "No, old sport, I'm not. But Miss Baker has kindly consented to speak to you about this matter."

I saw confusion and annoyance war over his face. I had half a mind to just tell him then and there, but another moment's consideration told me it was best not to deviate from my carefully laid plans. Mr. Carraway would understand. Miss Baker would make sure of it.

I couldn't believe it when Nick showed up for tea at the Plaza and still didn't know anything. He was just at lunch with Gatsby and Gatsby hadn't told him a thing.

I had politely inquired about what Gatsby had told him and Nick said he was told some outlandish things about Gatsby running to escape a sad past that I would enlighten him on. He also said Gatsby had told him I had a favor to ask him.

Gatsby was lucky I wanted this as badly as he did, otherwise I would have continued to drag out his misery, but as it was, I wasn't patient and I wanted this for Daisy.

I was about to start on the story when Nick held up a hand and asked, "Whatever fantastical request Gatsby put you up to, can it wait until after tea?"

I was shocked into silence for a moment. Nick wasn't anywhere near assertive, so I was surprised both by his abruptness and his request. I started to worry for the first time since Gatsby pitched his plan that this might not work. Nick might not go along with it.

The thought nagged me all throughout tea until we went for a romantic drive in Central Park. Night had fallen in the city, but it did nothing to quell the heat. The night was stifling, made more so by how close to me Nick was. He was looking at me with a tenderness that made me vaguely nauseous. Desperate to distract him from that look on his face, I told him Gatsby's story of how he and Daisy had met, fallen in love, and were ripped apart by first the war and then by her parents marrying her off to Tom.

I embellished the story a little to follow along with the way Gatsby believed it happened. I knew that even Nick couldn't have missed how tense things were between Tom and Daisy lately and hoped that would help him decide to help Gatsby.

When I finished their story, I waited to see what he would say. He had stayed mostly silent during, so I wasn't sure what he was thinking. Of all the things he could have said, he surprised me by pointing out, "You know, I think his home is right across the bay from the Buchanans."

"You're right, it is."

"It was a strange coincidence."

"But it wasn't a coincidence at all."

"Why not?"

It took everything in me not to sigh. It was taking far longer than it should for him to grasp the point. Apparently hinting wasn't going to work. "Gatsby bought that house so that Daisy would be just across the bay." I gave him a moment to let that sink in before finally arriving at the point. "He wants to know if you'll invite Daisy to your house some afternoon and then let him come over."

I held my breath as he considered. He couldn't say no. If he did, I would have to convince him.

"Did I have to know all this before he could ask such a little thing?"

I audibly exhaled, relieved. "He's afraid. He's waited so long. He thought you might be offended." So instead he had me doing the asking and offending for him. I had to admit, it was a rather brilliant plan though, since it was working flawlessly. I could only hope my own plan worked as seamlessly. "You see, he's a regular tough underneath it all." He was a regular baby making me do all the hard work with Nick for him, but that would hardly help my argument.

"Why didn't he ask you to arrange a meeting?"

Why indeed? It would have been so much easier if he had, but he had insisted it be Nick. "He wants her to see his house, and your house is right next door."

"Oh!"

The man was incredibly frustrating. I still didn't know if he was on board or not. I waited for him to say something, anything else, but he didn't. "I think he half expected her to wander into one of his parties some night, but she never did. Then he began asking people casually if they knew her, and I was the first one he found."

He hadn't found me exactly, but someone had said Daisy might be the one running around with that pro golfer girl. It didn't take a genius to figure out that meant me.

"It was that night he sent for me at his dance, and you should have heard the elaborate way he worked up to it. Of course, I immediately suggested a luncheon in New York - and I thought he'd go mad. 'I don't want to do anything out of the way!' he kept saying. 'I want to see her right next door.'" I had tried to change his mind since I wasn't sure that Nick would go along with the scheme, but Gatsby had been frustratingly insistent.

"When I said you were a particular friend of Tom's, he started to abandon the whole idea. He doesn't know very much about Tom, though he says he's read a Chicago paper for years just on the chance of catching a glimpse of Daisy's name."

Instead of responding, Nick snaked his arm around my shoulders. I tensed, before reminding myself this was for Daisy and relaxing into his arm as much as I could. I could have screamed when he changed the subject to ask me to dinner.

I agreed and brought the conversation back to Daisy. "Maybe we ought to invite Daisy to dinner with us. I'm sure she'd love to see you and heaven knows she's always alone while Tom is gallivanting around who knows where with whatever her name is. You know," I added almost as an afterthought, "Tom has a good thing going for him." I looked off into the night, taking a dramatic pause before turning back and driving my point home. "And Daisy ought to have something in her life," I said quietly.

"Does she want to see Gatsby?" I could have jumped up and danced my victory right then and there, but I stayed seated and calm.

"She's not to know about it. Gatsby doesn't want her to know." That was true, but it also worked well for my plan. I didn't want Nick accidentally talking Daisy out of the meeting and didn't want Daisy accidentally revealing too much to him before Gatsby and her had a chance to meet. It was better Nick and Gatsby both think she was in the dark. "You're just supposed to invite her to tea."

He finally agreed that he would. The relief and excitement were swiftly washed away a moment later when he drew me closer to him, and pulled his lips to mine. I fought my instinct to pull away and let him kiss me for a few moments before pulling away. He wasn't the worst kisser, but the kiss did nothing for me. It wasn't something I would welcome happening again, but it was a small sacrifice to make for my plan to rescue Daisy.

CHAPTER TWENTY-SEVEN
Daisy

"Are you sure this is a good idea?" I asked Jordan for the hundredth time that morning.

"For the millionth time, yes, I'm sure. He'll be a perfect gentleman and if it goes terribly, you won't have to see him again. I'll make sure of it."

"I'm really worried," I admitted.

She sighed and turned me to face her. "If you're really not comfortable, we can call it off." I considered it for a moment. I had been up all night tossing and turning, knowing today would be the day that I would be face to face with Jay again. It was almost too much.

I didn't know how I was going to feel seeing him again. I knew nothing could change the way I felt about Jordan, but I wasn't sure if I was going to be meeting with the Jay that sent me the threatening letter or the Jay from before the war, the sweet one from before he left. I didn't know what to expect, and it worried me, but Jordan was right. It was worth a shot. Even if he was terrible, whatever he said or did couldn't be any worse than Tom's worst.

"No, that's okay. I can handle it. If I can handle Tom, I can handle Jay." I squared my shoulders back and tried not to notice the pained expression on Jordan's face. I hated bringing up Tom's behavior, but it was the truth. I handled him on a daily basis, so I was sure I could handle whatever Jay threw at me for the hope of a better future far away from them both with the woman I loved.

Nick phoned right on schedule. I was worried he might sense I was acting off or ask questions, but he didn't. He just invited me to tea and made sure to warn me to come alone. When I told him I didn't understand, he clarified, "Don't bring Tom."

"What?" I asked, feigning confusion.

"Don't bring Tom," he simply repeated.

I put him out of his misery by playing along, "Who is 'Tom'?"

A minute later, we were off the phone, and the plan was in motion. I was amazed at how easy that was. I just hoped the actual afternoon went just as smoothly.

CHAPTER TWENTY-EIGHT
Gatsby

The day was finally here. I was finally about to be reunited with Daisy Fay, the one that got away, and it was almost too much to bear. It had to be perfect. I sent a man to mow Mr. Carraway's lawn and even more of my staff over with flowers, and then some more flowers when I didn't feel those would be enough.

Today had to be perfect. If there weren't enough flowers, she would laugh at me and walk away. If the grass was too long, she would think I still wasn't good enough for her. She would turn her nose up at me if I wore the wrong suit. I changed five times before I made it to Mr. Carraway's house. When I did, I was in a crisp white flannel suit, perfect for the summer heat. Underneath, I was wearing a silver shirt and a gold tie. I needed her to know I could afford anything now. If I didn't look flashy enough, she wouldn't be impressed, and she needed to be impressed. If I couldn't even impress and win back the love of my life, then there was no hope of me gaining anyone's respect. No one in society would respect a new money nobody who couldn't win back the girl that had already been promised to them. Without Daisy, I was nothing and after today, I refused to be nothing again.

I would do what I had to, but I was going to win her back.

She wasn't coming. I had been waiting for ages. She was late and wasn't coming. I couldn't wait around all day. I wouldn't. I wasn't going to be made to look like a fool. I jumped up from the couch and belted out, "I'm going home."

Mr. Carraway startled and asked, "Why's that?"

Why? She wasn't here and she clearly wasn't coming. Mr. Carraway might have fooled himself into thinking she was coming, but I was no fool and clearly I was being stood up. "Nobody's coming to tea. It's too late! I can't wait all day."

"Don't be silly; it's just two minutes to four."

Silly? I wasn't the one being silly; he was. He was the one still clinging to hope that his little tea party was happening. I looked at him again and saw he still believed it. I thought about leaving anyway, but thought better of it. Mr. Carraway was doing me a favor, I shouldn't abandon him. I sunk back on the couch in misery, but shot back up a moment later when we heard the sound of a motor outside.

Mr. Carraway smiled at me before rushing out the door to go get her. Daisy was here! I was finally going to see her. The car came to a stop and so did my heart. I couldn't do this. I couldn't see her again, not like this. Not wearing a silver shirt and a gold tie. What was I thinking? And not in this tiny house that smelled stiflingly of flowers. It was over fifty percent greenhouse now, more flower than house. I couldn't do this. I needed to leave.

Before Mr. Carraway made it to the door with Daisy, I let myself out the back.

The rain finally let up when the car pulled into Nick's drive. The drive was lined with lilac trees past their prime, but they still looked beautiful. Their gentle fragrance mixed with the smell of the rain and fresh cut grass soothed some of my nerves.

I was incredibly glad I already knew Jay was going to be here, but I still hadn't the faintest clue what to expect. I was still looking for the house when Nick came jogging out of a structure roughly the size of one of our garden sheds. I realized a few moments later that it was his house.

I took another look at it. It certainly was quaint and looked structurally sound at least. By the time he reached the car, I had regained what I could of my composure, but my nerves were fighting me. I pushed them down further and beamed down at him from under my lavender hat. "Is this absolutely where you live, my dearest one?"

He just smiled and helped me from the car. He hadn't said anything yet but I couldn't stay quiet. My nerves wouldn't let me. "Are you in love with me?" I murmured to him. "Or why did I have to come alone?"

He gave me what I supposed he meant to be a mischievous grin, but looked more apologetic and said, "That's the secret of Castle Rentrack. Tell your chauffeur to go far away and spend an hour."

I thought for a moment about changing my mind, about getting back in the car and leaving without seeing Jay again. I wanted to run, but Jordan was right. This could be worth it, and it was certainly worth a try. "Come back in an hour, Ferdie."

As I watched him back the car up the drive, I felt the panic rise in my gut, but it was too late now. I needed to be here, and I would be lying if I said I wasn't curious to see Jay. I wanted to know how he had changed, and why he had left, and what happened to make him as rich as he was. I had questions that I hoped might get answered, and there was no escape now. Like a cat whose curiosity fuels its early demise, I had gone too far to turn back. Forward was the only option.

I turned to Nick and gestured to the retreating car and chauffeur and said, "His name is Ferdie."

He seemed to understand my feelings of awkwardness and I was touched when he tried to make me feel more at ease by asking, "Does the gasoline affect his nose?" It was sweet of Nick to try to make me laugh with one of our inside jokes.

"I don't think so. Why?" I responded innocently and then laughed when he gave me a pointed look.

We had made it into the house by then. Nick led me to the living room and stopped cold. I looked around. I was looking for Jay and didn't see him but with the amount of flowers in the room, he could have been behind a bouquet and I might have missed him. From Nick's confused face, though, I didn't miss him. I wondered why he wasn't here. Maybe he had changed his mind and didn't want to see me after all.

"Well, that's funny," he said, more to himself than to me.

"What's funny?"

Whether or not he would have responded, I don't know. He was saved from having to come up with an excuse by a light knock on the front door. Nick moved to get the door, and I fought to compose myself. I was going to see Jay again. I could do this. I could act normal. I could do this. For me, and Jordan, and my dear Pammy, I could do this.

I stood there for what must have been moments, but felt like it stretched into hours, waiting for Nick to reemerge with Jay. Unable to stay still longer, I took a step toward the door and then heard quick footsteps. I looked over and my eyes locked on his. I thought I had prepared myself, but seeing him again, alive and well after all these years, was too much for me.

Unable to remain upright, I sunk back into the chair behind me. Seeing him took me back to the last time I saw him, to what we did in my car, and him leaving. To the letters he sent, all of them, not just the threatening one I was still angry about, but the sweeter ones too. But if he cared so much, why had he left without saying goodbye?

I just stared at him dumbfounded as my emotions raged. I felt like I was seeing a ghost. He was certainly pale enough to be one, but the water dripping in beads off his damp white jacket told otherwise.

I simultaneously wanted to cry from relief that he had made it through the war intact and rage at him for leaving me and threatening me. I took a deep breath and tried to remind myself that none of this mattered. You couldn't change the past, and I wouldn't want to. The past, as terrible and complicated as it was, had brought me Jordan and Pammy, and I wouldn't trade that for the world. I wouldn't have wanted a charmed life if that meant I didn't have them.

He was still staring and as I watched him, some of the life seeped back into his face. He lost some of his ghastly paleness and took on the more tanned tone of the boy I had known. His hair, while a mess from the rain, was still the same straw shade it had been and his eyes held the same intense look they had all those years ago. I cleared my throat in what sounded like a choking noise and forced myself to break the silence. "I certainly am awfully glad to see you again."

I waited for a reply as his face flickered through emotions faster than I could decipher them. He stayed silent, and I started to worry. Was he not happy to see me? He had arranged the meeting, but if I wasn't how he remembered or he was still angry with me about my being married, this was going to be a lot harder than Jordan had assumed.

The words from his last letter still haunted me. I wouldn't soon forget that he told me he would make sure I came to regret marrying Tom. I hadn't understood what he meant by that and still didn't, but I was no stranger to how volatile angry men could be so, to say the least, I was concerned.

It would be a lie to say I felt nothing at seeing him, though. I had cared about him and seeing him alive and well was a relief, but I didn't feel anything more than that. I was glad for it. There had been a tiny part of me that worried that with the anger I felt for him that some feelings would come back. I had thought it would be harder to be in the same room as him. I had thought I would feel far more than I did. Instead, I just felt anxious waiting for him to break his silence.

I looked up at his face again and tried to catch his eye, but he wouldn't meet mine. As I watched, his eyes roamed over my body with an air of appraisal. He must have liked what he saw, because a smile spread over his face. I couldn't help the shiver that ran through my body at his look. If he thought I was still the same girl who had let him touch me how he had, he was sorely mistaken. I was about to tell him so when I remembered myself and the plan. If I gave him a piece of my mind, this meeting would have been for nothing. If I was going to really give this a shot, I needed to play along for a little while.

He leaned back, seeming perfectly at ease while I was anything but. Unable to endure the continued silence while I could feel his eyes crawling over my body, I looked around for any distraction. It was then that I remembered where we were and thought to look for Nick. I moved to the edge of my seat, intending to go find him and drag him in here, but I didn't even get to stand before he entered the room. I shot him a look that screamed 'you owe me an explanation'. He would have expected me to be blindsided by the encounter. It wasn't hard to act annoyed that he had set me up since he had left us alone. I waited for him to say something, anything. Unfortunately, he was as at a loss for words as I was. After a few more moments of me and Nick pretending not to notice Jay's gaze on me, Jay finally spoke. He looked at Nick and explained, "We've met before."

With our history, that had to have been the biggest understatement he could have made. He tried to casually lean against the mantle, but in doing so, he bumped into the clock. It started to fall, but he turned quickly and caught it before it smashed. I was glad it took his attention from me for a moment.

I tried to collect my thoughts, but they were too disarrayed to be tamed. I was struggling to separate how I was feeling from how I needed to be acting. Jay finally sat down, putting himself at my eye level and also what I considered to be dangerously close, but he still didn't address me.

Again, he spoke to Nick. "I'm sorry about the clock."

Damn the clock. I desperately needed some inkling of what he was thinking, and all he deigned to speak about was my cousin's stupid clock. Nick was trying to shrink into the background. I don't know what he expected in arranging this little meeting, but it was clear he would rather be anywhere else right now than standing here with me and Jay.

"It's an old clock," was all Nick said.

I had dealt with more skirting around the awkwardness than I could handle and brought the conversation back to Jay and me, hoping it would get him to give me some indication of how he was feeling. "We haven't met for many years."

Without missing a beat, he replied, "Five years next November."

I hadn't thought things could possibly get more awkward, but that certainly did it. I couldn't believe he still remembered so exactly when we had parted. Then again, it wasn't a night I would ever be likely to forget either.

He still wouldn't meet my eye, but if I wasn't mistaken, some tenderness had seeped into his tone. Assuming I hadn't imagined it, I could work with that. All our unasked questions loaded the room with a suffocating feeling that had me wishing for more air. The boys must have felt stifled as well, since neither was able to muster up any conversation.

After what felt like ages, Nick blurted out that he should get the tea. Desperate for something, anything, to do, both Jay and I jumped at the suggestion, offering our help and hurrying toward the kitchen. However, the relief was short-lived when the tea was brought in already prepared for us. Despite being stuck in the room again, the tea was a welcome distraction. I was grateful to have something to busy my hands and mouth with.

Nick sat in the chair I had vacated, forcing me to the couch, meaning if Jay were to sit, he would have to sit right next to me. I wondered with how weird he was acting if he would and wasn't surprised when he chose to remain standing. I forced Nick into conversation, but as distracted as I was by Jay's presence hovering in a shadowy corner of the room, I hardly knew what to say.

Every once in a while, when I felt Jay's eyes land on me, I felt his displeasure. That worried me. It didn't bode well for mine and Jordan's plan, but more than that, I didn't understand it. He seemed miserable, and if he was so miserable, why was he still here? He had arranged the meeting. If he didn't wish to be in my presence, he was welcome to leave. After all, I hadn't invited him. He had invited himself and me to Nick's.

Not for the first time, I wondered just how much Jay and Jordan had told Nick about my past with Jay. I knew Jordan would have been discrete, but I wasn't sure if Jay had been. While these thoughts bounced around my mind, Nick and I made mindless small talk. Eventually, with all the safe topics exhausted, the room again fell to silence. After a few suffocating moments, Nick jumped up and excused himself, but to my surprise, before Nick could leave the room, Jay jumped up and demanded, "Where are you going?"

Judging by Nick's face, him and I were united in our confusion at both the intensity and volume of Jay's question.

I expected Nick to acquiesce to his friend's appeal, but to my surprise, he didn't. "I'll be right back."

Before Nick cleared the room, Jay interjected, "I've got to speak to you about something before you go." He was incredibly on edge, which was making me nervous. I was glad when he followed Nick out and gave me a moment to myself. I knew if the plan was going to work, I was going to have to be alone with him, but I didn't know if I was ready for that.

The boys were speaking in low voices that I couldn't quite make out, but when I heard my name, I didn't hesitate. I moved quickly and quietly closer to the door to try to hear what they were saying. I heard Jay ask, "She's embarrassed?"

I felt some relief at the surprise and tenderness in his tone. If him and Nick were reading my awkwardness and discomfort as embarrassment, I could work with that.

"Just as much as you are," Nick assured him. I felt even more relieved at that. I wasn't sure how to take the tension. I wasn't sure if he was still angry with me, but apparently he was feeling as awkward as I was.

"Don't talk so loud," Jay cautioned Nick, unaware of the futility of the request.

Nick did lower his voice before saying, "You're acting like a little boy. Not only that, but you're rude. Daisy's sitting in there all alone."

The words brought me back to my senses, and I hurried back to my seat on the couch. I settled back just in time for Jay to come waltzing back in. This time, his eyes met mine and he smiled. His smile was the smile of the man I had fallen for, the same smile that gave him the boyish charm I had so easily fallen for. It was the smile of an ambitious young officer who was going to make a name for himself or die trying. Judging from the little I knew about his life now, he had really succeeded in making a name for himself.

I couldn't help admiring how much he had grown up and come into his own. Looking into his eyes and seeing his smile, it was hard not to get swept back up into the past. For a moment I was eighteen again, a young girl floating from party to party, from man to man, searching for something, for someone, to make me feel something. For a moment, I was that young girl who found a life raft in this ambitious officer, the first of his gender to treat me with what felt like genuine care and affection, who made me feel passion for the first time.

It took me another moment before I remembered myself. He wasn't the young man I had known anymore, and I wasn't the same girl anymore. That story didn't have a good ending, but my story did. I was better off for having met him since it led me to where I was now. It led me to Jordan and gave me Pammy, and I could never be sorry for that.

I smiled at him, letting some of that gratitude show on my face. I was lucky to have felt what I did for him in the past and even luckier to have found what I had now with Jordan. She was my world, my stars, all I could ever need. Some of that must have shown on my face, because his own smile became more hopeful as he crossed the room to me and took a seat a couple feet from me on the other side of the couch.

"It's really so good to see you," I offered up. "I'm so glad you came out of the war okay."

"My Daisy, my darling Daisy," he said, savoring my name as he said it. I didn't know what to say. Years ago, I would have longed to hear him call me his darling again, but things had changed. I had grown up and wasn't anymore his darling Daisy than he was my lieutenant. I held no claim to his man anymore, nor did I want to.

I moved a little further away from him, but hit the end of the couch. I couldn't think of what to say and settled for, "It's so good to see you again. Tell me, how have you been?"

He didn't respond right away. Instead, he scooted closer to me. I let out a nervous giggle and had to fight against my instincts to stand up and bolt from the room. He moved his hand to my face and brushed a strand of hair out of my eyes. I startled a little and giggled, before trying again to draw him into conversation. "We haven't spoken in a long while. What have you been getting up to?"

He still didn't answer. His hand moved down from my cheek to cup my chin. I leaned back as far as the couch would allow. I felt a moment of short-lived relief when he moved his hand from my cheek, but he moved it to my upper arm and moved his other hand to my other arm, caging me between his arms. I was trapped between him and the end of the couch, and I knew that look in his eye. I gulped. I had exactly ten seconds to figure out how far I was willing to go for the plan. If I didn't do or say something, he was going to kiss me.

Either way, if I let him or if I didn't, it would feel like a betrayal to Jordan. If I let him, it would feel like I was betraying her. It didn't matter that I didn't want anyone but her and didn't want anyone but her lips on mine. If I let him kiss me, it would feel like I was going behind her back. On the other hand, if I didn't let him, if I shut him down here and now, it would kill our plan. He wouldn't care enough to help me if he didn't think I returned his feelings. I knew how much Jordan wanted to help me, and this was the best plan either of us could come up with. I didn't know what to do. Letting him kiss me would be both the easiest and hardest thing in the world.

I tried to stall him by saying, "Where have you been-" but he cut me off, saying, "-all this time? I know, my love. It's been too long, but we can forget all that now. I'm here now."

He leaned in and I moved back a little further, but there was no more space to go. I could move or push him away, but that would ruin everything. He moved toward me deliberately with a desperate look in his eye. I took a deep breath and let him come. I didn't lean closer, but I didn't move either.

When his lips met mine, for a moment, I forgot myself. I let myself go and gave into the feeling of the past colliding with the present. I was a young girl again, and it was me and my lieutenant against the world. For a moment, I was his again.

Then I remembered.

I remembered giving myself wholly and completely to him and how devastated I was when he left me without so much as a goodbye. I had felt worthless, a shell of my old self, and he was the reason. He was the reason I was in the situation I was in. I certainly wasn't blameless, but he was older and should have known better. I should have known better, but so should he.

I was rushed into marriage because of him. I was married to my abusive husband because of him. I was powerless to be with the woman I loved because of him, and I wasn't going to let him play with my heart again. This time, he would be the one devastated. He pushed me into this mess, and him and his money would get me out. I leaned into him harder, pressing my lips against his and letting him feel a taste of the desire I didn't have. He put us both in this position and if I had to use him to get out of it, I refused to feel guilty. I kissed him for a moment longer before pulling away.

I could feel my cheeks were flushed and knew it gave me the look of a blush. I giggled a little, acting out of breath, trying to give myself a moment to figure out what my next move was. I hadn't thought this through. Until now, I wasn't even sure I was going to actually go through with this, but now I was committed and wasn't sure what to do next. He tilted his head to the side and leaned in closer.

I pulled back a little further, and it finally registered to him that something wasn't right. He looked puzzled and slightly concerned, asking, "What is it, my sweet?"

I didn't know how to answer that. Honesty was out, but I needed to say something that would give him pause before kissing me again. I let some of the conflict I was feeling show on my face and said part of what was on my mind. "I can't believe we just did that."

"I know. I never stopped thinking about you. Thinking of you and this inevitable moment is what got me through the lonely days and nights of the past five years. I never stopped thinking about you."

I had to stifle my disbelief and anger at that. He abandoned me and now he was trying to sweet talk me with sweet nothings. I wasn't that easily swayed. "Jay, I-"

He interrupted, "Hearing you say my name again is one of the sweetest sounds I could imagine. A pleasure I have been dreaming about, but even my dreams of you pale in comparison to the real thing."

"Jay," I started again, "please let me finish. This is important."

"I know, my sweet, we have so much to catch up on. It's crazy, when I'm with you, it feels like no time has passed at all."

"As good as it is to see you, I can't pretend to be the woman I was. Things have changed."

"I know, I know. I'm grateful life has brought you back to me, but now that I've found you again, there will be plenty of time for talking. Right now, there are far more pleasant things we could be doing."

"I really must insist. You know I care a lot about you, but things are different. I'm a married woman now."

He looked surprised a moment before taking my hands in his and saying, "It's alright. You made a mistake and I can help you fix it."

I fought the smile wanting to play across my lips. He was making this incredibly easy. I almost felt bad, but reminded myself he was the reason I was here. He set the events in motion that got me to this point. He hadn't done right by me, and the least he could do was help me out of the mess I found myself in now. But I couldn't make it too easy. If I seemed too willing, this might not work.

I sighed. "I'm married now, Jay. There's no fixing that."

"You would be surprised what money can fix. I know you don't love him. How could you when you've always been mine."

I felt my anger and frustration well up at that. He had no right to talk about me like that. I wasn't his. I belonged to myself, but if anyone had a right to call me theirs, it was Jordan. Jordan had always been by my side and in my corner when I needed her. She was there for me when she had nothing to gain from it and when the rest of the world had turned its back on me.

"I know you must feel trapped, but now that I have you back, trust that I don't intend to let you go again. Now that you're back in my arms, I won't let anything tear you away from me."

The hard edge of insistence in his voice gave me chills. I knew he meant it to be reassuring, but it was anything but.

"I don't know how much money you have now, but I don't know how money can solve my problems. There's not enough money in the world to separate what God has joined together."

"My love, I have more money than God and defy even God to try to keep us apart. I lost you once and I won't lose you again."

"You really think there's something that could be done?"

"Of course. There's always something to be done. It won't be easy to get your marriage dissolved but I certainly have the money to throw at the right people."

I breathed out a sigh and looked at him with pleading eyes. "I couldn't ask you to do that."

"You don't have to ask. I have connections. It might take a little time, but I'll fix things for you. You'll see, it'll be just like it never happened."

"But Jay-"

"What is it now?" he asked, exasperation seeping into his voice. I shrunk down a little into myself at his tone and had to remind myself this was Jay. This wasn't Tom. Whatever Jay was thinking or feeling, he wouldn't hurt me. He never had, and I was sure he wouldn't start now. I tried to tell myself that, but despite the deep breaths, the tears started to fall.

CHAPTER THIRTY-ONE
Daisy

The annoyance on his face instantly morphed into concern as he pulled me into him. He held me tight as I cried and I let him. It was easier than talking because I was feeling too much to explain myself. He was so quick to try to swoop in and rescue me, like he could erase his past mistake. He wanted to give us a do-over, but even if I didn't have Jordan and still felt the same way about him, it wasn't possible to just pick up where we left off. So much had happened since he left. Besides, it wasn't just me. I had Pammy to think about, too. I didn't know if he knew about her and was hesitant to bring her up. If he didn't know, there was a chance it might change things for him. I wasn't sure if I could risk that. It might be better to ease him into it. Maybe it was best to spend more time with him before letting him know. I would have to let him know eventually, though. I couldn't keep it from him.

I pulled away from him when my tears slowed and said, "I don't know why you want to help me. I don't deserve it."

He softened further at that. "Please know I don't hold this against you. I got your letter. I know you didn't want to marry him. It was a mistake, but I understand. I know he must have forced you. You must have been too scared to say no. I know how you feel about me. For you to ignore my pleas and marry him anyway, he must have forced your hand. But please don't worry. I'll make sure no one takes you away from me again. I promise I'll never let you go again."

I knew the girl I was at eighteen would have loved to hear it, but the woman I was now was struggling not to roll her eyes. We had been separated for five years and I was a married woman with a child and he kissed me once and suddenly was pledging his undying love for me. Where was he five years ago when I needed to hear that? Where was he when I would have welcomed his advances? He was more of an arrogant fool than I realized to think I would simply jump at his offer now that he was around again. It pained me to have to play right into his hand and that he was so quick to believe me. It showed he never knew me at all if he truly believed I would be this easily swayed without him even bothering to offer any apology or explain why he never came back in the first place.

"You really don't think Tom will be a problem?"

He shook his head vigorously. "He won't be a problem, more of a minor inconvenience, and certainly something I can handle. And if he won't agree to let you go, I have ways of making him. I know people that could take care of him if he does prove to be a problem. Say the word and I can make the problem of him go away."

I couldn't decide if he was serious. He seemed to believe what he was saying, though. I wasn't sure if he was implying what I thought he was, but apparently Jay had become something of a dangerous man. I would have to be extra careful with how I played this. Tom wasn't a good person, but he was still the father of my child and I had loved him at one point, or thought I did. I didn't want to be around him or want him around Pammy, but I didn't want him to disappear, either.

"I don't think that'll be necessary. He's a scoundrel and a cheat. I don't think it'll take much to pay him off." I wasn't sure that was true, but I didn't want him dead. "I don't need him to disappear. I just want him away from me."

"You can be sure of that. I promise you I'll do whatever it takes to separate you from him. I'll make sure no one stands in our way again. I fought a war for you and made it out with my life with just one purpose in mind: to come home and claim the hand that was rightfully mine. I knew you were waiting for me. Even married to that scoundrel, you were waiting for me. I'm just sorry it took me as long as it did to find my way back to you. Every minute without you was agony."

I put my arms around him and pulled him into a hug so I could hide my face. I wasn't in control of my racing thoughts and wasn't sure what might show on my face. I didn't want to give him the opportunity to see something he shouldn't. I wasn't sure what to say next but was saved from having to decide by some loud banging coming from the direction of the kitchen.

I stiffened and pulled back from Jay, wiping what remained of the tears from my face with my handkerchief. When I looked back, Nick had reappeared from the kitchen and was looking back and forth between us. He looked questioningly at Jay, who was smiling so widely it would have been visible for miles. I was glad the plan didn't hinge on keeping this from Nick, because Jay was being anything but subtle. I could only hope Nick could be more subtle when it came to Tom. I hadn't thought Nick knowing would be a good idea, but Jordan had promised she would handle him, and I trusted her.

Neither Jay nor Nick paid me any mind while I took a moment to straighten my appearance and, more importantly, straighten out my thoughts.

"Oh, hello, old sport," Jay finally said to Nick.

Ever the conversationalist, Nick gave us the weather report, "It's stopped raining."

"Has it?"

I agreed with Jay. I had been so wrapped up in our reunion, I could hardly recall it had been raining in the first place. He turned to me with a meaningful look and said, "What do you think of that? It stopped raining."

I didn't know what to say or what he thought he was communicating. Whatever it was was lost in translation, but Jay was looking at me as if I were the sun and he had been in the dark for years, so I supposed it didn't matter what I said.

Nick was trying to be subtle about his disapproving look, but subtilty was not his specialty. I couldn't help wondering what it was he disapproved of. Was it his loyalty to my husband that had him conflicted? Or was he being protective of Jay? Could he already sense I was using Jay? I supposed the reason behind his feelings didn't matter much either way, but I knew this was going to change our relationship. I would have to be more careful around him.

I realized they were both staring at me and said, "I'm glad, Jay."

It was apparently enough of a response to encourage Jay, since he rushed on, turning to Nick, "I want you and Daisy to come over to my house. I'd like to show her around."

I was confused and relieved that Jay wanted Nick to come with us. I had thought he might try to get rid of him and was glad he hadn't, but that didn't change the fact that going to see his home was a terrible idea. His house was much bigger and would have much more space for us to be alone, away from Nick. I didn't want to go, but wasn't sure how to get out of it. Not wanting to betray any of my worry, I just nodded. Jay, if possible, beamed even wider and turned to Nick expectantly.

Nick gave Jay a questioning look and asked, "You're sure you want me to come?" I prayed he would say yes.

"Absolutely, old sport."

I was relieved I would be able to delay the inevitable alone time with Jay. I excused myself to freshen up, but really just needed a moment away from Jay. The emotional whiplash was too much for one girl to handle. After taking as long as I felt I could delay, I joined the boys outside.

Daisy

I knew Jay and Nick were neighbors, so we wouldn't be going far, but I still expected there to be a car waiting. There wasn't. The boys were both looking at the enormous mansion next door. I lived in what most people would consider to be a mansion and had lived in mansions all my life, but the house next door belonged in a class of its own. If my home was considered a mansion, this was a palace.

The boys continued to look at it and it sunk in that they were implying that was Jay's home. Jordan had said it was huge, and she wasn't prone to exaggeration, but this was far more than I expected. It made mine and Tom's home seem comfortably cozy by comparison. "That huge place there?" I asked.

Jay smiled hesitantly and asked, "Do you like it?"

I was glad to not have to lie. "I love it!" From what I could see, his home was a marvel. I might actually enjoy a tour. Even the McCormick's Chicago mansion paled in comparison, and that was just the part I could see from Nick's lawn. The palace next door was fit for a king and could fit an entire kingdom. There was no way he filled all that space himself. "But I don't see how you live there alone."

He laughed a little and said, "I keep it always full of interesting people, night and day. People who do interesting things. Celebrated people."

The mansion was right across the lawn, but instead of walking directly toward it, Jay had us enter the long way from the road. He insisted it was the only right way for me to see his home for the first time, the way it was meant to be seen.

As the three of us walked, Jay described his elaborate parties and the noteworthy people that attended them. To hear him tell it, his home was always full of the world's best performers, athletes, and scholars. Jordan certainly hadn't given that impression, but as an impressive athlete herself, she wasn't easily impressed.

I couldn't help but be impressed as we entered the drive and the palace sprawled out before us. It was reaching in every direction as if Jay's ambition had infected it, too. The sheer size of the home was overwhelming. How anyone could afford to live there was incomprehensible.

The gardens stretched out in all directions over the grounds. There were flowers of every color, shape, and size. A medley of floral aromas greeted me. I wanted to spend time looking at them all, but if I did that, I was sure I would never leave. Truly looking at and enjoying all the flowers in the garden would take at least a week, if not longer. Jay continued to watch me, waiting for approval and asking me how I liked it. In this at least, I didn't have to lie or disappoint him. The grounds were beautiful, and I couldn't imagine what was waiting inside.

Before we reached his home, though, he stopped us. "As much as I long for you to see my house, I must insist it wait a few minutes longer. There's a special part of the garden I need to show you," he said, looking at me. Then he nodded in Nick's direction and asked, "What do you say, old sport? Are you up for a detour?"

Nick nodded his ascent, but I suspected Jay barely noticed. He was already leading us away from the stairs and around the side of his home. I wondered what it was he was so insistent on us seeing, but I wasn't left wondering for long.

When we rounded another bend, I was greeted with a sea of daisies for as far as I could see. As I took in the scene, he turned back to me and said, "One for every day we've been apart. I had a new one planted every day until today. Today's the first day of the rest of our lives."

I looked out at the flowers again. They were even more overwhelming now that I knew their significance. I couldn't believe he had gone through all this trouble for me. A moment later, my thoughts caught up to reality. He didn't think about me every day. At least he wasn't thinking about me enough to say goodbye before he left. He might want what's best for me now, maybe, but that certainly wasn't always the case. And he didn't even plant the flowers himself. If it was such a labor of love, why did he have them planted? Why not do it himself? And even if he had hand planted each flower each day as a shrine to me, it didn't matter. I wasn't the girl he had known, and he certainly didn't know or care to get to know the woman I had become. If he wanted to swoop in and play the lovesick hero returning home, if he really wanted to save me from my husband, I would let him, but that was all I would let him do. I wasn't his now anymore than I ever was.

He reached out and took my hand, holding it in his as he caressed it with his thumb. "Tell me, what do you think?"

I smiled coyly and said, "There certainly are a lot of flowers."

"I'm certain I will never tire of looking at them, but I am glad there won't be any more."

I let him hold my hand as he led me back to the house. Nick followed along behind us, a welcome but easily overlooked presence. I continually forgot he was there, but I was grateful nonetheless because I was sure his presence was keeping Jay on his best behavior and I had no desire to see him on his worst behavior.

As Jay led us through room after room, giving the grand tour, I lost track of what we had seen and where we had been. It would have been incredibly easy to get lost there. It was also shockingly quiet for such a large home. We didn't pass by anyone else. I knew he lived alone, but we didn't run into any of his staff either, which was highly unusual for a normal-sized home. For a home of this size that had to be run by a small army, it was nearly impossible we hadn't encountered anyone. He must have given them the afternoon off so we would have the place to ourselves.

It was probably for the best. I didn't want word getting around about me and Jay before Jordan and I figured out what the next step in the plan was, but it was eerie being alone in a home so large.

The last room he brought us to was the one I was most curious about: his room. His apartment doors opened into a sizeable study.

"Care for a drink, old sport?"

Nick nodded his assent.

He didn't ask me and I wasn't sure if I should be touched he remembered or annoyed he was living in the past enough to assume that my not drinking hadn't changed.

Jay moved behind his large, highly polished desk and turned his back to us before spinning back around with a bottle of whiskey and two glasses. Where he got them from, I hadn't the faintest idea. He stepped closer to the desk to pour the glasses, and I saw what had previously been part of the wall was actually a hidden cupboard, perfect for storing illegal liquor. I wondered how many other secret hiding places there were built into this place.

Jay took his glass and my hand and led us to his bedroom. Again, I was thankful for Nick's presence. I did wonder how he was feeling, though. Being there with me and Jay had to be awkward for him, especially because he was a friend of Tom's, but Nick seemed supportive. I couldn't help wondering if that was because he cared about Jay or if maybe I had gotten through to him the other night. Maybe he understood how much I was suffering with Tom and was supportive of this because he thought it would make me happy. I hoped that was the case, but I wasn't so sure. He had clearly been uncomfortable with me discussing my feelings, but maybe he had considered it and arranged this for my benefit. I hoped so.

Jay's room was surprising in how plain it was. It wasn't that it didn't show expensive taste, it did, but there was nothing personal about it. Nothing new to be gleaned about Jay from the objects there. My eye swept over the room, stopping on a golden hairbrush on his dresser. It reminded me of a more ornate version of the one I used often. I moved to it and picked it up, looking more closely at it. Mine was silver with pearl embellishments, but the design could have passed for the same. I tried to recall if he had seen mine before, but didn't think he had. It was an odd coincidence. I stroked the brush through my hair and sighed in delight at how smoothly it ran through.

I turned around mid brush-stroke when I heard Jay start looking. He was laughing with the air of a man gone mad.

When he spoke, despite staring at me, he addressed Nick, "It's the funniest thing, old sport. I can't- When I try to-" He didn't finish either of the thoughts, but his laughter died down. It seemed he was feeling the same unreal quality of the afternoon that I was. Me being here in my lieutenant's room, who was now rich enough to have a golden lady's hairbrush just lying around, felt like a strange dream.

Even more so when he pulled open two large cabinets full of suits, dressing gowns, ties, and shirts, so many shirts. I gaped at the display, the quality and quantity. He clearly had more money than he knew what to do with.

"I've got a man in England who buys me clothes. He sends over a selection of things at the beginning of each season, spring and fall."

He started pulling them out one by one, letting them flutter to the ground. He had shirts in every color, pattern, and fabric imaginable. Silk, linen, and flannel in coral, apple-green, and lavender flew by, followed by striped shirts and plaid shirts and monogrammed shirts. Even if he wore two different shirts a day for the rest of his life, I was sure he could never wear them all. My amazement slowly started to turn to resentment as each new shirt flew by.

He had more money than he knew what to do with. The kind of money I needed from him wouldn't even make a dent in what he had. If I believed he really cared about me and my happiness, I could have just asked him for it, but I knew him better than that. I knew he wouldn't give me the money for the sake of my own happiness if it didn't include him. He claimed to love me, but only loved me if I fit his expectations and did what he wanted.

That wasn't love.

The frustration built over into tears. A strained sound came out of my mouth as I hid my head in the nearest pile of shirts and started crying.

I was angry, not sad, but the tears wouldn't stop. I couldn't imagine what the boys were thinking and tried to find an excuse. After a few moments, I was still coming up blank and decided it hardly mattered what I said, anyway. They would draw their own conclusions. "They're such beautiful shirts. It makes me sad because I've never seen such - such beautiful shirts before."

Neither of them called me out on the flimsy excuse and eventually I ran out of tears. They were both too wrapped up in their own thoughts to think of comforting emotional, crazy Daisy. If I had any belief left that Jay loved me, it died in that shirt pile.

He had used me for all I was worth, and I was going to return the favor.

CHAPTER THIRTY-THREE
Daisy

Jay intended to show us more of the grounds, but the return of the rain interrupted that plan. It didn't stop him from bringing me to the window to point out his pier, though. "If it wasn't for the mist, we could see your home across the bay." I thought he must have been speaking more generally that his pier looked toward my home, until he added, "You always have a green light that burns all night at the end of your dock."

To mask the shiver that ran through me at that, I laced my arm through his. He barely noticed, and I was glad for it. I didn't enjoy the idea that he had been over here for God knows how long staring across the bay imagining reclaiming me.

He was lost in a daze and stayed that way until Nick drew him into conversation.

Before we knew it, night had fallen and Nick was making his excuses, leaving me feeling trapped. Nick hadn't offered to take me home. Of course, he was walking home, but him or Jay should have offered to get me home. Neither did. Jay barely paid Nick any mind when he announced he was leaving.

"Darling, don't you think I should be going?" I whispered into Jay's ear. If he wouldn't take the hint, maybe I could push him into realizing he was ignoring chivalry.

He turned back to me sharply, saying, "Nonsense. The day is still young and I've just found you again."

I turned back to Nick for some help, but he was watching Jay. Jay didn't even notice. I waved to Nick, hoping he would understand the request, but he nodded back and took his leave.

So much for subtle.

"Jay, I really must be going. I don't know what might happen if I'm missed."

"You mean to say you miss him?" he asked sharply.

I quickly shook my head. His tone made me nervous, but the statement was ridiculous. Of course I didn't miss Tom, I just didn't want to be alone with Jay. This was more than I had bargained for. "Not at all. That's ridiculous!" I thought for a moment before softening my tone and putting a pleading expression on my face. "You can't mean to say you believe I would want to leave if I had a choice. I don't miss him, but if he notices I'm gone too long, I hate to think what might happen."

That seemed to satisfy him, although he was looking at me more carefully now as he asked, "What do you mean? What might happen?"

I debated how much to tell him before opting for some of the truth. "He has a temper, and he gets violent sometimes."

"God damn it!" Jay yelled, banging his fist against the now closed door. I jumped at the noise, my heart racing. He immediately looked remorseful and softened his tone. "I'm sorry, darling," he said, stroking my face. "He hurts you?"

I nodded weakly. "Sometimes."

"Damn him to hell! I promise you I'll find a way to free you from him."

Perfect, I thought, *but it couldn't hurt to lay it on a little thicker.*

"I can't believe that after all these years that here you are again swooping in like some dashing prince here to save me."

He smiled at that. "I will. I promise."

He leaned in and, more softly than he ever had, kissed me. It wasn't urgent or demanding. It was soft, pleading, and I lost myself for a moment. It almost made me forget what needed to be done. Almost.

I pulled away, and with sorrowful eyes, he said, "I suppose you must be going."

"We'll see each other again soon," I promised. I intended to ensure I was around him frequently enough that he remembered his feelings and his desperate need to rescue me.

It turns out Nick had sent my car and driver to pick me up. I silently thanked him for facilitating an easier escape.

As the car drove away from the mansion, I couldn't help but look back. The glittering palace all lit up in its splendor was hard to look away from. It stood solitary by the sea. Like its sole inhabitant, it appeared to be sitting there waiting for life to begin. It gave the impression that if you looked away for too long, both the house and its inhabitant would cease to exist. I kept my eyes trained on the mansion until we turned the bend and as I watched, the lights started to wink out one by one.

CHAPTER THIRTY-FOUR
Jordan

Daisy's tea with Gatsby was both a blessing and a curse. She had barely been around him for a minute before he was already pledging to help her dissolve her marriage. I was grateful he was going to help her, but hated that I wasn't able to. I hated her having to make herself uncomfortable by being around him longer, but it was the quickest way to get her away from Tom.

We had been lucky that with Tom spending all his time with his mistress, he wasn't around to derail our plans. Unfortunately, the plan hinged on Daisy spending more time than I would have liked with Gatsby. She was strategic about cutting their meetings short using Tom as an excuse and always leaving Gatsby wanting more, but the unintended consequence was that I barely saw her.

That wasn't just Gatsby's fault, though. My part of the plan was also keeping me quite busy. Keeping Nick away from both Tom and Gatsby had turned out to be much harder of a task than intended. If I wasn't keeping him occupied nearly every moment he wasn't working, he would bring up visiting Gatsby. I was starting to wonder if there was more to his feelings than friendship, but as long as he continued to be attracted to me, and therefore easily distracted by me, I supposed the nature of his feelings toward Gatsby didn't really matter.

I took Nick everywhere with me. When I called on friends or colleagues, he came. When I golfed, he observed. When I visited with my aunt, he came with. The way she perked up at the presence of my gentleman friend was amusing. I tried my luck at telling her we could use some money for a nice getaway, but she nearly had a stroke at the implication I would vacation alone with a man as an unmarried woman. I would have used any extra money she deigned to give me for myself, Daisy, and Pammy, of course, but she wasn't willing to part with any.

On the rare occasions Nick was working and Daisy was out, I dropped in on Pammy. I liked to surprise her with visits and check in on the nanny. I worried about the nanny, but so far, her only fault was that Tom had chosen her. Thankfully, she cared a lot for Pammy and was highly attentive to her. I tried to bring Pammy little presents when I could. Hearing her call me Auntie Jo warmed my heart and made me that much more determined to get her and her mother away from here as soon as possible. Daisy didn't deserve to be separated from Pammy as much as she was. It was painful to watch how distant they had been forced to become and the longer it went on, the harder it would be on the both of them when this was over.

No matter the cost, I had to get them both out of here as soon as possible. As much as I hated that Gatsby was the best shot she had at the moment, if things went according to plan and he got her her freedom, I would be forever grateful to him, scoundrel or not.

CHAPTER THIRTY-FIVE
Jordan

I missed Daisy so much, that even stolen little moments with her felt like heaven. We had scarcely seen each other over the past few weeks as busy as she and I both were.

I had thought I might feel some jealousy about Daisy spending so much time with Gatsby, but she was clear about how much she would rather be with me. She was doing this for us, for me, for our little Pammy, and for herself.

I would be lying if I said I wasn't growing impatient with Gatsby, though. "Gatsby certainly is taking his sweet time helping you," I grumbled as I held her to me. Her floral perfume wafting off her made me want her even closer. I never wanted to let her go.

She groaned. "You'd be surprised how much he's had that same complaint. I promise you he's working on it. I worry what he might do if his connections continue to struggle to meet his demands, though."

"What do you mean?" This was the first time she had mentioned any concerns about him. "You don't mean he'd take it out on you, do you?"

She shook her head quickly, and I relaxed a little. "Hardly. I mean I'm a little worried he might try to make me a widow instead of a divorcee."

I pulled away from her, holding her back so I could look at her face. "You can't be serious."

"He's alluded to it, but nothing concrete enough that I feel certain he's planning something."

I couldn't help considering it for a moment. Having Tom permanently out of the picture didn't sound like a terrible idea the more I thought about it. He would never be able to hurt her again. She would inherit his money by default, and she wouldn't have to worry about fighting him in what was sure to be a brutal divorce case. She wouldn't have to worry about losing Pammy in the divorce. "Are we sure-"

I didn't finish before she playfully shoved me, laughing. "Yes, we're sure. I'm not signing off on anyone's murder. He's an awful person, but he doesn't deserve to die."

"You know I don't like to disagree with you, but if I thought I could get away with it, I would have killed him long ago myself for him hurting you. He's a coward for how he physically pushes you around and tries to intimidate you, and the world would be a far better place without him in it."

She sighed. "You're not wrong, but we're not doing the wrong thing just because it's more convenient."

"I love you deeply, but my life would be far easier if you were a worse person."

She laughed at that and grinned, moving closer to me, pulling my mouth to hers. I melted into her kiss.

I couldn't wait until we could drop the ruse. Having to let Nick kiss me and knowing she was doing the same with Gatsby was making me even more impatient for this to come to an end. The silver lining was that Tom was staying away from her, and Gatsby still seemed harmless enough, so at least I didn't have to worry about her physically.

I let her kiss me for a few more moments before pulling back. "We don't have much longer."

She groaned. "I know, but it's been ages. Are you sure we'll be missed?"

"By Nick? Absolutely."

She laughed at that. It wasn't a secret that he was as wrapped around my finger as Gatsby was Daisy's. I didn't love having to deceive him, but the outcome was well worth the method to get there. If the price of Daisy and Pammy's freedom and safety was a couple of broken hearts, I would gladly pay it. I had been willing to pay the price when it had been my heart on the line, so I was more than willing to sacrifice Gatsby and Nick's hearts as collateral damage.

Daisy and I hardly spent a day apart when it could be helped now, except for when my parties happened. It was an unfortunate necessity for my business. I had to keep hosting influential people in my home, entertaining them. Unfortunately, she refused to be anywhere near the parties, saying she couldn't be seen with me. I had tried to argue that she wouldn't be with *me* per se, but at my party with hundreds of others, but she hadn't relented, saying her husband couldn't know about us.

It was really starting to sink in that she was actually here to stay, that we were back to being an us. The only thing standing in our way was the small inconvenience of her being a married woman; an inconvenience I was hoping to resolve sooner rather than later.

Most of the time she wasn't here, when I wasn't called away to mind business concerns, I was reaching out to my contacts looking for a way to get her out of her marriage. Of course, I could afford the best divorce lawyers in the country if it came down to that, but I hoped to spare her the pain. I had everyone dependable that I knew looking for any loopholes in the marriage contract or anyone that could be bribed to make the problem go away. Unfortunately, I had been coming up blank so far, but it was a temporary setback.

She was mine in all but name, and I was growing impatient to change that. I was sick of sharing her with that no-good bastard she called husband, sick of her having to split her time between me and him.

Today she couldn't even make it out because she didn't know where he was going to be for the day. It was infuriating. I invited Mr. Carraway to my home to attempt to distract me from going to find her. I knew it would make things worse for her, so I wouldn't, but it was tempting. I was growing more and more impatient by the day. I hated having to hide our love, hated that she was being forced to pretend she loved another. It was sickening.

Mr. Carraway's presence would be welcome, though. I hadn't seen him in quite a while. Miss Baker had been keeping him quite busy. I envied him and his ability to do anything with her, to be seen anywhere with her. He wasn't having to sneak around and hide like he was anyone's dirty secret. I loathed feeling like Daisy was hiding me. I felt no better than the penniless lieutenant I had been when I met her. I had come up in the world, but having her hide our love brought me right back there, right back to feeling unworthy.

Unfortunately, what might have been a pleasant afternoon with a good friend took a turn for the worse when some uninvited guests came trotting in. It wasn't uncommon for people to come and gawk at me and my home, but usually they had the decency to wait until one of my frequent parties. These three arrived unannounced, uninvited, and unwelcome during the middle of the afternoon.

The feelings of annoyance gave way to anger when I recognized one of the men from the papers. It was Tom Buchanan, the no-good low life who had stolen my Daisy from me. Here he was arriving on horseback like some wayward prince here to debase himself by partaking in my drink and hospitality. I saw red, but took a couple of deep breaths as him and his companions dismounted.

"I'm delighted to see you," I forced out, not that it mattered. The people that came to see me never cared if they were welcomed by me. They only cared that they got what they came for, my alcohol and a good story. Well, who was I to deny them? "I'm delighted you dropped in. Sit right down. Have a cigarette or a cigar," I said, ringing the service bells. "I'll have something to drink for you in just a minute."

Tom and the woman took my drinks. The other man with them didn't. Tom met my eye and downed the drink before putting it violently down on the table. The server hadn't even left the room yet. I gestured to him to bring Tom another. He did.

Tom nodded his approval and I couldn't decide if he was taunting me or genuinely approved. Either way, I didn't like it.

"Did you have a nice ride?" I asked, directing my question to Tom.

"Very good roads around here."

"I suppose the automobiles-" Mr. Carraway tried.

"Yeah."

Apparently they weren't here for idle conversation. I introduced my-self to the party, and Tom had no recognition of me. It was unthinkable that he held such an important part in my life, but to him I was nothing. I was sure I had seen him in the city before, and said as much, but he brushed it off. I hated that he was able to forget my face when his haunted me.

The thought of him touching Daisy, *my* Daisy, consumed me with anger until I blurted out aggressively, "I know your wife."

"That so?" he asked, unphased.

I tried to rein in my rising anger at his arrogance. His dismissal of me when he turned to Mr. Carraway almost had me doing something regrettable, but I held onto my last shred of control.

"You live near here, Nick?"

"Next door," Mr. Carraway confirmed.

"That so?"

The conversation continued much like that, with me trying not to punch Tom in the face and Tom making inane comments and looking around haughtily judging me and my home. How dare he look down on me when I was worth more than him? Even with all the money I had, he still had the nerve to turn up his nose at me. It infuriated me. I could only hope they would soon leave now that they had what they came for. They had seen my home, and me, drank my alcohol, and were leaving with a story of how impolite of a host the notorious Gatsby was. I was sure they would laugh about it with their friends over less expensive drinks. I could imagine it now, them talking about the silly fool who drinks away his money chasing a dream he could never have. My grip tightened on my glass until the woman spoke, startling me out of my thoughts.

"We'll all come over to your next party, Mr. Gatsby." As an after-thought she phrased it as a question. "What do you say?"

"Certainly; I'd be delighted to have you."

It hardly made a difference to me who came to those parties anyway, since Daisy wouldn't.

The other man said something about leaving. I was grateful, but did as etiquette dictated and invited them for dinner.

"You come to supper with *me*," the woman suggested, looking at me and Mr. Carraway. "Both of you."

The party started to get up and leave. I looked to Mr. Carraway, who replied, "I'm afraid I won't be able to."

"Well, you come," the woman said to me. The last thing I wanted to do was leave, but she had just partaken in my hospitality. It felt rude to deny her. "We won't be late if we start now."

"I haven't got a horse," I said, trying to excuse myself, before realizing that was something that separated me from them and explaining, "I used to ride in the army, but I've never bought a horse." I hated the thought that they might be thinking they were better than me for having horses. What did I need horses for? I had a car. "I'll have to follow you in my car." I insisted, determined to show them that my car was superior to any horse. "Excuse me for just a minute."

I took my time picking out a hat and coat, and thankfully, when I came out the door again, they were gone. Mr. Carraway made their apologies and excuses to me, but I couldn't have been happier. If I never saw Tom again, it would be too soon.

I had been avoiding Jay's parties for as long as I could, but after Tom came home raving about that lunatic Gatsby who had more money than sense and claimed to know me, I had no choice. He insisted we go and when I tried to say I didn't want to, he told me he was sick of me running around town without him. He snidely told me that if I didn't want to go out with him, I didn't need to keep going out at all. I couldn't lose the freedom I was quite enjoying, so I agreed and prayed that Jay would behave.

Mr. Carraway stopped by one morning out of the blue to inform me that Tom and his party had been serious. They were coming to my party tonight. Thankfully, Mr. Carraway also brought the most welcome news that Daisy would be coming, too.

I was ecstatic. She had seen my home, but she hadn't seen it the way it was meant to be seen, full of life and interesting people. She hadn't seen me in my element as master of the house and master of revelries. I was the party king of New York City and I knew that once she saw how I was worshipped, she would know once and for all if she didn't already, that she had made a mistake marrying Tom. She belonged with me. Together we could be the reigning party king and queen of New York City. No one threw a finer party than I did, in either West or East Egg. No one could compare. But when Mr. Carraway left, and the silence creeped in, the thought invaded my mind, 'what if she hated the party?' What if she had a miserable time?

I wallowed in despair for a little while before jumping into action. I couldn't let that happen. This would be the best and brightest Gatsby party of the summer. This would be the party that every party aspired to be. Anyone who was anyone would be here and anyone who wasn't would despair.

Only the best would do for Daisy.

I set to work right away, phoning every connection I had throughout the city. I didn't normally bother spreading the word about my parties, since people always showed up, anyway. In New York City, if you threw a party, invited or not, people would come. Tonight, though, I needed them all there. Tonight, the random guests wouldn't do. This needed to be spectacular.

CHAPTER THIRTY-NINE
Daisy

The very moment we entered the party, Jay was there to greet us. Nick had told me and Tom in no uncertain terms that at a Gatsby party, it was rare to actually see the host. I wished he hadn't said that, since it must have been making Tom more suspicious that Jay came over to specially greet us.

I wished that Jordan was here, but she had a golf fundraiser she couldn't get away from. She insisted that sending Nick along was just as good, though. She promised me that without her, Nick would be glued to my side and wouldn't leave me alone with either of the men. She hadn't actually told him anything, but she said he could be counted on to follow me around since he didn't like being alone at parties. I hoped she was right.

Nick reintroduced Jay to me and Tom, and then an uncomfortable silence pervaded the group. Tom was surveying the scene, and I let myself take a look around, too. The party was already in full swing even though it was just barely twilight and I knew from what Jordan told me that it would only get crazier. There were already people tripping all over themselves and slurring their words from the drink. I hoped Tom wouldn't get sloppy tonight in front of all these people. I didn't know what Jay might do if he did.

"These things excite me so," I said, and then loudly whispered to Nick, "If you want to kiss me any time during the evening, Nick, just let me know and I'll be glad to arrange it for you. Just mention my name. Or present a green card. I'm giving out green-" I was still trying to joke the tension into easing when Jay cut me off.

"Look around."

"I'm looking around," I said, making it more obvious as I again surveyed the scene. "I'm having a marvelous-"

Again, he didn't let me finish. "You must see the faces of many people you've heard about."

Sick of not being allowed to finish a sentence, I let Tom answer for me.

"We don't go around very much. In fact, I was just thinking I don't know a soul here."

Jay's eyes narrowed for a split second before his party host smile returned. "Perhaps you know that lady." Jay pointed out a beautiful woman sitting under a flowering plum tree. I was surprised to find, on closer inspection, that I did recognize her. She had starred in one of the movies that had hit big recently.

"She's lovely." She had a regal air to her that reminded me a little of Jordan.

"The man bending over her is her director," Jay told us.

He walked us from group to group, showing me off. I grimaced at the gesture. I didn't like being made a spectacle of, and being personally introduced to each drunkard on his grounds was too much for me. I was thankful he was trying to be discrete, though, since he remembered to introduce me as "Mrs. Buchanan." I hadn't ever heard him call me that.

It was always Daisy or Miss Fay. As much as I hated being called Mrs. Buchanan, I was grateful he remembered to address me properly in front of Tom and the rest of the partygoers.

It also amused me watching Tom's scowl grow as he was introduced to person after person as Mr. Buchanan, the polo player. Despite his protests, that's how Jay continued to introduce him for the rest of the evening. I was sure he objected to having his identity diminished to just being a polo player, but since I was diminished to just being his wife, I had no sympathy.

Tom was quick to start drinking and, much to my relief, we quickly lost sight of him. Thankfully, I wasn't left indecently alone with Jay either, since Nick stayed glued to us.

Jay made a couple of comments to Nick about how he should go meet this person or that person, but Nick stayed with us, ever the faithful shadow. In what had to have been an excuse to get me alone, Jay suggested a dance. I listened for a moment and, hearing a foxtrot score start to play, I agreed. The foxtrot wasn't an intimate dance and would look innocent enough to anyone watching.

No matter how much had changed in the last five years, he was still a lovely dancer. If anything, his dancing might have improved. It was easy to lose myself in the dance. It was the most fun I had had so far that night.

After our second dance, Jay whispered in my ear, "Let's go somewhere quiet," and gently guided me away with a hand across my back.

Luckily, Nick had been watching us and when he saw us making an escape, came bounding over and followed. Jay hid his displeasure well.

The downside of large parties is there's always someone around. I desperately wanted to get Daisy alone, but knew she wouldn't be willing to risk getting caught with me. While we were dancing, I saw Mr. Carraway watching us and got an idea. Mr. Carraway's house was close enough we wouldn't be missed, and I was sure he would be a good sport about lending me his home for a little while. After all, I hadn't had a moment of privacy with Daisy because of him.

He was agreeable enough, but followed us. Even worse, Daisy refused to enter his house.

"I need to stay close, just in case."

"In case of what?" I asked, frustrated. Didn't she want me as badly as I wanted her? Why was she keeping up this pretense when we were alone?

"I can't be missed, Jay. If he finds out about us, I don't know what he might do to me."

Rage coursed through me at that, but it quenched a little when I saw how concerned she looked. She needed me to calm down. I tried, telling her, "Don't worry about him, love. He won't lay a finger on you. I'll make sure of it."

"I trust you. I really do. I'm just scared." The thought that she had been living in fear of him for years was enough to drive me to the brink of madness. I wondered again if she might come around to him disappearing. Her being a rich widow would be quicker and easier than getting her marriage dissolved, but so far, every time I mentioned it, she shot the idea down.

"You don't have to be scared with me. I'll protect you." She was mine to protect, and I would make sure no other man touched or hurt her. I wouldn't let anyone else have her.

I tried again to get her to enter Mr. Carraway's house to have some fun with me, but she wouldn't go further than the front steps where she insisted on sitting, saying she wouldn't walk another step. I offered to carry her, but she wouldn't budge.

Even more aggravatingly, she had Mr. Carraway stand watch within earshot in the garden. I told her she was being paranoid and was told he was watching for a fire, or a flood, or any act of God. *Ridiculous*, but I made the best of it. Taking her lips to mine the second his back was turned.

I kept trying to push her further, but she wouldn't do anything more than kiss. She kept looking back at Mr. Carraway, saying, "We can't, Jay. He might hear us."

I would have killed Mr. Carraway on the spot if I thought she would let me take her right then and there with him gone, but I knew her better than that. She was anxious and, despite my insistence that making love would calm her nerves, she wouldn't be persuaded.

I hadn't been with her again since the first time five years ago and I was yearning to claim her again, but she continued to protest. I sighed and forced myself to be content with just kissing her for the time being. She was right. She deserved better than to have our carnal reunion on the front steps of her cousin's house.

A short time later, she pulled herself away and got up, saying we really should get back. Frustrated as I was, I let her lead on, back to the party. I supposed I was happy she was at least enjoying herself at my party.

I hadn't thought I would have ever been happy to see Tom, but when Nick, Jay, and I returned to the party, it wasn't long before he found us. I was pleasantly surprised that he was still at a pleasant level of drunk and hadn't yet tipped the scales into being the angry drunk I knew he was after a few more drinks.

I was glad he was pacing himself and not embarrassing himself or me. From the way he was looking over his shoulder at a short little blonde, I was sure I wouldn't have to worry about him bothering me tonight. I was grateful for his presence forcing Jay to keep some level of distance and decorum, though.

A few moments after Tom came over, Jay was called away on business. The butler told him the call couldn't wait. He looked dismayed but took the call. After Jay left, Tom made excuses and went back to his new friends, leaving me alone with Nick and his incredibly drunk friends. It was better than being around Tom, but I still couldn't help wishing I could be anywhere else right now.

When it was finally time to go, I couldn't wait for the car to pull around and take me away from here. Jay looked pained I was leaving, though, so I tried to assure him I had a good time, but I don't think I succeeded. I knew he wanted to impress me and that I should have tried harder to convince him he succeeded, but nothing about the drunken debauchery he called parties appealed to me. Tom didn't shy away from loudly proclaiming the superiority of East Egg parties to the wild West Egg parties. To me, it wasn't that the party wasn't as exclusive and proper as an East Egg party that bothered me, but how the people conducted themselves.

They turned up almost every night uninvited and reigned chaos all over Jay's home. They drank like it was going out of style and partied like the world was ending. If it were only on occasion, I could forgive it, but they happened weekly, sometimes multiple times a week, and it was hard to excuse acting like a drunken fool that often.

Tom was drunk enough he didn't hold back from loudly criticizing Jay and the party before we had even left Jay's property.

"Who is this Gatsby anyhow? Some big bootlegger?"

"Where'd you hear that?" Nick asked, a surprising amount of annoyance in his voice.

It wasn't like Nick to be assertive. Besides, with all the liquor here, it wasn't a surprising conclusion. If Jay wasn't a bootlegger, he must have highly unsavory contacts to keep the supply flowing like he was. It wasn't hard to get ahold of a few bottles a week, but the volume he was serving was well beyond the scope that even my rich drunkard husband could procure.

"I didn't hear it. I imagined it. A lot of these newly rich people are just big bootleggers, you know."

"Not Gatsby," Nick snapped.

I wondered if I should try to cool the mounting tension, but I didn't and Tom didn't stop. "Well, he certainly must have strained himself to get this menagerie together."

Sick of hearing Tom complain, I interjected, "At least they are more interesting than the people we know."

Tom smirked at me. "You didn't look so interested."

"Well, I was," I shot back.

He laughed in my face. I couldn't decide if I was more angry that he was being rude or that he was right. He turned to Nick and asked, "Did you notice Daisy's face when that girl asked her to put her under a cold shower?"

I didn't care to continue to listen to him, so I started singing along with the music, and Tom fell blessedly silent. When the song I knew ended, I blurted out another defense for Jay. "Lots of people come who haven't been invited. That girl hadn't been invited. They simply force their way in and he's too polite to object." I didn't know why I bothered. Tom was right; the parties were tacky and tasteless. I didn't care for Jay, but I didn't care to hear him insulted either, especially not by Tom, who was no better than he was.

"I'd like to know who he is and what he does," Tom said, ignoring me. "And I think I'll make a point of finding out."

"I can tell you right now. He owned some drugstores, a lot of drugstores. He built them up himself." I was repeating the same lines he had fed me and even I didn't believe them. Looking around this place, it was clear this wasn't drugstore money. It was much more likely to be *drug* money.

CHAPTER FORTY-TWO
Gatsby

Daisy hated the party. I wanted to blame her misery on her scoundrel of a husband, but I knew I was lying to myself. He was partially responsible for her misery, but so was the party. I had wanted her to see how far up in the world I had come, but with her husband there sneering and looking down on me, I could hardly feel like she was impressed.

She tried. My sweet little Daisy tried to lie to me, but I saw right through her. The moment I found Mr. Carraway again, I pulled him aside and burst out, "She didn't like it."

"Of course she did," he said immediately. He was a good friend, but a terrible liar.

"She didn't like it. She didn't have a good time." I had hoped having her at the party would help her feel like she was part of my world, like our worlds could be intertwined like we were, but seeing her in the midst of the revelry made it all the more clear she didn't belong there. What did it say about me if I did? What did it say about our future if she couldn't fit into my world? Couldn't she see I had done all of this for her? "I feel far away from her. It's hard to make her understand."

"You mean about the dance?"

"The dance?" I quirked an eyebrow at him. Of course, I wasn't talking about the dance. I thought he was smarter than that and was surprised he wasn't keeping up. "Old sport, the dance is unimportant."

None of this was important, not really, but I had built every facet of my new life to appeal to her, and having her be ungrateful and unhappy at a party I threw in her honor had me feeling like maybe she wasn't the girl I used to know. "And she doesn't understand. She used to be able to understand. We'd sit for hours-"

I broke off as I paced, thinking. We used to sit just the two of us and talk for hours about what our future would look like. I hadn't imagined this as my future. Even in my wildest imaginings I hadn't thought to reach this high, but I knew I would do great things. She always believed in me back then. Why did it seem like she didn't now? Now that I had made something of myself, now that it would be easiest for her to stand by my side and support me, she felt so far away.

It was his fault, of course.

If she had come without her dolt of a husband, she would have enjoyed herself. It would have been better for her to come alone, but she didn't feel comfortable being seen with me in public without him. Once he was out of the equation, I was sure things would be different. She would see things my way again and we could get back to the people we were together.

"I wouldn't ask too much of her," Mr. Carraway cautioned. "You can't repeat the past."

"Can't repeat the past? Why, of course you can!" Once I got Daisy's husband out of the picture, we could pick up where we left off. It's what I'd been working toward since I decided I made a mistake leaving her. I shouldn't have left her the way I did, but it was hard to still truly regret it.

If I had stayed and married her and became Daisy's husband, I wouldn't be half the success I was today.

I had thought when I walked away from her that I could do better. It wasn't the right time, and I wasn't ready to commit to just one person, especially when women were throwing themselves at me. I wasn't ready to find myself tied down so soon without seeing what the world had to offer. When after a few more women I was still thinking about Daisy, I started to think I might have made a mistake.

I wrote to her, sure she was still pining for me, sure she would be waiting for me, but she never responded. That was when everything went wrong. She wasn't waiting for me like she should have been. She let herself get pushed into marriage instead of waiting for me, but we could go back. I could fix things.

Once Tom was out of the picture, things could go back to the way they were. I wouldn't feel distant from Daisy anymore. "I'm going to fix everything just the way it was before. She'll see."

With Tom out of the picture, she would come around to the life I had built for her. I was sure of it.

CHAPTER FORTY-THREE
Jordan

I was able to sneak away from the fundraiser before the night was over. I thought about dropping by Gatsby's party, but figured it was too far and that I would just be in the way. I didn't want to distract Daisy, especially with both Tom and Gatsby in the same place as her for the first time. Besides, I was sure Nick would make himself useful and glue himself to Gatsby and Daisy, so instead of heading over to spend time with my girl, I did the next best thing and went to check on *our* girl.

Pammy was fast asleep, but the nanny liked me well enough and let me duck in to check on her. She was sleeping soundly and as much as I wanted to hear her excitement to see Auntie Jo and hug her tightly, I wasn't cruel enough to wake her. I bent down and kissed her forehead before leaving the room.

Moving to the sitting room, I made myself comfy. Showing up at the party would have been a little dramatic, but there was no reason I couldn't wait here for Daisy. I hadn't spent much time with her lately and missed her dearly.

I had just settled in with a book when I heard the phone ringing sharply from the other room. I waited as it rang and rang, waiting for it to stop, but it didn't. There was a brief pause, during which I assumed the butler had answered, but then it began again.

It took me a moment to remember how late it was and that the Buchanan staff rarely worked this late. It was also unusual for calls to come through this late. I let it ring, and again it faded out. There was a moment of peace before it started again. This time, I put down my book. I was starting to worry. What if it was Daisy? What if she was in trouble? She had no way of knowing I would be here, but what if something had happened and she was calling home for help?

I rushed to the phone and picked up the receiver. Before I could even say hello, there was sobbing on the other end. My heart stopped, all my worst fears running through my mind for a second before the voice yelled, "Tom! Tom! You have to help me!"

I breathed out a quick sigh of relief. It wasn't Daisy. I was about to correct the person, but they continued, "He's saying we're going to move away. He's saying he'll take me away from here and then I'll be faithful. He threatened to beat the sin out of me. I can't stay here. I'm so scared. You have to help me. It's not just me. I'm pregnant, and I know it isn't his. You have to help me, for me and your son. He's going to kill me. I just know it."

A thousand thoughts ran through my mind. This had to be Tom's mistress, and she was pregnant and in trouble. No wonder she was with Tom; it sounded like she was in desperate need of help. It took me just a moment of selfish thoughts that this would complicate things to decide it didn't matter; I was going to help her. I would never leave a woman in trouble like that if there was anything I could do about it. It was also impossible to miss the parallels between her and Daisy's situations, and if this were Daisy on the phone pleading to some stranger, I would hope they would agree to help her. I couldn't let this woman stay suffering if there was anything I could do about it.

"This isn't Tom."

"M-M-Mrs. Buchanan?" she choked out a horrified gasp.

I quickly corrected her, "No, no. I'm not Tom's wife. I'm a friend of the family's. Tom's out at a party, but I'm willing to help however I can."

She choked on her sobs. "I'm so sorry. I was just looking for Tom. We're um," she paused and hiccupped, "old friends."

"It's okay. I'm not Tom, but I'd be happy to help. Let me meet you somewhere and we can talk things out."

"W-why would you want to help me?"

"Us women have to stick together." She didn't say anything, so I added more of the truth, "Besides, you remind me of a dear friend of mine. She's in a rotten situation and I'm helping her, but I would hope that if she didn't have me, that a kind stranger would be willing to help her out."

She again was quiet, so I repeated, "Let's meet somewhere. Can you get away?"

There was a pause, before she said, "I think so."

"Where are you?"

"In the pits of hell." I waited, before she continued, "The Valley of Ashes, where hope goes to die and money runs dry."

It took me a moment to understand where she meant; it wasn't so far from here.

"I can come pick you up."

"No!" she said quickly, the panic evident in her voice. "That would make him suspicious. I have a little apartment in the city, though. I'll take the train and meet you there, but I can't stay long."

"Why not?"

"He's already angry. I can't make him more suspicious. My sister's in the city, so I'll say I'm visiting her, but he'll expect me back by morning."

I took down the address and hung up the phone. I moved back to the other room to get my coat. I looked longingly at my book for a moment before heading to the car. I wasn't sure what I could do for her, but I needed to at least hear her out and see if there was a way I could help.

CHAPTER FORTY-FOUR
Jordan

When the woman who introduced herself as Myrtle opened the apartment door, I was surprised to notice she was a good deal older than myself and Daisy. I hadn't expected Tom to have gone for an older woman. She was pretty enough, but she didn't hold a candle to Daisy. It was a rude thought that I immediately dismissed as being unnecessary, especially because I was biased. Gatsby and I agreed on just one thing, that Daisy was the most beautiful girl in the world. I loved her fiercely, but none of that was this woman's fault.

She didn't ask to be pitted against Daisy for Tom's affection. I wondered what she saw in him in the first place. Trading one bad situation for another didn't seem like an improvement.

She turned and went to the kitchen to get herself a drink. She offered me one, but I declined and made myself comfortable on a chair in her living room. The space wasn't as large as the apartments I was used to, but it wasn't cheap to live in the city and her having an apartment in the city in addition to her home outside of it must mean she was doing okay financially. The furniture, if tacky, was at least good quality and the place was clean and well taken care of.

She swept back into the room and I noticed her makeup was running. She plopped down onto her couch and some of the whisky sloshed out of her glass onto her dress. She didn't even seem to notice and took a big gulp of the stuff. I grimaced as I watched her drain half the glass. She set it down roughly and turned to me, "So you're Mrs. Buchanan?"

I cocked an eyebrow at her. Hadn't we already been over this? "I'm not. I'm a friend of the family's."

"Okay 'friend of the family's'", she said, emphasizing each word with evident distrust, "if you're not Mrs. Buchanan here to warn me off of her husband or pay me off to disappear, then who the hell are you and what do you want with me?"

I took a breath. I wasn't sure how I expected this to go, but I hadn't expected this. Although, her suspicion made sense. "I didn't lie to you. I suppose I should have clarified, though. I'm not Mrs. Buchanan, but I am her friend. I'm no friend of Tom's."

She sighed, picked up her glass, and took another large swig. "Ah, there it is. She sent you instead. So what is it Mrs. Buchanan wants with me?"

"She actually doesn't know I'm here, but I'm curious what you see in Tom."

"He's not my husband."

"He's not a good man."

"Maybe not, but a bad man with money is a better than a bad one without."

I looked around the place, not understanding. Sure, it wasn't my taste, but anyone who could afford a city apartment of this size clearly wasn't hurting for money. "Things can't be that bad. This is a really nice place."

She laughed ruefully before saying, "My point exactly. My husband could never afford this," she said, gesturing to the room.

It took me a moment to realize what she was saying. "Tom's paying for this?"

"Being his mistress has its perks. He needs somewhere to store me when he wants to get away," she said ruefully. "He gets a little rough sometimes, but at least he doesn't leave as many marks as my husband does."

I felt a mixture of anger and disgust rise up at her words. I wasn't upset with her, of course. She was just doing the same thing Daisy was, trying her best to get herself out of an impossible situation. Some of my anger was for Tom. It wasn't about the money. They had enough to spare that the apartment didn't make a dent. I was more angry that he not only treated Daisy like shit, but he was doing the same to his mistress. This woman didn't deserve that, and Daisy sure as hell didn't.

"He's despicable."

"He might be, but he's the only chance I've got. I wasn't lying on the phone. I'm scared about what George might do to me."

"Your husband?"

She nodded. "I've been spending more and more time out of the house lately and he's been getting suspicious. He's been threatening to lock me up and move us away. I can't do that. If he moves me away from here, I wouldn't have anyone. Right now, I at least have my sister. Maybe I should stop seeing Tom, but I don't know if that would stop George from spiraling. He's always been an angry, suspicious man. Of course, it hasn't helped that Tom's been wanting to see me more and more lately. I would be flattered, but he's constantly complaining his wife is never around and available to him. I'm not stupid. I know Tom doesn't care about me, but I need him. He promised to help get me out. He kept saying he would divorce his wife, but that she's Catholic and won't let him."

"Daisy's not Catholic," I blurted out.

"Figures. I didn't actually believe him. If he wanted out of the marriage, it wouldn't matter that his wife didn't-"

I cut her off. "No, you don't understand. It's not just that Daisy's not Catholic. She isn't, but that's not the point. Daisy isn't the one that wants to stay married. If she could divorce him tomorrow and walk away with their daughter Pammy and a bit of money to let them live comfortably, she would in a heartbeat."

She was gaping at me and I watched her process before she asked, "She wants a divorce?"

"Of course she does. He's an abusive ass."

Myrtle looked thoughtful for a moment before nodding. "I can see that. He hasn't been nearly as bad as George is, but Tom did slap me around the other day for saying Daisy's name."

I couldn't have heard her right. "You mean you insulted her and that pissed him off?"

"No. I literally mean I said her name, and he hit me for it."

I don't know why it surprised me, but it pissed me off even more. "I knew he was quick to anger, but that's something else entirely."

She shrugged. "He warned me about it, and I kept pushing him. He hadn't hurt me much before that and I didn't believe him, but at least he warned me. George doesn't anymore."

I hated the thought of this woman being helplessly pushed around, especially with her being pregnant. "Wait, Tom knows about the baby and still hit you?"

She looked sheepish at that, picked up her glass and went to drink, but it was empty. "I should get some more. It's a bit of a long story that I refuse to be sober for."

She went back into the kitchen with the glass and a minute later came back with just the bottle, no glass in sight. She plopped back down on the couch, taking a swig directly from the bottle and said, "I suppose it's not long of a story, but I definitely don't want to be sober for it."

She took another swig before putting the bottle down on the table where her glass had been. "I've been pushing Tom to help me get away from George. The apartment was the most he was willing to do, but some help that is. I can't come here too often without having hell to pay when I go home. It was more for Tom than it was for me. Now that things with George are getting worse, I'm desperate. I hoped that maybe if I told Tom I was pregnant that he would care more about my safety and get me away from George."

"Are you pregnant?"

"Unlikely, but not impossible. He certainly isn't careful."

"So you thought that Tom would leave Daisy for you to protect you?"

"Hardly. If that was what he chose to do, I would have learned to live with it. Even if he turned out to be as bad as George, at least he has money, but that's not what I wanted. I was hoping he would give me enough money to get away from George and set myself up comfortably. If he hadn't offered, I wasn't above threatening to tell his wife. He wouldn't have taken kindly to that, but I'm desperate and thought there was a chance it would work. To be honest, I still might have to. George is getting worse and worse by the day."

I gave into my anger for a moment thinking about all the women out there who were likely trapped in the same way Myrtle and Daisy were and all the men who got away with hurting them just because they were men. Society gave men license to commit a number of atrocities as long as they were against women. It was despicable.

"What if we could get you away from both George and Tom?"

"We?"

"Me and Daisy."

She cocked her head at me, clearly confused. "Daisy Buchanan?"

I nodded.

"Why the hell would Daisy Buchanan help the woman who's been sleeping with her husband?"

"Because you're a woman in need of help. There's a million reasons, really. She doesn't want to be married to him. She understands what it's like to be trapped in an abusive marriage. She understands what it's like to feel like you have no options and to have to pick the one that you're most able to live with. She knows a lot about the sacrifices women have to make in this world to survive. But even if none of those were true, it would be enough that you're a woman in need of help."

"She's really that altruistic?"

"She cares about others, and it's clear to me that you didn't choose to be with Tom to hurt her."

"I didn't, but I can't say that I would have made a different choice. If it came down to a choice between my safety and hurting another woman's feelings, I would choose myself."

"And neither of us would blame you. Even if her feelings were hurt, which I can assure you they aren't, neither of us would want you to endanger yourself to spare her feelings."

"So, what do you propose? Do you have the money to spare to help me?" She looked at me with the first stirrings of hope I had seen on her since I had walked in. I didn't, though. If I had the money required, I would have already paid Daisy's way to freedom, but I did have an idea.

If I could get Daisy on board, there was a certain man with more money than sense who would be willing to do just about anything Daisy asked.

"I don't, but I know someone who does, and I have a plan."

"A plan?" she asked with some derision. "A plan is all I have right now. Is yours better than mine?"

"I think it is. Besides, my plan doesn't involve Tom, so if my plan doesn't work, there's nothing stopping you from trying yours."

"But you know I'm not pregnant," she pointed out.

"But he doesn't."

"You would let me lie to him and use him for his money?"

"I would encourage it. Tom doesn't deserve either of you, and while getting Daisy out of his clutches is going to take longer, you have a chance right now to get away, and I want to help you in any way I can."

"And you're sure Daisy will agree."

"I'm sure. I'm quite close with her."

"If you're sure," she said slowly, "I suppose my plan can wait a little while."

I ran some quick calculations and said, "Give me a couple weeks. If you're not on your way to freedom by then with enough money to be reasonably comfortable, you can try your plan."

She nodded slowly. "Okay, I can do that." After a moment she added, "But please don't take much longer than that. I'm not sure how much longer I can hold George off and survive in that house. It's getting worse by the day. I can survive two weeks, but after that, I'm not so sure."

"I promise you, if my plan doesn't work, I'll do everything in my power to help you with yours. I won't leave you alone and in danger."

"Thank you," was all she said.

She didn't ask for details of my plan, and I didn't offer them up. I didn't want to expose Daisy any more than I had to without talking to her first, since my plan hinged on her using Gatsby. I left Myrtle's that night intent on talking to Daisy about it the first minute I could get her alone.

CHAPTER FORTY-FIVE
Jordan

The next morning, the very first second I could, I pulled Daisy away up to her room. Thankfully, I had caught her before she left for Gatsby's, but Tom was due back soon and she needed to leave before he returned, so I didn't have too long. I intended to tell her about Myrtle the moment she shut the door, but the second she did, she pulled me to her and kissed me. I took me a minute to remember myself and pull away.

"Jord-" she half whined, half pleaded, trying to pull me back to her.

It took all my willpower to not let her, but this was important.

"I actually didn't pull you up here for that."

She pouted. "Maybe that wasn't the reason but it should be."

I frowned, hating that I couldn't play along. "I'd love to, trust me, I would, but this is important."

She sighed and moved away from me to flop down on her bed. "Okay, okay. What is it?"

I paced the room as I told her everything I learned last night. I watched her go through all the same emotions I did, and wasn't the least bit surprised that when I finished explaining, her first questions, rapidly fired at me the moment I finished, were, "So what can we do? How are we helping her? What's the plan?"

It warmed my heart that she didn't hesitate. Even I had hesitated a little at first, but not my girl. She heard another woman was in trouble and it didn't matter that that other woman was cheating with her husband or that it would complicate our own plans. She still wanted to help her without question, and I loved her all the more for it.

"I'm thinking we can get Gatsby to help."

She considered it a moment before asking, "How? He wasn't been able to get me away from Tom yet, despite being incredibly motivated. How could he help Myrtle?"

"Well, with you, it's a bit more complicated. You need it to be legal because of Pammy. It doesn't matter as much with Myrtle."

"Okay, so she can skip a messy divorce and just disappear?"

"Sort of." I paused, trying to think of how to explain my thought so it wouldn't sound crazy. "She needs to disappear, but in a way final enough that her abusive husband wouldn't be hunting her down."

She stared at me, blinked a couple of times, and said, "I don't get it."

"What if we could make everyone think she had died?"

"You want to help her fake her own death?" she asked incredulously.

"I know it sounds crazy, but I think with Gatsby's help, we could do it."

"Do you think he would help?" she asked slowly.

"I think he would if you asked him. We would need some money and some of his connections, but I think we could pull it off."

"I might be able to convince him with some time."

I hesitated for a moment before saying, "We don't really have time. I told her we would give it a shot in a couple of weeks."

"A couple weeks?" she exclaimed. "Two weeks isn't enough time for me to get Jay on board subtly."

"I know! I know, but I didn't know what else to do. If she tells Tom she's pregnant, he might hurt her and even if he doesn't, he might insist on staying in her life, and what happens then when there's no baby?"

She groaned. "You're right. He wouldn't like being lied to and would probably get violent. So we're really doing this?"

"I think we have to. I know it's more than we planned on taking from Gatsby, but it wouldn't be enough that he would even miss it."

"I'm not worried about Jay's money. I'm worried about having to convince him to help us, especially with me still needing his help, too."

"He's mad about you, Dais. He'll help if he sees how upset you are about Tom abusing another woman. He'll help and, if anything, it should push him to be even more motivated to get you out of there."

She smiled a little at that. "Okay, I'll see if I can find a way to bring it up to him."

She started for the door, but I pulled her back to me first, crushing her into a fierce hug. "I love you," I told her softly as I held her to me.

"I love you, too, more than words can express." She pulled back and kissed me gently before backing out of my hold and leaving the room.

CHAPTER FORTY-SIX
Gatsby

I couldn't stop thinking about how much Daisy hated my parties. It plagued my thoughts. I hardly slept at all after she left. Watching him take her away would have been bad enough, but I was sure she was the reason they had left early. She hadn't enjoyed herself at all. Tom, on the other hand, had been plenty busy with his wandering eye and hands. He would have stayed far longer, so she must have wanted to leave. I knew she would never leave my side voluntarily, so she must have really hated my guests.

The parties were important for my business. I needed the connections and legitimacy the parties afforded me to continue operations. I also needed the parties for the distraction they provided. Yes, they drew attention to me, but inviting people in to gawk at and ask about my fortune and circumstance made it easier to control the rumors about me.

I knew I needed the parties, but it was hard to feel like they mattered at all when Daisy hated them. They were a necessary evil, but if she hated them, maybe I could pause them for a while. There wasn't much about myself I wasn't willing to change to make her happy. I was sure if I paused the parties that she would spend more time here.

Yes, I thought, *I'll tell her first thing when she shows up. That'll really make her understand the extent of my love. She'll be happy enough that she'll launch herself into my arms and make love to me for the first time in five years.* I couldn't wait to see her.

I was nervous enough about the afternoon, knowing I was going to have to spend ample time lying to Jay about how I had felt about the party. Now, having to find a way to bring up Myrtle made things that much more complicated.

I walked in and he swept me into a hug, spinning me around the floor. I laughed as he did. His energy was infectious for a moment. When he stopped, he said quickly, "I'm stopping the parties."

"You're what?" That was the last thing I expected him to say.

"You hate them, and while they'll have to start again eventually since they're good for business, you hate them so I'm stopping them for now."

"You don't have to do that," I said hesitantly, unsure what he wanted from me.

"I know I don't have to. I want to. I want you to know how much I care about you and your happiness. Putting a stop to the parties for now is within my power and anything within my power that would make you happy is as good as yours."

Maybe this wouldn't be as hard as I thought after all. "Well, there is one thing-"

He either didn't hear me or didn't mind cutting me off since he kept talking. "Besides, without the parties, you'll be able to spend a lot more time here."

I paled at that. "A lot more time?" I squeaked out, feeling the panic rise. I was already here for a little while almost every day. The last thing I wanted was to have to spend more time with him. Especially time alone. I was having a hard enough time putting him off. He was already begging me to be more physical with him. He kept telling me I must not really love him if I wasn't willing to.

Those were the same words he had used to get me to relent five years ago, but I was older and wiser now. Besides, he was right. I didn't really love him, and I certainly wouldn't be getting physical with him. I regretted it enough from the first time that even if I didn't love Jordan and still cared about him, I doubted I would let him talk me into it. It was what had gotten me into this mess in first place.

"Without the parties and the strangers wandering around, you'll feel a lot safer coming here. You won't have to worry about being seen with me."

I was fully panicking now. I needed an excuse. I needed to say something, anything. I heard a clatter coming from somewhere else in the house.

One of the staff most have dropped something, I thought.

The thought struck me with a new excuse. "I can't. If you stop the parties, the staff will talk. The staff will know it's because I'm here and word will get around town."

He frowned at that. "I hadn't thought about that."

I had been counting on that. It wasn't a problem that could be easily solved. "There's something else I wanted to talk to you about," I said, unsure of how to bring up Myrtle.

"Of course, darling, you can tell me anything."

"I need your help with something."

"Anything at all in my power is yours."

"I'm not sure," I said slowly. "It's a big favor and I'm worried it's too much."

"There isn't anything I wouldn't do for you."

"Maybe it's not doable, though." There was a chance it was too big for him to accomplish, but I hoped I was wrong.

"Nonsense. There's nothing my money can't fix."

"I have this friend who needs to disappear."

He quirked an eyebrow. "Disappear permanently?"

I nodded slowly. "Ideally, yes."

"Does it have to look like an accident?"

"What?"

"Does their death have to look accidental?"

"No! No, I just meant she needs to get away. Her husband is abusing her, and she needs to get away."

He looked at me sympathetically. "I promise I'm doing everything I can to get you away from him. You don't have to run. I'll protect you."

I should have seen that coming. Of course, he wasn't getting it. "I'm not talking about me. I'm actually talking about my friend. She needs help getting away from her husband."

He nodded in understanding. "Ohhh, so he's the one who needs to disappear. I can handle that."

"What? No!" I couldn't understand why he was always so quick to jump to the idea of murder, and why he seemed so okay with it. "She had just wanted some money to start a new life, but I didn't think that would work. I don't think that if she just left that her husband would let her go."

"So, let me get this straight. If you don't want either of them killed, what is it you're asking for?"

"I want to help her fake her death, to get her away from him and give her some money to live comfortably, away from him. If he thinks she's dead, he won't go looking for her and she'll be free from his abuse and from worrying about him tracking her down."

"Who's this friend that you are looking to go to so much trouble to help?"

Jordan had been looking into Myrtle since their conversation and had given me the information we needed.

"Her name is Myrtle Wilson. She's married to George Wilson. He owns a gas station outside the city. Myrtle tried to get Tom to help her, but he refused, so she seduced him. He slept with her and still wouldn't give her any help, so she came to me."

He looked angry, and I was worried for a moment before he said, "That no good two-timing bastard! He cheated on you and didn't even have the decency to help the poor woman."

"He's such a monster, but she believed him. I feel bad for her. I don't want anyone to have to suffer at his hand."

"If you'd like him to disappear, just say the word."

I shook my head quickly. "No, no. I want her safe and somewhere that George and Tom can't hurt her, which is why she needs to be presumed dead. Otherwise, George or Tom might go looking for her."

"Faking someone's death isn't an easy task. What's your plan?"

I didn't really have a plan. "I hoped you might have an idea. I know how smart you are. I didn't think there was any problem too big for you."

I was laying it on a little thick, but I wanted him to give this his all. I didn't have a plan and needed him to try his hardest to help her. If I couldn't save myself right now, at least I could save her.

"Well, that certainly isn't easy. You've given me quite a lot to think about," he said slowly, "but you know I would do anything for you."

I stayed a little while longer, talking with him about how important it was to me before making my excuses and returning home. I hoped he would take my request seriously, because if he didn't, I had no idea how else to help Myrtle.

It felt like Daisy had given me a couple of impossible tasks. I thought about them for most of the night and was ecstatic to figure out they had the same solution. I needed help to pull off the ruse she wanted, and I needed staff I could trust.

There was only one solution. The very next day, I let go of the entirety of my staff and replaced them with people on the payroll of one of my business partners. I needed people I could trust, and the people I trusted, trusted them. They assured me none of my new staff would speak a word about Daisy coming over or a word of my affairs in general to anyone. It was the perfect plan, since I would need people I trusted to execute the other part of my plan.

I was going to have to get creative. It wasn't easy to make someone disappear without arousing suspicion. I went through several options, but all of them would require extensive police investigation, which would quickly reveal she wasn't actually dead. That wasn't an option, but I was struggling with how to avoid it. One of my partners had an inside man on the force, but I would need more than that to help her disappear.

George and Tom both needed to find out. George was easy enough. As her husband, he would be notified if anything happened to her. Tom was more complicated. He had no public ties to her and they had no friends in common. He wouldn't find out unless it was made public. So whatever happened either had to catch the attention of witnesses or be leaked to the press.

The problem was, every possible solution I came up with would result in an investigation. There was no way to make her death look accidental without her body being examined by the police.

Unless it didn't look like an accident. If the cause was clear enough and they were busy chasing a culprit, they wouldn't need to examine her body. If it were gruesome in nature, it would be easily explainable that only the officer on my payroll looked at her before covering her up. George would, too, of course, but his judgment would be clouded by grief, so that hardly mattered.

I was going to have her hit by a car. Not actually, of course, but she needed to appear to be hit by one. If we could make it look like she was and give the police a responsible party to track down, we could get her out without anyone being the wiser.

The problem, of course, was the scapegoat. I could sacrifice one of the business's men, but that was hardly ideal. I pondered it for a couple of hours before the perfect plan formed. I did know someone I needed to get rid of, and what better way than to frame him for manslaughter? If he went to jail, the courts would hardly deny Daisy a divorce and no one would begrudge her from moving on from a monster who would plow down an innocent woman with his car, especially when they found out it was his mistress he had killed. It could be said she was blackmailing him, threatening to come clean about their affair, and rather than let the truth come out, he silenced her.

It was the perfect plan. I decided to leave out the part about using Tom to Daisy, though, in case she got cold feet or a conscience. I just told her I had a foolproof plan. She was ecstatic and continually told me how proud she was of me and how much it meant to her that I was doing this for her.

She would be even more thankful when she found out the plan was going to get rid of her Tom problem as well.

CHAPTER FORTY-NINE
Jordan

"He figured it out!" Daisy exclaimed, grinning.

"Who figured what out?" I asked. I was glad to see Daisy looking happy. More often than not nowadays, she looked anxious. Happiness was a rare but welcome sight.

She grinned wider. "Jay! He figured how we're going to help Myrtle."

She told me Gatsby's plan to fake a car accident, and I had to admit I was somewhat impressed. It was a much more elaborate plan than I had expected, but maybe that was for the best. It might be so elaborate that no one would question it. After all, who would be crazy enough to fake getting hit by a car in order to disappear?

"So, when are we doing this?"

"Jay wants to spend the day with all of us. Him, me, you, Nick, and Tom. He said he needs Tom there, too, to make sure he's not with Myrtle when this happens."

"How does he propose that?" I asked skeptically.

"Everyone will come to lunch, of course."

"And how do you propose we get everyone there?"

"Easy enough. When you see Nick tonight, ask him how Jay's been. I guarantee he'll go over there. The new staff, on Jay's orders, will turn him away and then I'll have Jay phone him and invite him to lunch. He won't say no."

"And Tom?"

"I'll tell Nick to make sure he's there. Between me and Nick, he won't be able to say no."

I nodded slowly. Daisy hardly ever asked anything of Tom and if all she was asking was that he attend a lunch, I didn't think even he would deny that request.

"Are you sure his plan will work?" I asked her.

"As sure as I can be. He said he has inside people to make sure it runs smooth. I'm hoping it does, and I trust he's put effort into it. I've been using this as my latest excuse not to be there too often. I keep telling him I'm worried about my friend and won't feel at peace until I know she's safe. It's true, I'm worried about her, but even when she's safely gone, I'm not spending any more time over there than strictly necessary."

I took her hands in mine. "You're doing such an amazing job and I promise you it'll be over before you know it. If he can successfully pull this off, I have no doubt he'll be able to get you away from Tom soon."

"I keep telling myself that, but it's hard to believe that's going to happen. It's hard to believe that there's a future for me that Tom's not in, as much as I want that for you, Pammy, and me."

It was breaking my heart to see how little hope she had left. I wished with everything in me that there was something, anything, I could do to help, but I was already doing everything I could.

Chapter Fifty
Daisy

I stopped at Jay's for what I hoped was going to be a short visit. I was happy with how well things were going so far. Myrtle knew the plan. We were going to be getting her out in a couple of days. Tomorrow, Jay was going to invite Nick to lunch with me, Tom, himself, and Jordan, and then the plan would be set in motion. I just needed to get through tonight without anything happening to upset Jay. I needed his help on this or the whole plan fell apart.

When I knocked, one of his new men answered gruffly, but pulled open the door when he saw it was me. I asked where I could find Jay and he pointed me in the general direction of the West Wing. I headed that way, but couldn't find Jay in any of his usual spots. We normally spent time together in one of his various sitting rooms and drawing rooms, but I didn't see him anywhere. I was going to turn around and look somewhere else, hoping to either bump into him or flag someone else down who could help me find him, but as I turned another corner, I noticed there were flower petals on the floor.

I knelt down and picked one up to look at it; it was a daisy petal. With a sigh, I looked to see where the trail went. It rounded another corner. How anyone could navigate this palace was beyond me. I turned another corner and saw the petals continued down the hall. As I followed them, I found myself even more lost. I had only explored the entire home once when Jay had given Nick and me a tour, so I had no idea where I was or how to get back outside. I was just thinking about how terrible it must be for his new staff, who certainly must have been frequently getting lost, when I recognized where I was.

The petals stopped abruptly at the door to Jay's bed chamber.

I considered turning around and going the other way, but I didn't know my way out. I could wander around for hours without finding my way out. I used to be able to count on encountering one of his staff to help me, but the new people weren't nearly as helpful. Besides, I needed him to want to help me.

I needed to march in there and tell him to get any ideas he might have out of his head. I needed to tell him I was too overcome with worry about Myrtle and couldn't possibly do what he wanted with her fate hanging in the balance, and then I needed to get out of here.

I took a couple of steps closer and the anxiety took root. I wanted to turn and run, but I knew that wouldn't help anything. I needed him, but I was starting to wonder how long I could keep this up for. I wondered if Jordan would understand if I put a stop to this after we helped Myrtle. I didn't think I could keep this up much longer, and I was starting to think he might be dragging out helping me on purpose, so he had something to hold over me.

I opened the door gently, worried about what I might find. I should have expected what I did. He was sprawled out on his bed in his old uniform, looking every bit the dashing lieutenant I had met and fallen for five years ago. My heart raced a little at the memory before the reality hit me. We were alone in his bedroom. I hadn't been here since he first showed me and Nick around, but we hadn't been alone then. Now, we were very much alone and from the look in his eye, he had expectations of me that I wasn't planning to meet.

Kissing him was one thing. I had been kissing him plenty. Jordan and I had agreed to do whatever it took, but this was too much. Kissing him wasn't unpleasant. I wouldn't be doing it if I didn't feel like it was necessary, but I didn't hate kissing him. Jordan was doing the same with Nick. We both knew our plan would require keeping them busy, but all Jay and I had done was kiss and this was a line I wasn't willing to cross. He grinned at me and gracefully moved off the bed and crossed the room to me.

I had two options. I could turn on my heel and walk out now, or I could try to convince him to wait, try to make it seem like his idea not to go through with this.

I didn't want to have to cajole and beg this man, who clearly knew nothing about me or what I actually wanted, but this wasn't just about me. I had Pammy to look out for, and there wasn't much I wouldn't do to ensure her happiness and safety.

"Darling, you found me," he said pulling me toward him. He moved to kiss me, but before his lips even reached mine, I could smell the alcohol on his breath. I flinched away from it. Whisky kisses were dangerous ones. Before he could feel I was slighting him, I pulled him into a hug instead.

"The flowers were a lovely touch."

I pulled back and was surprised when he let me. "Ah." He grinned wider. "I'm glad you found them. You deserve to never sully yourself by walking on common ground. You should float on flower petals wherever you go."

He was in a flowery mood. "They certainly helped me find your room. Your home is so large it's quite easy to get lost in here."

"My darling, you could never be lost. I wouldn't let you. Wherever you go, I promise I will always find you."

He had only affection in his voice when he said it, but I still had to suppress a shiver. That was one of my fears. After he helped get me and Pammy extricated from Tom, Jordan and I planned to take Pammy and disappear. We wouldn't leave a trace since the last thing I wanted was Tom finding us, but Jay's words produced a new fear.

I hadn't worried about him following us, which now seemed naïve. Of course, I knew he would be upset, but I didn't imagine he would track me down. Maybe this wasn't a good idea after all. If I were trading my shackles for chains, it might be better to stick with the shackles I was used to. After all, I had traded one prison for another before when I agreed to be married, and I had quickly come to regret that.

"Jay, I-"

He didn't let me finish, snaking his arms around my back and pulling my lips to his. It wasn't sweet like some of his kisses, or eager like others, or even passionate. The kiss was frenzied and fierce. He was forceful in a way he hadn't been with me since the last time I was with him five years ago. I felt myself freeze up as the memories took hold of the misery I felt after he used and abandoned me. The feelings of hopelessness washed over again as my body stopped feeling like my own. I knew he was touching me, kissing me, but I was so numb I didn't feel it. It wasn't until I felt his hands on my chest that I came back to myself and jumped away from him.

"Jay!" I clutched my dress back up in front of my chest, trying to cover myself, to shield myself from his prying eyes and wandering hands. "I'm a married woman!" I exclaimed, looking for a rationale that he could understand. The truth, that I didn't want him to touch me, didn't feel safe. I wasn't sure if he would stop just because I asked. My asking might just make him angry. I had too much experience with angry men to take that risk lightly, especially since he was drunk. I didn't know what kind of drunk he was and I wasn't eager to find out.

He groaned. "In the eyes of the law only. I'll have it dissolved in no time, but it was hardly a legal wedding. You can't be legally his, because you're mine." He closed the distance between us and caressed my cheek. "You've always been mine. From the first day we met, I knew I had to have you. You were the most beautiful woman I had ever laid eyes on, and I wasn't worthy of you, but knew I would be some day. You were the best, and only the best would do for me." His hands trailed down, meeting mine where I was holding my dress. He slowly removed my fingers one by one.

Under his spell, I let him. My dress fell, and he caressed my now bare shoulders and said, "I've dreamed of this moment since our last night together. How I've longed to touch you again."

He pulled me to him, crushing my chest against his. My breath hitched. He ran his hands over my back, causing me to shiver.

"How I've longed to hold you like this."

He planted kisses on my neck, one by one, lower and lower until he was kissing my collarbone and then my bare shoulder.

I went to pull back again, but he held me in place with his hands. I sucked in a breath as his lips sunk lower. I pushed back against him more insistently, but he held tight. "Jay- please."

He chuckled. "I love it when you say my name."

"No, Jay, please stop."

He paused for a moment and looked up at me. "Too much teasing? Very well."

I sucked in a gasp as I felt his lips on my now bare chest. I felt my body respond to him, but as good as it felt, this was the last thing I wanted.

"Jay-" I gasped louder when he sucked harder. "Please, we can't."

I tried again to move back, but he wouldn't let me go.

He paused long enough to say, "Darling, I know you want this. I can feel how your body is responding to me. You don't have to put on a show, it's just us here. I won't tell if you don't."

I was starting to get angry now, scared still, but the anger was rising. How arrogant a man he was to think that he knew me better than I knew myself.

"Jay, stop. I don't want this."

"I know, I know." He murmured into my chest, "You're such a good loving wife who would never cheat on her husband. I promise you, if your divorce goes to court, no one would ever believe you were capable of adultery."

"That's not what I'm saying."

"Oh, so you are capable? Duly noted," he said, redoubling his assault against my chest with renewed vigor.

"Jay, stop. I'm being serious. I don't want this."

He did stop for a moment and I felt relief that he was finally listening. I didn't care what I had to say to get him to understand; I just needed him to stop. Jordan was the only one I wanted touching me like this. I didn't know why he wasn't understanding that I didn't want this.

"Are you saying you don't love me?" he asked, finally raising himself back up to my face. He pulled me tighter to him and with one hand took my chin and turned my eyes up to meet his. "You did the same thing to me last time. I really thought you wanted to prove your love for me. Maybe I've been too generous. Why am I trying so hard to get you out of your marriage if you don't love me? I told you you would regret marrying him. I'm trying to be generous and help you fix the mistake I warned you against, but I don't have unlimited patience."

I didn't know what to say. He was right; I didn't love him. I was using him, but now I wasn't so sure I was the only one trying to manipulate the situation. The way he was talking to me, it was like I was the eighteen-year-old girl again who was so enamored with him she would have done anything he asked. He had told me the same thing then, that I had to prove my love for him with my body, and I had listened. It had been the worst mistake of my life. I had let him push me into it, let him manipulate me into feeling like I had to give myself to him. I wasn't going to let him do that again.

I tried again to push away from him, but his grip on my chin tightened to a point just shy of pain. I flinched. "Jay, I-"

"Stop," he commanded, and the cold look on his face was enough that I listened. "If you're going to say anything except that you love me, I'd rather hear you moaning."

I blinked at him, not understanding, but a moment later his hand was gone from my face and trailed over my chest. I sucked in a breath at the contact before he moved lower, his other hand pulling me tight to him. He snaked his hand under my skirt and I saw red. Our plan be damned, he was going to regret that. He wasn't Jay anymore; he was just another man trying to use and abuse me. He wasn't any better than Marcos or Tom, but I wasn't the scared little girl I used to be.

I jabbed my knee up as hard as I could into his groin and was rewarded with his touch immediately stopping. He yowled in pain and crumpled to the ground. I didn't waste a second securing my dress and running from the room. In my haste, I made a few wrong turns, but by the time I found the exit ten minutes later, he hadn't found me and none of his staff had even seen me.

I let myself out and jumped into my waiting car, not looking back. As far as I was concerned, the plan was dead. I refused to be alone with him again. We would just have to find another way.

That night, I hardly slept, tossing and turning with nightmares I couldn't keep at bay. After another hour, I gave up on sleeping all together and just stared at the ceiling, thinking. That was how Jordan found me that morning.

"What you are doing still in bed?" she asked as she swept into the room. "The day is young, but we-" She stopped abruptly when she saw me and rushed over to me. "What's wrong?" She gently cupped my face in her hands when I didn't look at her and turned my head. "What happened?"

"Jay happened," I forced out. I didn't want to talk about it, not really. I was worried she would think I was weak, worried she would be right. I was weak. Yes, I had gotten myself out of the situation, but only after letting him escalate things way past what I was comfortable with. I didn't want her thinking less of me or thinking I might actually want him.

"What did he do and how badly does he need to hurt?"

I blinked at that. "He was drunk and didn't stop when I told him to. I stood up to him, but I think I ruined our plans. There's no way he's going to help me after that, and Pammy, and Myrtle, poor Myrtle." I started crying at that and she pulled me into her and held me tight while I cried.

"No matter what you did, I'm sure he deserved it. Don't worry about the plan; we'll figure something out. It's not worth you putting yourself at risk like this. What did he do?"

"He tried to pressure me into letting him have his way with me. He was saying things like how I must not love him if I was trying to stop him and that I didn't deserve his help if I didn't love him."

"That bastard!" she yelled and started to move away from me.

"Where are you going?"

"To kick in his door and teach him some fucking manners. I don't care if you were using him. He's a grown man who should know better than to pull that crap."

I pulled her back to me quickly. "It's okay. I got him pretty good before I left, right in the groin. He probably won't be fit to have his way with anyone for a little while." I grinned when I saw her surprise, and then she chuckled.

"I love you so much."

"And I love you."

After a moment, she added, "I'm so proud of you."

"Thank you," I said more seriously. "It wasn't easy, but I'm proud of myself, too. In a way, I'm grateful I was using him, because if I still cared about him, I might have given in like last time."

"Wait, he said that to you before?" she asked slowly.

"Some of it. He convinced me that giving myself to him was the only way to prove my love for him. He kept telling me that if I didn't, it meant I didn't love him and was saving myself for someone else. I really cared about him, and thought I loved him. I was so scared that he was going to go off to war and die thinking I didn't love him. The thought terrified me. I couldn't let him leave thinking that, so I let him have me."

She was quiet for a minute before growling out, "I'm going to kill him." She moved to get up again, but I held her arms.

"Jord, please."

"No, I love you, but no. I'm going to rip his arms off his fucking body so he can never violate anyone again."

"It's not like that, though," I said, half trying to explain and half trying to calm her down. "I didn't try to stop him that time."

"You shouldn't have had to! He shouldn't have used your feelings as a weapon to get what he wanted! He shouldn't have made you feel like you had to prove yourself. You were a fucking kid, Dais. You were an eighteen-year-old child, and he was a twenty-seven-year-old man. He fucking knew better, and he used your feelings against you. I don't give a fuck how much money and influence he has; none of that is going to save him from what I'm going to do to him for hurting you."

"Wait, Jord, stop, please. I need a minute."

She seemed to sense how much I needed her to listen, so she did. I needed to think a moment. I had regretted that night with him, sure, but only because he had left the next day. I had been beating myself up for making a bad decision. I had never stopped to think about how he had talked me into it. How he had manipulated me.

"He manipulated me, used me, and then left me," I said slowly.

"And they won't find his body."

"You don't understand. All this time, I thought I was naïve and should have known better."

"Of course you were naïve; you were just a kid! He knew better, and he still used you. He pressured you into relenting and letting him have you."

"He didn't love me," I said slowly. I had never really thought to question that. Sure, I didn't think he loved me now, but I had always thought he had back then. I knew he left, but I had never questioned his feelings for me. Now I wasn't sure what to think.

I didn't feel sure of anything, except the gorgeous blonde sitting across from me who was swearing vengeance on my behalf. Even if nothing else made sense, she did.

"All this time, I thought I had done something wrong to make him leave after that night. I had held onto the thought that I wasn't good enough and something about me made him leave. Maybe a part of me is still a little naïve, because I should have known that I didn't cause him to leave. I couldn't make him stay, but I didn't drive him away. He got what he wanted from me and he left." The clarity that things were never going to go differently, that I couldn't have done or said anything to make him stay, was freeing. "I couldn't have made him stay."

"There's absolutely nothing wrong with you. He was crazy for leaving, but it was his insane choice and there was nothing you could have done to change that. Besides, if he had stayed, we'd probably be right where we are now but with you trying to get away from him instead of Tom."

The truth of her words was undeniable and for the first time, I granted myself forgiveness.

I pulled her into a tight hug and whispered, "Thank you, so much. I don't know what I did to deserve you."

"I'm the lucky one, and even though I'm sure you're about to say something about how violence isn't the answer and ask me not to harm him, I would do anything for you."

"Even leave Jay alone?"

"Begrudgingly," she replied. "He doesn't deserve the mercy, but for you, I'll extend it."

I smiled at her and pulled her lips to mine, wanting to thank her and erase the memories of unwelcome kisses with her very welcome ones.

I woke up with an aching groin and aching head, and the memories from the previous night slowly came back to me. I had created quite a mess for myself. I had wanted her so badly and was so sure she wanted to give herself to me again, but maybe I was wrong. Maybe she was serious about not breaking her marriage vows until I helped her out of her marriage. I had tried and failed to convince her to let me make love to her. I was trying to dissolve her marriage, but I was growing impatient of waiting for her. She was worth the wait, but the waiting itself was incredibly frustrating.

As the pain started to fade, I came to my senses. It was Daisy, and she was worth the inconvenience of waiting for. She was the best, and I deserved nothing but the best.

Sure, she was angry with me, but that could be fixed. I penned a letter to her and, before the ink dried, gave it to my butler to have delivered to her. It was risky having a letter delivered to her home, but if her no-good husband happened to read the letter, I made sure there was nothing objectionable in it. In fact, I was simply suggesting I should come dine with her and her husband tomorrow and to write back if tomorrow didn't work.

She seemed to really care about helping out her friend, and I was sure going forward with the plan would help to get me back in her good graces.

I couldn't believe my eyes. Jordan was reading over my shoulder and looked just as confused.

"He still wants to go forward with the plan?" I asked.

"It sounds like it," she said slowly. "Could it be some sort of trick?"

"I don't think so. Unless he's angry enough to side with Tom, but I don't think that's possible."

"Well, there's one way to know for sure."

"What's that?"

"Phone Nick. If Gatsby's truly going through with it, he'll have invited Nick, too. If this is just an excuse to see you again or to try to get alone, he wouldn't have invited Nick."

"You're brilliant!" I exclaimed, rushing for the phone.

It rang several times before my cousin's voice came through. "Hello?"

"Nicky dear, it's Daisy. Tell me you're coming to lunch tomorrow. I might perish if you don't."

He let out a breathy chuckle. "I did receive a rather manic invitation from Gatsby earlier, and I wouldn't dream of missing it."

The relief floated into my voice, "You're truly wonderful. I'm delighted that we won't be parted much longer."

The rest of the conversation was brief. I didn't have much else to say and didn't want to talk long for fear of giving something away. If I was too eager for his presence, he might form some sort of suspicion. I had no idea what thoughts and connections his mind would form if he did and didn't want to find out.

I grinned at Jordan as I hung up the phone. "Nick's coming."

She looked surprised, but tentatively happy. I couldn't help riling her up a little. "Look a little happier, dear. Your suitor is coming to lunch."

She leveled me with a glare that had me doubling over in laughter. I couldn't help myself. When I looked up, she was begrudgingly smiling. "I can't stay annoyed with you when a laugh or smile from you is enough to brighten the darkest day."

I loved her fiercely and told her as much through stolen kisses the entirety of the day.

CHAPTER FIFTY-THREE
Jordan

The tension in our unlikely party was boiling over as surely as the heat was. It was fitting our plan was coming to fruition on the hottest day of the year. Nick and Gatsby had arrived together and intruded simultaneously upon the little slice of shade Daisy and I were lounging in. Neither of us had a desire to move. The heat was a convenient excuse. It clouded over everything today, making the simplest of movements feel oppressive.

"We can't move," I said at the same time that Daisy did.

They both moved closer to us, and Nick took my hand in his for a moment before relinquishing it. I thanked the heat for enforcing a distance I wasn't sure he would have maintained on his own.

Nick looked around the room and asked, "And Mr. Thomas Buchanan, the athlete?"

I laughed at the little moniker, and was about to answer when we all heard Tom's voice in the hall. He sounded angry. Wonderful. Our little party was tenuous enough without him already being in a bad mood.

Nick was looking at me with a question in his eyes, and I didn't feel the need to hide the truth. I was sure it was Myrtle Tom was talking to. "The rumour is that that's Tom's girl on the telephone."

Daisy had been giggling with Gatsby, but that quieted her, so we all heard Tom's next words clearly. "Very well, then, I won't sell you the car at all... I'm under no obligations to you at all... and as for your bothering me about it at lunchtime, I won't stand for that at all!"

I stiffened at that. Myrtle had filled me in briefly on Tom's plan to sell her husband George one of his cars. George was going to use it to take Myrtle away from here. That he was calling up bothering Tom for it now was a very bad sign.

I shot Daisy a look. Her eyes reflected my own worries, but for the boys' benefit she said, "Holding down the receiver."

I wondered if that was a common occurrence for him to do if she was so readily able to come up with the lie. Did he often lie to her about his dealings and take fake calls?

"No, he's not," Nick rushed in. "It's a bona-fide deal. I happen to know about it."

That Nick was acquainted with Myrtle wasn't something I expected. Before I had time to worry about how that might impact our plan, Tom came hurrying into the room.

"Mr. Gatsby!" He held out his hand to Gatsby and violently shook it. Gatsby returned the gesture. I wondered if they were going to stay like that until one of their hands fell off, but Nick cleared his throat and they seemed to realize themselves and both dropped their hands. "I'm glad to see you, sir," Tom said to Gatsby and turned and nodded to Nick, "Nick."

Daisy didn't let them say anything else. She cut in with an authority I didn't recognize but was proud of. "Make us a cold drink," she told Tom. I was shocked when he turned and left the room to do just that.

The moment the door was closed behind Tom, she grinned and leapt up and crossed the room to Gatsby and kissed him hard.

It was part of the plan. I knew she was testing the waters, making sure he was still our ally and still under her influence, but it wasn't fun to watch, especially when she murmured, "You know I love you."

Even knowing she meant it for me, the fact that she was saying it to him was too much for me to handle without comment. "You forget there's a lady present," I said. Hoping it would pass for playful scolding.

She met my eye with a mischievous look in hers as she looked around, as if looking for the lady in question. I longed to chuck a pillow at her, but suppressed the urge.

"You kiss Nick, too," she suggested.

She was devious, and from the look in her eye, she knew it. "What a low, vulgar girl!" I cried out.

"I don't care!" she cried and jumped up, flouncing away from Gatsby before sighing and settling back next to me on the couch.

A moment later, we were interrupted by Pammy and her nanny rushing into the room. It was about the last thing any of us expected, but Daisy quickly opened her arms and crooned at her, "Bles-sed pre-cious." Pammy didn't move and I saw hurt flash across Daisy's face before she added, "Come to your own mother that loves you."

Pammy did as she was bid and rushed across the room. As she did, she noticed the strangers and when she got to Daisy's side, tried to hide herself in Daisy's skirts. I would have laughed at her skittishness and how adorable she was, but I was too concerned about how Daisy was feeling to truly be amused.

"The bles-sed pre-cious," Daisy drew out her words, trying to draw Pammy out of her shell, but it wasn't working. "Did mother get powder on your old yellowy hair? Stand up now, and say - How-de-do."

She did she was bid and adorably clutched Gatsby's and then Nick's hands in greeting. Gatsby, even after having let go, continued to stare at Pammy in wonder.

"I got dressed before luncheon," Pammy said quietly. Her eloquence startled me. I knew she was incredibly smart, but it had been a while since I had heard her speak in polite company. Truthfully, it had been a while since I had heard her speak at all. The last few times I had seen her had been brief visits while she was asleep. I had been so preoccupied with our plans and with Daisy that I had been failing to notice just how much time was passing and how much little Pammy was growing up before my eyes.

"That's because your mother wanted to show you off," Daisy said, beaming at her. "You dream, you. You absolute little dream."

Pammy looked at me and grinned, saying, "Yes. Aunt Jordan's got on a white dress, too."

She shyly waved to me, and it felt bittersweet. I couldn't help missing the way she used to call me Jo or Auntie Jo. She was growing up way too quickly for my liking.

"How do you like mother's friends?" Daisy turned her in Gatsby's direction and continued, "Do you think they're pretty?"

She looked around before asking, "Where's Daddy?"

She was anxious, and I wondered if it was because of the company or because of Tom.

Daisy chose not to answer and instead filled the awkward silence with the disclaimer to Gatsby, "She doesn't look like her father. She looks like me. She's got my hair and shape of the face."

I looked over and saw Gatsby was looking at Pammy with an unreadable expression. I didn't know what he was thinking, but I didn't have to to know I didn't like it.

The nanny stepped forward and called for Pammy, who was quick to go to her and was led out of the room just as Tom reentered carrying four glasses of gin. The ice clinked in the glasses as he moved.

Gatsby was the first to grab one. I went next taking mine and handing the other to Nick, leaving no room for Daisy to have to refuse it. Tom took his and we all busied ourselves with drinking. It helped with the heat a little, but the main advantage was that it was a balm for the tension in the room.

"I read somewhere that the sun's getting hotter every year," Tom supplied, breaking the silence. "It seems that pretty soon the earth's going to fall into the sun - or wait a minute - it's just the opposite - the sun's getting colder every year."

The room stayed silent. A few moments later, he turned to Gatsby. "Come outside. I'd like you to have a look at the place."

He took Gatsby outside, and Nick dutifully followed. The moment they were outside, Daisy and I exchanged a look before we both hopped up and ran to the window, looking in their direction.

"What do you think they're talking about?" she asked nervously.

"I'm not sure," I said carefully. "Probably nothing important. Maybe he wanted to give them a closer look at the dying sun."

She chuckled at that. "I truly don't know how he comes up with some of the things he says."

They didn't stay outside long and lunch was served shortly after. When we were almost done, the silence seemed to have fully suffocated Daisy, who didn't have the benefit of alcohol to numb the discomfort. She burst out, "What'll we do with ourselves this afternoon? And the day after that, and the next thirty years?"

She was really panicking. I understood and hated that she was in this position at all, but in order to get her out of it, I needed her to keep a cool head.

"Don't be morbid," I told her. Hoping she would understand my meaning, I added, "life starts all over again when it gets crisp in the fall."

I hoped it was true. If Gatsby could be counted on, which was a big if, but if he could be, it was possible she would be a free woman by the fall.

"But it's so hot," she cried out, and I could see she was close to tears. More quietly, she added, "And everything's so confused." I wasn't sure what to do. Having Tom and Gatsby together in the same place was too much stress for her, especially with how they had both been treating her. I hated that I couldn't do anything to help. "Let's all go to town!"

I was about to agree, when Tom loudly chuckled. "I've heard of making a garage out of a stable," he was saying to Gatsby, "but I'm the first man who ever made a stable out of a garage."

"Who wants to go to town?" she asked louder. Gatsby turned to her. "Ah, you look so cool."

He met her eye, and an understanding passed between them. Whatever happened next, he was agreeing to be by her side if she would be his. She was telling him she would be if only she could. I hoped that would be enough to keep him motivated to help her. "You always look so cool," she repeated.

I glanced at Nick and saw he was watching Tom. I quickly looked at Tom and felt my blood run cold when I realized he was seeing too much. He looked astounded as he gazed back and forth between Daisy and Gatsby.

I nudged Daisy under the table with my foot as discretely as I could. She broke eye contact and more innocently said, "You resemble the advertisement of the man." She looked around for help, but Tom was busy staring at Gatsby and Nick was busy staring at Tom. I was going to jump in but she continued, "You know the advertisement of the man-"

"All right," Tom cut in, "I'm perfectly willing to go to town. Come on - we're all going to town."

He jumped up quickly with a manic look in his eye. None of us moved. "Come on!" he burst out, "what's the matter, anyhow? If we're going to town, let's start."

Daisy rose gracefully, and we all followed suit. Once outside, she turned to Tom and challenged, "Are we just going to go? Like this? Aren't we going to let anyone smoke a cigarette first?"

"Everyone smoked all through lunch," Tom said, not willing to budge.

"Oh, let's have fun," she said with a pleading in her tone. "It's too hot to fuss."

He didn't respond.

CHAPTER FIFTY-FOUR
Gatsby

Daisy and Ms. Baker left Mr. Carraway and me outside alone with Tom. I was of two minds, unsure whether to be amused or worried by Tom's outburst. It was clear he had seen too much pass between me and Daisy. I don't know how she had managed to hide her feelings as long as she had. On the one hand, I was happy he was finally realizing that she wasn't his. He couldn't treat her however he wanted to. She might be his wife in name, but she wasn't his. He didn't hold her heart, he never had. Her heart was mine, but the manic look in Tom's eye when he realized what was happening had me worried for her.

I hoped they would hurry up. I had no desire to be around Tom without her. I looked at Mr. Carraway, but he just continued to shuffle pebbles on the driveway with his foot. I started to say something and thought better of it, but I must have made some sort of noise, because Tom whipped around to face me.

I asked the first thing I could think of. "Have you got your stables here?"

"About a quarter of a mile down the road."

"Oh."

I hoped Mr. Carraway might say something, but he didn't.

"I don't see the idea of going to town," Tom burst out. "Women get these notions in their heads-"

"Shall we take anything to drink?" Daisy called from an open window upstairs.

"I'll get some whisky," Tom said, turning and marching inside.

I was grateful for the reprieve. This was a bad idea, though. I shouldn't have come to Tom's home. I turned to Mr. Carraway. "I can't say anything in his house, old sport."

Mr. Carraway nodded thoughtfully, adding, "She's got an indiscreet voice." I knew what he meant. It wasn't so much what she said, but the air and manner with which she said it. "It's full of-" He trailed off, but I knew what he was getting at. It was rich in feeling, in underlining meaning. She spoke with an air that belied her upbringing. You could almost hear the privilege in the richness of her voice.

"Her voice is full of money," I finished for him.

He nodded in understanding, but I wondered if he truly did understand. From his humble abode, it was clear he had never really felt the siren song of wealth. If he had, he would be dashing himself time and time again on her shores like I was. Again and again I rammed myself against the harbor that was ultimate notability, but each time the shore seemed to move further and further away.

Until I found Daisy again, the goal kept moving, but now that she was back, it was clear she had always been what was missing. I had her now, but it wasn't enough yet. She wasn't completely mine the way I needed her to be. If I could just reach a little higher, pull her away from him, make her just mine, I would be happy. I would be respected. I had been naïve before, but the money didn't mean anything without the respect I craved and that couldn't be bought. If it could have been, I would have already had it.

Tom came out of the house, followed by Ms. Baker and Daisy, my shining sun, my golden rays of hope.

"Shall we all go in my car?" I asked, moving to it. I thought Tom would object but he was silent. For the plan, I needed him to object. I touched the seat and felt the green leather of the seats had warmed quite a lot in the sun. "I ought to have left it in the shade." He wouldn't want the ladies to be uncomfortable and would insist on taking his own car.

Instead, he demanded, "Is it standard shift?"

"Yes."

"Well, you take my coupe and let me drive your car to town."

His entitlement made me angry, but more than that, he was ruining the plan. It was supposed to be his car that he drove. He had already used my girl now he wanted to drive my car, too? I would be damned if I let him do that. Besides, it would muddy up the plan. "I don't think there's much gas."

"Plenty of gas," he said with a glance at the gauge. "And if it runs out, I can stop at a drugstore. You can buy anything at a drugstore nowadays."

I don't know what he thought he knew, but he couldn't possibly know the truth. I looked at Daisy, but she was just frowning at Tom. At least she wasn't taken in by his implications that were inching a little too close to the truth for comfort.

"Come on, Daisy, I'll take you in this circus wagon," he said, gesturing to my car.

I crossed my arms, but before I could say anything, Daisy spoke up. "You take Nick and Jordan. We'll follow you in the coupe."

She walked over to me and trailed her hand lightly over my arm. I could live with the arrangement. I wanted to be alone with Daisy anyway, and we could make it work for the plan. As long as Tom's car was on the road, I could still make this work.

We moved to the car as the others got into mine. In a low voice, Daisy breathed out, "This way we can be alone," and suddenly I couldn't care less about the car. I had been worried I was losing her, worried I pushed her too far. I would be more careful going forward, of course, but I hadn't lost her. She still wanted me. I would've let Tom drive my car as often as he liked if it meant she would continue to look at me like that.

CHAPTER FIFTY-FIVE
Jordan

I settled in between Tom and Nick in Gatsby's car. I worried that things didn't appear to be going exactly to plan, but Gatsby hadn't seemed worried so I was hoping he was able to adapt his plan to these new circumstances. I leaned back in the seat, hoping for a smooth ride at least, but it was clear in the first moment that Tom was unfamiliar with the controls. Of course, he was too stubborn to admit it. He would rather kill us all than admit that Gatsby was more schooled in cars than he was.

We lurched off into the afternoon, and my stomach lurched with the car, but my heart stopped when Tom demanded of Nick, "Did you see that?"

"See what?" Nick asked.

He took his eyes away from the road to look incredulously at Nick and me. I watched as the dawning came into his eyes that we weren't surprised because we had already known.

"You think I'm pretty dumb, don't you? Perhaps I am, but I have a - almost a second sight, sometimes, that tells me what to do. Maybe you don't believe that, but science-" He trailed off, sensing he was losing us. After another lurch of the car, he tried again. "I've made a small investigation of the fellow. I could have gone deeper if I'd known-"

"Do you mean you've been to a medium?" I asked, trying to throw him from whatever rant he was gearing up for and lighten the mood. From what I knew of Gatsby, anyone who really knew him before he became the party king of New York City had likely died in the war.

"What? A medium?"

No surprise my humor went over his head as well as the fact I was poking fun at him.

"About Gatsby," I clarified.

"About Gatsby! No, I haven't. I said I'd been making a small investigation of his past."

"And you found he was an Oxford man." I didn't really know why I was defending him, except that I didn't want Tom to be right about anything.

"An Oxford man! Like hell he is! He wears a pink suit."

That I didn't really believe Gatsby was an Oxford man was irrelevant. If Tom didn't believe it, I would die before admitting I felt the same. "Nevertheless, he's an Oxford man."

"Oxford, New Mexico," he snorted, "or something like that."

I wondered if he had actually found out something useful. I desperately wanted to know. My curiosity about Gatsby hadn't yet been sated, but letting Tom ramble wouldn't be good for anyone today. "Listen, Tom. If you're such a snob, why did you invite him to lunch?" I asked, letting my annoyance show. This whole thing had been a bad idea in the first place. If Myrtle wasn't dependent on us, I would have shot the idea of the gathering down in a heartbeat.

"Daisy invited him; she knew him before we were married - God knows where!"

He stayed mercifully quiet for a few minutes after that. We were deep into the Valley of the Ashes, when I recognized a billboard Myrtle had told me about. Doctor T.J. Eckleburg's eyes were baring down on us and it gave me an idea. Myrtle's husband George ran a gas station. I was about to mention Tom's previous comment on the waning gas when, surprisingly, Nick piped up, "Aren't we low on gas? Maybe we should stop."

"We've got enough to get us to town," Tom objected.

"But there's a garage right here," I said quickly as the building Myrtle had described came into view. "I don't want to get stalled in this baking heat," I added.

With an irritated sigh, he slammed on the brakes. I lurched forward, colliding with Nick's arm that he had shot out protectively in front of me. If a certain little brunette didn't have full possession of my heart, his caring gesture might have moved me. It didn't, but it was thoughtful nonetheless. He really was a sweet boy.

The man, George, that emerged from the garage was every bit as Myrtle had described him. Short, balding, on the heavy side, and walked with a hunch. I had thought she must have been exaggerating and was shocked to see she hadn't been. I expected him to move with some arrogance like other abusive men did, but he shuffled along as if in a dream, as if he was hollow and just going about the motions.

"Let's have some gas!" Tom cried, and George moved faster. "What do you think we stopped for - to admire the view?"

I couldn't believe that Tom had the audacity to berate the man whose wife he was sleeping with, but I shouldn't have really been surprised.

"I'm sick," George said, coming to a stop. "Been sick all day."

"What's the matter?" Tom barked out.

"I'm all run down." He sounded fine enough, but I was sure what we were planning for later would leave him actually sick. I felt a little guilty looking at this listless man before reminding myself that, no matter how he looked now, he had been hurting Myrtle for years. He was bad enough that Tom had been a better alternative for Myrtle. That hardened my heart against him.

"Well, shall I help myself?" Tom spit out. "You sounded well enough on the phone."

He moved slowly, wheezing, to the car, and I started to wonder if something was actually wrong with him. His face was tinged green.

"I didn't mean to interrupt your lunch. But I need money pretty bad, and I was wondering what you were going to do with your old car."

"How do you like this one?" Tom asked, and then shocked me by claiming, "I bought it last week."

"It's a nice yellow one," he said, considering.

"Like to buy it?"

I couldn't understand what he was getting at. There was no chance Gatsby would sell it to Tom in the first place, unless Tom intended to sell Gatsby's car out from under him as payback. It was underhanded, and I hoped Nick would object to it so I didn't have to.

"Big chance," George said thoughtfully, considering, before shaking his head. "No, but I could make some money on the other."

"What do you want money for, all of a sudden?" Tom demanded.

"I've been here too long. I want to get away. My wife and I want to go West."

I paled. We were running out of time quicker than I thought then. It was a good thing we were getting Myrtle out tonight. I looked around for any sign of her, but didn't see her. I hoped she wasn't worried. I hoped she knew we were coming for her.

"Your wife does," Tom repeated, startled.

"She's been talking about it for ten years, and now she's going whether she wants to or not. I'm going to get her away."

I was more grateful than ever that our plan was already in motion. We had to get her out before things had a chance to get any uglier.

The coupe raced by in a flash of dust and a wave of Daisy's petite hand.

Tom saw them, too, and his anger intensified. "What do I owe you?" he barked out.

George must not have heard his remark and continued, "I just got wised up to something funny the last two days. That's why I want to get away. That's why I been bothering you about the car."

He knew. I had half a mind to storm in there and bring Myrtle with us now, but I knew the risks of running away as a married woman, and we had a better plan. We were going to get her out, and if the plan didn't work, I would come back and drag her out myself.

"What do I owe you?" Tom repeated.

"Dollar twenty."

I wondered for a moment if George suspected Tom, but if he did, he was holding that back.

"I'll let you have that car," Tom said finally. "I'll send it over tomorrow afternoon."

I looked at Nick and saw he was looking up at the upstairs apartment. As I watched, the curtains rustled, and I saw Myrtle peek out and even from the car I could see the fear in her eyes as she looked at me. I tried to smile reassuringly, but I was starting to doubt the plan myself. It hardly mattered, though. One way or another, she was leaving tonight because I would be damned if I let her spend another night in that sort of terror when it was in my power to help her.

Tom was speeding faster than even I was comfortable with. I resorted to trying to distract him but hardly knew what I was saying. Thankfully, the coupe finally came to an abrupt stop and when Daisy waved us over.

She stuck her head out the window and called, "Where are we going?"

"How about the movies?" I suggested.

"It's so hot," she complained. "You go. We'll ride around and meet you after. We'll meet you on some corner. I'll be the man smoking two cigarettes," she joked.

"We can't argue about it here," Tom snapped. "You follow me to the south side of Central Park, in front of the Plaza."

We rented a suite and took to the parlour after some tense argument between Daisy and Tom that made me incredibly anxious. I kept looking at Nick to intervene, but it was like the heat had stifled him into silence. He just allowed it to happen. I shouldn't have been surprised since it was what he had done all summer, but I had hoped he might say something, anyway. Once again, he disappointed me.

CHAPTER FIFTY-SIX
Daisy

The suite was large enough that it should have felt airy, but with Tom and Jay in the same room, I was suffocating.

"It's a swell suite," Jordan said quietly, trying to break the tension. It worked. Despite it not being funny, everyone laughed.

"Open another window," I said to no one in particular.

"There aren't any more," Tom responded.

"Well, we'd better telephone for an axe-"

Tom cut me off to say, "The thing to do is to forget about the heat. You make it ten times worse by crabbing about it."

I glared at his turned back as he unrolled his precious whisky and put it on the table.

"Why not let her alone, old sport?" Jay chimed in. "You're the one that wanted to come to town."

The room went silent until there was a sudden crash. I jumped, looking around quickly before seeing it was just the telephone book that had fallen to the floor and slumped in relief. Nick and Jay both went to pick it up, but I noticed Tom was staring at Jay with an anger that concerned me. "That's a great expression of yours, isn't it?" Tom asked him.

"What is?" Jay asked distractedly.

"All this 'old sport' business. Where'd you pick that up?"

I didn't know what Tom was getting at, but I didn't like it. "Now see here, Tom. If you're going to make personal remarks, I won't stay here a minute. Call up and order some ice for the mint julep."

Tom was surprisingly silent, and we all heard the wedding march carry in from the ballroom below.

"Imagine marrying anybody in this heat!" Jordan lamented.

"Still - I was married in the middle of June. Louisville in June! Somebody fainted. Who was it fainted, Tom?" I asked him, trying to distract him.

"Biloxi," he said curtly.

"A man named Biloxi. 'Blocks' Biloxi, and he made boxes - that's a fact - and he was from Biloxi, Tennessee." I hardly knew what I was saying now, just that I had to keep talking. If I stopped talking, who knew what would come out of Jay's or Tom's mouths.

We just needed to get through a couple more hours unscathed and then Myrtle would be free and I would have at least saved one girl from Tom, even if it wasn't me.

Jordan picked up my nonsensical conversation. "They carried him into my house, because we lived just two doors from the church. And he stayed for three weeks, until Daddy told him he had to get out. The day after he left, Daddy died." She paused a moment and added, "There wasn't any connection."

"I used to know a Bill Biloxi from Memphis," Nick chimed in.

"That was his cousin. I knew his whole family history before he left. He gave me an aluminum putter that I use today."

I was incredibly grateful for the two of them, more than they knew. I knew Nick was just trying to keep the peace more than help me personally, but I was grateful to him regardless.

The music continued to waft in. "We're getting old," I said with a sigh. "If we were young, we'd rise and dance."

"Remember Biloxi," Jordan said with a smirk. She was right, though, it was too hot to dance. "Where'd you know him, Tom?" Jordan asked.

"Biloxi?" Tom thought for a moment before saying, "I didn't know him. He was a friend of Daisy's."

"He was not," I insisted. "I'd never seen him before. He came down in a private car."

"Well, he said he knew you. He said he was raised in Louisville. Asa Bird brought him around at the last minute and asked if we had room for him."

Jordan grinned at that. "He was probably bumming his way home. He told me he was president of your class at Yale."

Tom and Nick exchanged a confused look.

"Biloxi?" Nick asked.

"First place, we didn't have any president-" Tom stopped when he noticed Jay was jiggling his foot and turned to him. "By the way, Mr. Gatsby, I understand you're an Oxford man."

Jay surprised us all by saying, "Not exactly."

"Oh yes, I understand you went to Oxford."

"Yes - I went there."

Tom paused, raising his eyebrows. With incredulity dripping from his voice, he continued, "You must have gone there about the time Biloxi went to New Haven."

There was a knock on the door that startled us all. A waiter entered with crushed mint and ice, but was gone before any of us could think of something to break the tension.

"I told you I went there," Jay repeated.

"I heard you, but I'd like to know when."

"It was in nineteen-nineteen. I only stayed five months. That's why I can't really call myself an Oxford man."

I looked around and saw that everyone else was looking at Jay surprised. Well, everyone except Tom, who was watching me.

"It was an opportunity they gave to some of the officers after the armistice. We could go to any of the universities in England or France."

It hardly mattered now, but I was still proud of him for telling the truth and keeping his head held high. He didn't let Tom intimidate him into lying, and despite my other feelings for Jay, that was commendable.

I rose with the ghost of a smile on my face. Let Tom and Jay make what they will of that. "Open the whisky, Tom, and I'll make you a mint julep. Then you won't seem so stupid to yourself." I looked down and saw the sprigs of mint were incredibly fresh and urged them all, "Look at the mint!"

No one did, because Tom wasn't done. "Wait a minute," he snapped. "I want to ask Mr. Gatsby one more question."

"Go on," Jay challenged.

"What kind of row are you trying to cause in my house, anyhow?"

"He isn't causing a row," I rushed to say, not ready for whatever was coming next. "You're causing a row. Please have a little self-control."

"Self-control!" Tom barked out. "I suppose the latest thing is to sit back and let Mr. Nobody from Nowhere make love to your wife." My heart dropped. I had suspected he knew, but suspecting and knowing were two very different things. I had to be incredibly careful how I played this. I was walking a very thin line balancing things with Jay and Tom and if I wasn't careful, I might get hurt. "Well, if that's the idea, you can count me out... Nowadays people begin by sneering at family life and family institutions, and next they'll throw everything overboard and have intermarriage between black and white."

He was turning red in his anger, a fact I found a little ironic since he was so proud of being white, but I kept my mouth shut.

"We're all white here," Jordan said under her breath. *God, I love that woman.*

Tom kept going as if he didn't hear her. "I know I'm not very popular. I don't give big parties. I suppose you've got to make your house into a pigsty in order to have friends - in the modern world."

I had no idea how he had turned his anger about losing me into a rant about the state of the modern world, but it would have been funny if my future wasn't hanging in the balance.

"I've got something to tell *you*, old sport," Jay started, but I knew where he was going and couldn't bear it.

"Please don't!" I interrupted. "Please, let's all go home. Why don't we all go home?"

I was surprised when Nick immediately chimed in. "That's a good idea. Come on, Tom," he said, getting up. "Nobody wants a drink."

"I want to know what Mr. Gatsby has to tell me," Tom said slowly.

It was a like a bad accident; I knew it was coming but couldn't look away, couldn't stop it, couldn't even blink.

"Your wife doesn't love you," Jay finally said. "She's never loved you. She loves me."

I held my breath, but was surprised when neither man turned to actually look at me.

"You must be crazy!" Tom exclaimed.

Jay jumped up, waving his hands, and loudly exclaimed, "She never loved you, do you hear? She only married you because I was poor, and she was tired of waiting for me. It was a terrible mistake, but in her heart, she never loved anyone except me!"

I saw Nick reach for Jordan and try to pull her to the door, but she stayed rooted to the spot and the movement caught Jay's and Tom's attention. They both swung to Nick, who sheepishly dropped Jordan's hand and stayed put. Then, Tom turned to me, a challenge in his eye.

"Sit down, Daisy," he said in what I was sure was supposed to be a gentle tone, but came out a bit patronizing. "What's been going on? I want to hear all about it."

I did sit down, but before I could say anything, Jay interrupted, "I told you what's been going on. Going on for five years - and you didn't know."

Tom had been looking at Jay, but turned back to me sharply and demanded, "You've been seeing this fellow for five years?"

My heart was beating out of my chest and I couldn't think. He was going to hurt me. He always got loud before, and he was going to do it here in front of everyone. I flinched. I couldn't help it.

"Not seeing," Jay answered for me. "No, we couldn't meet. But both of us loved each other all that time, old sport, and you didn't know. I used to laugh sometimes to think that you didn't know."

I had no idea what Jay thought he was doing, but if he kept talking, he was going to ruin everything. He was going to ruin me. Tom had Pammy. Jay had to know I couldn't leave, that I wouldn't leave her. No matter how angry Tom got, I still had to go home with him. I wouldn't dream of getting him angry and then sending him home alone with my daughter. I had to go with him, so whatever Jay thought he was doing, he was just making things worse for me.

It was even more clear than it had been before that he didn't love me. He might never have, but he certainly didn't now. If he did, he wouldn't be doing this. He wouldn't be risking my safety and the safety of my child. I wondered if Pammy had even crossed his mind once in all of this. In his plans to get me out, did it matter to him if she was collateral damage? I hoped it did, but if I was being honest with myself, I wasn't sure he would care. If there was a way he could get me out of Tom's grasp, I doubted he would stop to think about what that would mean for Pammy and keeping her safe, too. I wondered if that's what he was doing now. Maybe he thought that if he angered Tom enough, that I would leave Tom right here and now for my own safety. If Jay thought that, he truly didn't know me. I would never leave her.

"Oh — that's all," Tom said, tapping his fingers together before exploding, "You're crazy! I can't speak about what happened five years ago, because I didn't know Daisy then — and I'll be damned if I see how you got within a mile of her unless you brought the groceries to the back door. But all the rest of that's a God damned lie. Daisy loved me when she married me and she loves me now."

I didn't know how he could possibly believe that would still be true.

"No," Jay said, shaking his head violently.

"She does, though. The trouble is that sometimes she gets foolish ideas in her head and doesn't know what she's doing," Tom continued. I didn't know if he was trying to convince me, Jay, or himself. I looked over at Jordan, whose eyes were narrowed at him. I shook my head slightly, and she calmed a little. I hated that she was having to see this, but I couldn't have her getting involved. Things had already gone wildly off the rails. If I had any chance of recovering the evening, she had to stay out of it. "And what's more," Tom continued, "I love Daisy, too. Once in a while I go off on a spree and make a fool of myself, but I always come back, and in my heart I love her all the time."

A spree? That's what he was calling it now. I didn't give a damn what he did, truly I didn't, but for him to sit there spewing this utter bullshit about how he always loved me was too much. Did he love me when he was sleeping around? Did he love me when he put his hands on me? Did he love me when he forced me to stay away from our daughter? How dare he.

"You're revolting," I spit out. I turned to Jordan first but quickly pivoted my gaze to Nick. "Do you know why we left Chicago? I'm surprised that they didn't treat you to the story of that little spree."

Jay walked over and put his hand on my shoulder. I knew he was trying to calm me, but I tensed up.

"Daisy, that's all over now. It doesn't matter anymore. Just tell him the truth — that you never loved him — and it's all wiped out forever."

I blinked up at Jay, unsure what he wanted from me. "Why — how could I love him — possibly?" There was only one person in this room I loved and it certainly wasn't either of the brutes standing in front of me demanding my love.

"You never loved him," he prompted.

I hesitated. I wasn't sure that was true. I had at least thought I loved him when I married him. Jay was so desperate to hear it, and I didn't know why, but I didn't want to give him that satisfaction. I looked at Jordan and then Nick as an afterthought for any sort of guidance, but neither said anything.

"I never loved him," I repeated softly.

"Not at Kapiolani?" Tom demanded. Our honeymoon. I thought wistfully, the good part of the honeymoon before things turned sour, back when we were truly living in marital bliss.

"No," I said spitefully, but I couldn't shake the thoughts of the people we had been back then. I might have loved him then. If he had stayed the man he was then, I might have. I hadn't known then that he would turn into the man he was today. I had been happy then.

"Not that day I carried you down from the Punch Bowl to keep your shoes dry?" he asked softer, a pleading tone in his voice that was starkly reminiscent of how he used to talk to me back then, back when we first met and I was someone to be respected. Someone to be gentle with. I let myself get lost in the nostalgia for a moment before I heard him say gently, "Daisy?"

It woke me up. He had to know he was hurting me. The memory of the person he used to be hurt. "Please don't." I tried to snap, but my tone had lost most of its bite. I turned away from Tom, looking instead at Jay.

"There, Jay," I said, but I was shaking. Jordan handed me a cigarette. I tried to light it, but I was shaking too much. I threw it down, unlit, onto the carpet, exasperated. "Oh, you want too much!" I cried out, almost in tears.

The stress and emotion were getting to me. "I love you now — isn't that enough? I can't help what's past."

I started crying in earnest then, not for either of the men in front of me but for myself and Pammy, and Jordan. For all the hell we had been through and were continuing to be put through. I hated that I couldn't see it ending anytime soon. Jay couldn't even do that right. He was never supposed to have said anything. That wasn't part of the plan. The plan hinged on Tom staying in the dark, but Jay couldn't even do that right. "I did love him once — but I loved you, too."

Jay just slowly blinked at me. I almost wasn't sure he heard me until he repeated, "You love me, too?"

I started to nod, but Tom cut in. "Even that's a lie. She didn't know you were alive. Why — there's things between Daisy and me that you'll never know, things that neither of us can ever forget."

"I want to speak to Daisy alone," Jay insisted. "She's all excited now—"

I didn't let him finish. The fact that he wasn't even speaking to me anymore and was instead speaking to everyone else about me was enough that I didn't care to hold back anymore. "Even alone, I can't say I never loved Tom. It wouldn't be true."

"Of course it wouldn't," Tom agreed quickly.

I whipped my head to him. "As if it mattered to you."

"Of course it matters," he said with such strong conviction I almost believed him. "I'm going to take better care of you from now on."

Before I could say anything, Jay cut back in, "You don't understand, you're not going to take care of her anymore."

"I'm not?" he asked with a chuckle. "Why's that?"

"Daisy's leaving you."

I couldn't believe it, truly, that Jay would be so stupid. I couldn't leave Tom now. Jay had made damn sure of that with how royally he had just screwed things up for me.

"Nonsense," Tom said sharply.

They both turned back to me, and I half heartedly said, "I am, though."

"She's not leaving me!" Tom barked out at Jay. "Certainly not for a common swindler who'd have to steal the ring he put on her finger."

"I won't stand this!" I cried out. I needed this to stop. I needed to get out of here. The room was suffocating me. "Oh, please let's get out."

"Who are you, anyhow?" Tom continued to ream into Jay, ignoring my pleas. "You're one of that bunch that hangs around with Meyer Wolfsheim — that much I happen to know. I've made a little investigation into your affairs — and I'll carry it further tomorrow."

"You can suit yourself about that, old sport."

I hadn't the faintest idea what they were talking about, but I was happy they, momentarily at least, weren't focusing on me.

"I found out what your 'drugstores' were. He and this Wolfsheim bought up a lot of side-street drugstores here and in Chicago and sold grain alcohol over the counter. That's one of his little stunts. I picked him for a bootlegger the first time I saw him, and I wasn't far wrong."

What a hypocrite. He drank the alcohol, but was too good to associate with the criminals who sourced it.

"What about it?" Jay asked. "I guess your friend Walter Chase wasn't too proud to come in on it."

"And you left him in the lurch, didn't you? You let him go to jail for a month over in New Jersey! God! You ought to hear Walter on the subject of you."

It was like I didn't even exist to them. Jordan, Nick, and I might as well have not even been in the room.

"He came to us dead broke. He was very glad to pick up some money, old sport."

"Don't you call me 'old sport'! Walter could have you up on the betting laws, too, but Wolfsheim scared him into shutting his mouth."

Jay just let Tom keep going.

"That drugstore business was just small change, but you've got something on now that Walter's afraid to tell me about."

Jay seemed to realize then that they had been largely ignoring me. He turned to me and started making wild excuses, defending himself against everything Tom had said and things he hadn't even been accused of. If he was hoping that would win me back, he was wrong. Each forceful proclamation had me withdrawing further into myself. I knew I should be careful how I was acting, should be making him think he still had a chance so he would help me, but I couldn't force myself to.

In a single afternoon, he had stolen all my hopes of a quick escape, of a better life and even if I had still loved him, I was sure I would have never forgiven him for that.

He kept going and going. When I couldn't stand another second, I did the only thing I could think to do. I turned to Tom. "*Please,* Tom! I can't stand this anymore."

I made sure he saw the anguish and fear in my eyes. If I could count on one thing to never change about him, he loved rescuing a damsel in distress.

Unfortunately, he wasn't done getting back at me. "You two start on home, Daisy. In Mr. Gatsby's car."

I looked at him in shock. I had appealed to his kindness and chivalry, but I should've known better that it didn't exist anymore.

"Go on," he said with a satisfied smirk. "He won't annoy you. I think he realizes that his presumptuous little flirtation is over."

With that proclamation hanging over our heads, Jay and I made our escape out into the stifling summer night.

CHAPTER FIFTY-SEVEN
Daisy

I was hoping the ride would be a silent one, but Jay wasn't one for silence.

"Don't you see everything I've done for you? I have more money than all the Rockerfellers combined! How can that not be enough for you? How can I still not be enough for you?"

I stared at him in disbelief, frustrated at his utter lack of understanding. "It's never been about the money. Hasn't anyone ever told you that money can't buy everything?"

Now was his turn to look shocked. He let out a loud laugh and replied, "Money can't buy everything? That's rich! Why, of course it can! I sure do have enough of it."

"Well, it can't buy me."

I thought this would make a stronger impression on him, but he didn't miss a beat before replying, "Sure it can. Tom bought you, didn't he?" He said with a scoff. "What's your price? Name it and I'll double it. Can't you see, Daisy? We'll be so happy together." I stared at him. I am sure my jaw must have hit the floor in utter disbelief.

"For the last time, this isn't about the money, and Tom doesn't own me!"

"Well, of course not. We both know I owned you the second I took your innocence. You were mine then, just as you are now and always will be."

"I will never be yours, not then, not now, not ever." I was so angry I didn't think before speaking. Maybe if I had held back a bit more, things might have gone differently. I have never been said to be rash, but in my anger, I was.

I glared at him, but the look in his eye sent a chill down my spine. An involuntary shiver passed through my body. I held my breath, waiting for him to say something, anything, to break the deafening silence.

When he did speak, it was a little too calmly and all he said was, "You'll regret that."

I felt the swerve of the car before I could comprehend what was happening. I saw the headlights coming straight at us as he said, "If I can't have you, no one will."

I screamed his name and in a split second before the impact, managed to yank the wheel out from him and to the right. It didn't budge much, but it was enough. We missed the car by a fraction of an inch. I let out a breath as my tears started to fall.

The car came screeching to a halt as Jay yelled with triumph. Dumbfounded, I turned to see him grinning ear to ear. Before I knew what I was doing, I saw my hand shoot across the distance and strike his face with a deafening sound. "What the hell is the matter with you? You could have killed us both!"

He kept laughing, the grin never leaving his face. "I knew it! I knew it!" he said, more to himself than to me.

I prayed for the strength not to slap him again. "Knew what?" I asked out of some curiosity but more from concern, as he had clearly lost what was left of his mind.

"I knew it! You do still love me!"

"Have you lost your mind? What the hell makes you think I would ever change my mind? Especially after a stunt like that?"

He just kept smiling and said, "I knew you'd choose to be with me. I knew you wouldn't make me kill both of us."

I had never been more frightened by a man in my life. The fear Tom instilled in me was nothing compared to how I was feeling at that moment.

I knew there was only one way that I would safely walk away from this. "Pull the car over, Jay."

"Of course, my love. Do you want to drive? Maybe it will settle your nerves from that near miss we just had." I couldn't believe the nerve of this man, but I had regained enough sense to stay silent.

He came around to the passenger side and opened the door for me. As I exited the car, I looked around and quickly weighed my options. We were still miles from home and no one else was around. Getting back in the car was unfortunately the quickest and safest way back home. I prayed I wouldn't regret this as I hopped into the driver's seat. At least I would be in control from here on out, so nothing would go wrong.

CHAPTER FIFTY-EIGHT
Daisy

I pushed the car faster than I probably should have, but I wanted to get the ride over with. I needed to get away from him.

The car went speeding into the Valley of Ashes, kicking up a trail of dust behind it.

He put his hand on my arm and I startled so much I almost sent the car careening into a ditch.

"Daisy, love, you should slow down."

He was one to talk. He had almost killed us and now he wanted to talk to me about safety. I took a breath, pushing down my instinct to go faster to spite him.

He was right, of course, I should slow down, but I wanted to get home. Nothing tonight had gone even remotely to plan. We continued to blow through the valley when I saw the billboard approaching, the eyes that Jordan had told me about. That meant we were close to Myrtle's house. I looked at him, wondering if everything wasn't lost. "Myrtle's nearby."

He grinned. "I know dear, so take it easy a little. Wouldn't want anyone getting hurt."

"Are you still-" I trailed off, not sure what to ask since in truth I wasn't sure what his plan actually was. I knew he was planning to help her and that had been good enough for me. I didn't know the details.

"Yes, I just need you to slow down a little."

I immediately slowed. If nothing was going to go right for me, I could at least make sure one woman was saved tonight.

"My man's going to be waiting for us around the corner."

"So, what do you want me to do?"

"Just keep driving, love, you're doing great."

I did what he asked, and we started to approach a gas station. We weren't going nearly as fast as I had been, but still fast enough we would pass it quickly. I looked at Jay, who was looking around. "Keep going; my man should be here any second."

I didn't see anyone, but I did what he asked. It was too important not to.

I kept going. We were going to pass the gas station any second, when I saw headlights from the other lane coming at us.

"There he is!" Jay exclaimed. "Right on time!"

"Now what?"

His man slowed down but was still coming at us quickly. "Keep driving. It's not time yet."

The other driver was starting to swerve a little, and it was making me nervous. "Jay," I started to say.

"Not yet!"

They were all over the road; I didn't know what his plan was, but they weren't driving safely at all. "Jay."

"Still not yet!"

I held my breath for another few seconds, but I couldn't keep silent. They were almost in our lane and almost on us. "Jay!"

"Now!" he yelled and grabbed the wheel again, swerving left hard.

"Jay!" I screamed, trying to pull the wheel back. *Not again. Fuck. I was going to die. I was going to die and Jordan and my dear Pammy would never forgive me.*

"Trust me!" he yelled out.

I didn't, but it was too late.

"Forgive me, my love," I whispered as I closed my eyes and slammed on the brakes.

The impact was jarring, but I was surprised to find nothing hurt. I slowly opened my eyes and saw Jay grinning at me. "We're alive?"

He nodded emphatically. "We're fine, and better yet, your friend is going to be now, too. Look."

He pointed to the other car, and I saw two men get out with a woman quickly following. She was covered in blood.

"Oh God!" I screamed. "She's bleeding! She needs help!"

"Shhh! Love, it's fake. Myrtle needed to be convincing."

As I watched, the men came through the headlights and I could see one was dressed in a suit that was just shy of fashionable and the other was dressed as a police officer.

"Is he?"

"A policeman?" He nodded. "He's my man on the inside."

The woman, who must have been Myrtle, passed through the headlights and grinned at me. I was relieved she was okay, but so confused.

"What's happening?"

Jay didn't say anything. As I watched, the policeman looked around and gestured to a spot on the ground a little ways behind our car.

"We have to go," Jay said quickly.

"What? Why?"

"For this to work, we have to get out of here, now."

I slowly started to move the car. As we started to move away, I saw in the rearview mirror that Myrtle was now lying in the street.

"Faster," he said with an intensity in his voice that left no room for argument.

I did as he said, but still asked, "But what are they doing?"

"What did it look like?" he asked. "In another moment or two, people are going to rush onto the streets. The crash wasn't quiet. What they're going to see is a woman lying dead in the road and a man who witnessed the whole thing and saw a big yellow car speeding off."

"But- but-" I wasn't understanding. "If they think she's dead, won't they come after the car that killed her?"

"They can try," he said with a grin. "The car will be gone by morning."

"But won't they know she's not dead?"

"My man on the inside will cover her and tell everyone she's too gruesome a sight to look at. No one will bother looking, and if they do, they'll see a bloodied up woman and won't look closer."

"And then what?"

"Then, after the circus has died down, my man will take her body to the morgue. By the time anyone thinks to look for her, she'll be well on her way out of town with an already rotting corpse in her place."

I was stunned. "That's- that's so insane it might actually work."

He grinned. "Of course it'll work. I told you you could count on me."

As we drove off toward my home, he continued to talk about his plans for us and how he was going to rescue me like he rescued her. I didn't have the energy left to argue with him so I let him talk, but as soon as he got Myrtle safely out of here, I wasn't planning to see him again. Between his anger and his obsession, he was scaring me and I wasn't convinced anymore that he was any better than Tom.

CHAPTER FIFTY-NINE
Jordan

I was getting more and more worried the further we got without any sign of Daisy and Gatsby. They didn't leave too far ahead of us. We should have caught up to them by now, especially with how quickly Tom was driving.

It seemed like the moment he had them leave, Tom realized he made a mistake sending them off alone together, but it was too late now.

We were halfway through the Valley of Ashes when we saw a commotion. *Myrtle.* In the chaos of the night, I had forgotten she was counting on us.

"Wreck!" Tom cried out when it became apparent the source of the commotion was a car accident. "That's good. Wilson'll have a little business at last."

He slowed a little, but didn't actually stop until the stricken faces of the people in front of the garage came into view.

The car slowed to a stop. "We'll take a look, just a look."

With the car stopped, we could hear a heartbreaking wail coming from inside. I listened closer and heard the gasping sobs interspersed with "oh my god" over and over again.

"There's some bad trouble," Tom said quickly. He raised himself up to his full height, trying to see through the crowd, and I could feel the moment he saw whatever it was. A harsh sound came out of his throat and he shoved his way to the front. Nick and I followed a moment later, and I gasped when I saw it, too.

Myrtle was lying dead on a worktable in the corner of the garage. She was wrapped in blankets, but from her hair peaking out, there was no mistaking it was her. And the blood. The blankets were drenched in it. I felt the contents of my stomach start to rush up at the sight of all that blood. I looked down at my shoes and took a couple of deep breaths. *What the hell happened to her? What happened to the plan?* I started to panic, but felt Nick's hand on my arm and remembered myself and where we were. There would be plenty of time to spiral and feel guilt later.

I gave a small grateful smile to Nick and tried to breathe. Satisfied, he turned his attention to our surroundings. As he did, the wailing noises came back into focus and redrew my attention. I followed Nick's gaze and saw the noises were coming from George. I immediately felt both pity for him and anger. How dare he mourn her death like he hadn't caused her so much pain in life? But seeing him so broken, it wasn't something he could fake. Whatever he had done to her in life, he was a mess now that she was gone.

I was grateful when Tom pushed his way over to the police officer and interrupted him to ask, "What happened? That's what I want to know."

"Auto hit her. Instantly killed."

That poor girl. It wasn't enough that she had a tragic life; she ended up having a tragic death, too. At least it was a quick death.

"Instantly killed," Tom repeated, stunned.

"She ran out in the road. Son-of-a-bitch didn't even stop his car."

The man the officer had been interviewing piped in, "There were two cars, one coming, one going, see?" He made gestures with his hands until the officer nodded.

"Going where?" the officer asked.

"One going each way. Well, she-" he gestured to Myrtle under the blanket and lost his voice for a moment before continuing, "-she ran out there and the one coming from New York knocked right into her, going thirty or forty miles an hour."

The officer asked a couple more questions when someone stepped forward and said, "It was a yellow car, big yellow car. New."

There was no mistaking that. That had to have been Daisy and Gatsby. *What the hell happened?* I was trying to hold on to hope that this was somehow part of their plan, but looking over at Myrtle in the sheet and all that blood again squashed that hope.

"See the accident?" the officer asked the man.

"No, but the car passed me down the road, going faster than forty. Going fifty, sixty."

George heard some of the conversation and yelled over, "You don't have to tell me what kind of car it was! I know what kind of car it was!"

I saw Tom tense up and realized where this was going. George had only seen Tom driving the car. Tom rushed over to George and seized him roughly, trying to shake sense into him.

Nick and I moved closer to make sure to hear them.

"You've got to pull yourself together," he said sternly. The statement was ludicrous. The man had just lost his wife and Tom was telling him he was being too emotional. If it wasn't for the situation, I would have laughed out loud.

Tom held onto him, Tom's support seeming to be the only thing keeping George on his feet.

"Listen," Tom continued, "I just got here a minute ago, from New York. I was bringing you that coupe we've been talking about. That yellow car I was driving this afternoon wasn't mine — do you hear?"

I had forgotten he had told George he owned the car, even tried to sell it to him. I wondered if George was going to buy any of this.

"I haven't seen it all afternoon," Tom finished. Another obvious lie, but at least he didn't sell out Daisy, so I couldn't be too upset about it.

The police officer looked at them then and asked, "What's all that?"

"I'm a friend of his," Tom said quickly. Again, in any other context, the statement would have been laughable. He was secretly sleeping with George's wife. You could hardly call that friendship. "He says he knows the car that did it... It was a yellow car."

The police officer looked at him suspiciously. "And what color's your car?"

"It's a blue car, a coupe."

"We've come straight from New York," Nick added.

Tom moved George to a seat in the office, and we all quickly excused ourselves.

We jumped into the car and Tom inched away from the garage until we cleared the accident and he floored it, racing through the night.

I looked over and saw tears were streaming down his face and forced my own tears and guilt down. We should have helped Myrtle sooner. "The God damned coward!" Tom cried. "He didn't even stop his car."

I hated to agree with Tom, but Gatsby was going to have hell to pay when I found him.

Chapter Sixty
Gatsby

I dropped Daisy off after making sure she was okay. I meant to go home. I should have. The car needed tending to, but I couldn't leave her. He was going to come home raging mad after everything that had happened and after finding out about his mistress. I didn't trust him alone with her. I watched her for a while before they pulled up. Their car came skidding into the driveway and I ducked behind the bushes to stay out of sight.

I watched as Tom tried to get Miss Baker and Mr. Carraway to enter the house. Miss Baker did, but Mr. Carraway looked disgusted with them both and stayed outside. I knew I could count on Mr. Carraway. The moment the door closed behind Tom, I called out to him softly. When he came my way, I stepped out from between the bushes I had ducked behind. I brushed off some greenery from my bright pink suit and waved to him.

"What are you doing?" Mr. Carraway asked.

"Just standing here, old sport."

Mr. Carraway uncharacteristically narrowed his eyes at me.

"Did you see any trouble on the road?" I asked.

"Yes," he said without adding anything else.

I needed to know if the plan worked, though, so I asked, "Was she killed?"

That had to be why he was angry with me.

"Yes."

"I thought so; I told Daisy I thought so. It's better that the shock should all come at once. She stood it pretty well."

He looked like he wanted to hit me, which meant the plan had gone perfectly, but I still kept rambling. "I got to West Egg by a side road and left the car in my garage. I don't think anyone saw us, but of course I can't be sure."

I was sure, though, sure I was seen by the right people who would give the right story. The story that would point right to Tom.

"Who was the woman?" I asked.

"Her name was Wilson. Her husband owns the garage. How the devil did it happen?"

"Well, I tried to swing the wheel—" I stopped instantly. I hadn't meant to say it like that. That wasn't the story. I was supposed to have been driving, not her. Mr. Carraway shouldn't know differently. To everyone else besides myself, Mr. Carraway, Tom, Miss Baker, and Daisy, Tom would have been the one behind the wheel. I had made sure of it.

"Was Daisy driving?" he asked.

I slowly relented. I supposed it didn't harm anything if just Mr. Carraway knew that. "Yes," I said before adding, "but of course I'll say I was. You see, when we left New York she was very nervous, and she thought it would steady her to drive — and this woman rushed out at us just as we were passing a car coming the other way. It all happened in a minute, but it seemed to me that she wanted to speak to us, thought we were somebody she knew. Well, first Daisy turned away from the woman toward the other car, and then she lost her nerve and turned back. The second my hand reached the wheel I felt the shock — it must have killed her instantly."

His anger rolled off him in waves. "It ripped her open—"

"Don't tell me, old sport," I interrupted, wincing. It was ugly business, but it was what needed to be done. We needed people to believe she was dead so she could really disappear. "Anyhow — Daisy stepped on it. I tried to make her stop, but she couldn't, so I pulled on the emergency brake. Then she fell over into my lap and I drove on."

It was better he think Daisy was grief stricken than that she was driving and didn't bother to stop the car.

"She'll be all right tomorrow," I said, unsure if I was trying to convince him or myself. "I'm just going to wait here and see if he tries to bother her about that unpleasantness this afternoon. She's locked herself into her room, and if he tries any brutality, she's going to turn the light out and on again."

I really hoped it wouldn't come to that, but with how volatile he was right now, I refused to leave it up to chance. I couldn't leave her in case she needed me.

"He won't touch her," Mr. Carraway assured me. "He's not thinking about her."

"I don't trust him, old sport."

"How long are you going to wait?"

It was a good question, but I wasn't going to move until I knew she was okay. "All night, if necessary. Anyhow, till they all go to bed."

"You wait here," Mr. Carraway said. "I'll see if there's any sign of commotion."

He really was a good friend.

After a few minutes, he returned.

"Is it all quiet up there?" I asked, anxious for his answer.

"Yes, it's all quiet. You'd better come home and get some sleep."

I shook my head. She needed me tonight. Everything would work itself out tomorrow. The right stories would be told and traced back to Tom. He would be taken away and she would be safe. Until then, I could stand guard all night if I had to. I would protect her. "I want to wait here till Daisy goes to bed. Good night, old sport."

I felt Mr. Carraway walking away, but I didn't move. I would keep vigil all night if I had to.

Chapter Sixty-One
Jordan

I had been pacing in the sitting room for what felt like hours. I didn't want to interrupt her and Tom and risk making what had to be a volatile situation any worse, but my nerves couldn't take this. I listened for shouts every time I passed the door or any other sign of a commotion, but none came.

Five more minutes, I decided. If she wasn't out of there in five more minutes, I was going in. I couldn't wait any longer. I was getting more and more anxious for her by the second. I didn't think he would hurt her tonight, but with him I could never be sure of his intentions, and I was damn sure I wouldn't let him lay a finger on her.

With what I estimated to be a minute left, she came sweeping into the room. I looked at her for half a moment, saw the tears she had wiped away, and was across the room in a heartbeat. I pulled her into me and whispered to her it would be okay. She was shaking as I held tight to her.

When her breathing slowed a little, I finally asked, "What the hell happened? Is Myrtle-?" I trailed off, not wanting to say the word.

"Okay, I think."

"Okay?" I asked incredulously. Had she not seen the blood? "There was so much blood. There's no way she survived that."

"Oh, no! She's okay! That was all part of Jay's plan."

"His plan was to run her over?" I gasped.

"No, no! She didn't get hit; he made me hit the other car. She wasn't even in the road. She got out of the other car looking a mess covered in blood."

"Are you sure? She didn't look alive."

"I'm sure. They were going to take her away once things died down tonight. The officer on the scene was an inside man of Jay's."

I relaxed a little. "So she's okay?"

Daisy smiled weakly. "That part of things at least didn't get messed up."

"Are you okay?" I asked carefully.

"For now, but I don't want to see Jay again. I don't care what his money could do for me. I don't want to see him again."

I wasn't surprised. I had been ready to suggest we call off the plan many times myself, but now with both men behaving erratically and with Tom knowing she was with Gatsby, it wasn't worth it. Any benefit that Gatsby could have had came largely from the element of surprise. Now that Tom thought Myrtle was dead and that losing Daisy was a possibility, he wasn't going to let her go without a fight, and that was the last thing Daisy needed right now.

"Please don't be upset with me," she said, sounding defeated.

"I'm not," I rushed to say. "I swear I'm not. It's the right thing to do. I don't want you around him either. Especially after he assaulted you again."

"And the car accident."

I nodded. "I don't know why he was willing to risk your safety for his plan. I'm glad it worked for Myrtle's sake, but I hate that he made you be in the car."

She blinked up at me for a moment before saying, "That's actually not what I was talking about. Before the planned one, he scared the hell out of me and almost killed us."

"He did what?" I barked out.

She immediately shushed me and looked at the door. I stilled, watching the door with her, but nothing happened. Tom didn't come in.

"What did he do?" I asked more quietly. There was still an edge in my voice, but that wasn't going away anytime soon.

It took her a few minutes to explain and a few more minutes for my heart to slow down and the roaring in my ears to stop enough that I could force out, "He would rather you dead than not with him?"

She nodded slowly. "I thought he was better than Tom, but now I know I was wrong. Tom has so many faults, but I can say with certainty he wouldn't murder me for trying to leave him. He would be vindictive and cruel and maybe abusive, but he wouldn't take my life, just any ounce of my dignity and happiness that he could."

The fact that she was having to choose between a man who would literally kill her for not wanting to be with him and a man who would simply berate and beat her for not wanting to be with him enraged me. The feeling that I was helpless to free her from that choice had me almost in tears. "I promise the literal moment I can safely get you and Pammy out of here, we'll leave and never look back."

She smiled weakly. "I know you will. I love you. I promise I can wait longer. However long I need to, you're worth it."

I knew she would, but she shouldn't have to. To hell with a society that thought being beaten was better than being in a loving relationship with someone from the same gender. It incensed me that if word were to get out, the shocking and upsetting part of the story wouldn't be that Tom beat Daisy, but that Daisy was cheating on him with a woman.

One day, I would get her away. I couldn't change society on my own, but I would be damn sure to shield the woman I loved from it as best as I could.

CHAPTER SIXTY-TWO
Gatsby

Mr. Carraway came over the moment I arrived at home and tried to urge me to leave town. The idea was preposterous. I wasn't going to leave when things were almost fixed. Daisy was almost mine, and I wasn't going to leave anything to chance. I had to stay here to see it through. Mr. Carraway was worried I was going to be caught. I hated lying to him, but the stakes were too high. I wasn't going to be caught, because the woman wasn't dead and the car was going to belong to someone else by the time the police went looking for it.

I had arranged the paperwork to be found that the vehicle had been sold to Tom Buchanan weeks ago and had a witness that would swear it was him behind the wheel. Daisy wouldn't say anything, of course. She would be relieved to see him hauled off in handcuffs, and if he tried to implicate her or me, who would believe him? The evidence was stacked against him. I had made sure of that. The only thing bothering me was that she was still in that house. She didn't have to return last night. She could have stayed out. I would have kept her safe. I didn't know what was keeping her there.

It seemed Mr. Carraway wasn't going to leave anytime soon, so I started to talk to him about myself. I hadn't told anyone in my new life about my past and where I had come from and I don't know what possessed me to tell him, but he was a good listener. I told him all about my past and how I met Daisy. I hadn't meant to fall for her, but I had and had never been able to shake her as much as I tried.

It was hard to believe that after all these years, I was just a few more hours away from her being mine again. It almost didn't feel real, but all the pieces were in place. The car was being moved to Tom's stables later today and an anonymous tip would be delivered to the police that that's where they could find the yellow car.

Mr. Carraway stayed all morning, although I was sure he had places to be. I was just about to tell him to leave when we were interrupted by the gardener.

"I'm going to drain the pool today, Mr. Gatsby. Leaves'll start falling pretty soon, and then there's always trouble with the pipes."

I looked out at the pool and noticed for the first time that he was right. Summer was quickly coming to an end. I felt like I had hardly enjoyed it, and now it was almost over. The thought filled me with some dismay. I looked at the pool again and thought that I couldn't make summer come back, but I could at least enjoy the pool. "Don't do it, today. You know, old sport," I turned to Mr. Carraway and explained, "I've never used the pool all summer?"

Mr. Carraway stayed a good deal longer. It was clear he was concerned, and I understood why, but I couldn't explain myself to him. It would ruin everything if anyone found out, so I had to let him worry.

When he finally left, it was reluctant.

"I'll call you up."

"Do, old sport."

"I'll call you about noon."

"I suppose Daisy'll call, too." I was sure she would. It had been a late night. I supposed she would sleep late and then she would give me a call.

"I suppose so," Mr. Carraway agreed.

"Well, goodbye." I shook his hand and watched him leave.

Before he reached the edge of the lawn, he turned around and shouted to me, "They're a rotten crowd. You're worth the whole damn bunch put together."

I wasn't sure if he meant the people who came to my parties or New York in general. It didn't matter much, though. Once I had Daisy, I would be content anywhere. I would leave New York tomorrow if it was with her on my arm.

I killed a little time writing in my journal. It was an old habit from when I was a boy that I hadn't ever stopped. I had found it helpful to write down my schedule and little reminders. Now I wrote down most of my thoughts. It was a productive way to clear the mind to think of other things.

I looked at the clock and was surprised to see it was already two. Still no call from Daisy. I wanted to go check on her, but I knew better than to be seen over there today. I couldn't look like I was caught up in this, because I was sure Tom would accuse me when they found him guilty. I knew all of that, but it was still hard to stay away from her.

I needed to distract myself. I looked outside and noticed the weather was still nice enough for the swim I wanted to take. It couldn't hurt. I hadn't swam all summer, and there was no time like the present.

CHAPTER SIXTY-THREE
Daisy

I slept fitfully that night, but every time I woke, I glimpsed Jordan keeping watch by my door. I tried to persuade her to come to bed, but she kept saying it was too risky. I knew she was right, but that didn't stop me from longing for her to lie with me.

When I gave up on sleeping altogether, she was still awake. I begged her to get some sleep, but she kept telling me she could sleep later once things were more sorted.

She was being stubborn, but she wasn't wrong about it. Tom and I had talked on and off through the night, but we hadn't come to an agreement. I wanted to leave. I didn't feel safe here where Jay could easily find me, but Tom was too deep in his grief to be willing to leave.

I felt a little guilty for that, but it was hard to empathize too deeply with anyone besides her. She had been desperate for Tom's help and he had kept her trapped like he did with me. I didn't enjoy seeing him miserable, but her happiness was more important than his temporary grief. If one thing about Tom was dependable, it was that he would forget her when the next pretty woman crossed his path.

I hoped this morning he would be a little more amendable to getting away.

"I can't stand it here. I won't stay another minute. We need to get out of the city."

"Trouble in paradise?" he asked snidely, but with none of the venom he would have had yesterday, so I opted for the truth.

"He's got it in his head I'll run away with him. He's crazy and I don't know how to convince him I'm not going anywhere with him."

"So you want us to pack up and ship out and run away from your problems?"

"It would be a novelty for once to be leaving somewhere because of me." It slipped out before I could stop it and I tensed, waiting for his anger.

Surprisingly, he gave me a small smile. "Maybe we're more alike than you want to admit."

It was far from the truth, but having him smile was too much of a relief to pass up by arguing with him.

"So, can we?"

"Can we what?"

"Pack some bags and get away. Me, you, Pammy, the nanny, we'll all go on a trip, just us. It's been too long since we've spent some family time together."

The moments dragged on in the wake of his silence, but finally he said, "That's not a half bad idea. We'll go tomorrow."

"Today," I countered, not hiding the pleading in my voice.

He paused again, before relenting, "Okay, today. We can be gone in a couple of hours."

As much as I hated to leave Jordan again, I was relieved.

She and I decided I would send word to her when we got to where we were going and she would come join. I wanted her to come right away, but even as I asked I knew that wasn't a good idea.

"Are you sure you can't come?"

"I can't. One of us has to stay here and make sure things end up okay."

I knew she was right. With Jay and Myrtle and the police investigation, there was still so much that might go wrong. I needed to get out of here before things got worse. I knew that, but I couldn't stand to be parted from her. "Are you sure?" I asked again.

"Absolutely sure. I'll make sure Gatsby doesn't get any funny ideas of following you and make sure Myrtle gets settled okay, and then I'll come find you."

"Promise?"

She smiled softly at me. "I promise, wherever you are, wherever you go, I'll always find you. You're my home."

I felt myself start to tear up. "I love you."

Always able to sense what I needed, she grinned. "Don't get all sappy on me. We have to get you packed."

I laughed as she bumped her shoulder into mine and directed me toward the wardrobe.

After a tearful goodbye, Tom, the nanny, Pammy, and I were gone within the hour.

CHAPTER SIXTY-FOUR
Jordan

With Daisy gone, I resolved to do what I could to keep things calm here until she was in the clear.

With that in mind, I called Nick. The first thing out of his mouth was asking about Daisy.

"I've left Daisy's house," I lied. I knew whatever I shared with him would be told immediately to Gatsby and he couldn't know she had left yet. She needed more time to get further away. "I'm at Hempstead, and I'm going down to Southampton this afternoon." He didn't say anything and his silence started to bother me. "You weren't so nice to me last night."

"How could it have mattered then?"

I knew what he meant, and I was being unfair. He thought Myrtle was dead. Of course, he was upset. I tried to soften my judgment by adding, "However — I want to see you."

I wanted to keep an eye on Gatsby, and the easiest way was through Nick. I did want to see him, too. I had grown fond of him.

"I want to see you, too."

"Suppose I don't go to Southampton, and come into town this afternoon?"

"No — I don't think this afternoon."

"Very well." There was nothing else to say.

"It's impossible this afternoon." He went on to list various excuses until eventually the call was over. I resolved to try again later. I figured if I gave him some time that later he would be better reasoned with.

I didn't get that luxury. Late that afternoon, when I returned to Daisy's to check on the home and staff, I was given a message that Nick had frantically phoned from Gatsby's. I tried phoning him back, but the line was busy.

I made a couple of calls until I started to get bits and pieces of the story.

Gatsby was dead, murdered by Myrtle's husband, George. The facts were still few and far between, but somehow George had found out that the car belonged to Gatsby and showed up at his mansion with a gun. He shot Gatsby before turning the gun on himself.

People were saying Gatsby had been having an affair with Myrtle and had ran her down when she tried to leave him, and then George killed Gatsby for killing her.

It wasn't too far from the truth, so I couldn't feel too bad that the headlines were wrong or that all of this started because we helped Myrtle escape. I couldn't feel sorry about the loss of either of the men either. The world was free of Gatsby, who would have killed Daisy for not loving him, and George, who had been abusing Myrtle for years.

What mattered most was that Daisy and Myrtle were safe and even though I wouldn't wish death on anyone, I couldn't say I wasn't happy knowing they would both sleep sounder for it.

I tried Nick a couple more times, but wasn't at all surprised he didn't answer. I knew he would be blaming this on Tom and Daisy, and by extension, me. Nick idolized Gatsby, and I was sure Gatsby's death was destroying him. I felt some sympathy for Nick, but that was where my sadness ended. Gatsby had been terrorizing Daisy, and I wasn't sad to see him go.

CHAPTER SIXTY-FIVE
Jordan

It was no surprise that I didn't hear from Nick. I thought about going to Gatsby's funeral, if not for the man himself, then just to be a friend to Nick, but decided against it. I wasn't sure Nick would want me there. After all, he hadn't called.

Besides, there was no place for me at the funeral of a man who I was glad wasn't around anymore.

My loose ends in the city almost all ended when Gatsby died. I hadn't been able to find out where it was Myrtle had gone to, but I knew wherever she was, she was better off. I had no idea if Myrtle even knew that her husband was dead. I wrote to her sister, knowing Myrtle had planned to reach out to her when things were safe. I hadn't heard anything back yet, but that was hardly surprising. My letter was incredibly, necessarily vague that I was an old friend and was leaving an address in case she wanted to talk about her sister.

I gave her my aunt's apartment address. One of my aunt's many faults was how nosy she was, so I was sure that even when I left, if a letter came for me, she would know how to find me.

I was readying to leave, knowing any day now I would hear from Daisy and go meet her, when Nick surprised me by reaching out saying he wanted to talk. I hoped it was what I was thinking. I hoped he felt bad about how we had parted ways and wanted to make the breakup, if that's what you could call it, official. We hadn't really been together, but we had shared an understanding that I disliked him less than most other people in a room, and I was sure he felt the same.

I had been on my way out to the course, but agreed to meet with him. I felt like I owed him that much. I wanted to close that chapter in my life, too.

He sat me down and talked to me about all the reasons we weren't going to work out. I let him talk and say what he needed to. It didn't matter to me anyway, so I hoped he was getting what he felt he needed out of the conversation. He told me about Gatsby's death and finding him in the pool. He told me about how disillusioned he was with New York and how everyone had preyed on Gatsby's hospitality when he was alive, but no one had shown up for his funeral. That got to me, and I felt a sliver of remorse at not having gone. I knew it was for the best I didn't, but the thought of Nick suffering through that alone was hard to bear.

When he got to the end of his speech, he said in a condescending tone I hadn't expected from him that he hoped we could stay in touch and that I would be okay.

I so badly wanted to tell him I was fine. In fact, I already had someone, but clearly I couldn't mention Daisy. Before I knew what I was saying I blurted out that I was already engaged to another man. I wasn't sure he believed me, but he was polite enough to act like he did.

He paused for a long moment where I thought he might say something, or maybe even try to change his mind, but eventually he just stood up and thanked me for meeting with him. I felt like I owed him more than I had given him, so I told him, "Nevertheless, you did throw me over. You threw me over on the telephone. I don't give a damn about you now, but it was a new experience for me, and I felt a little dizzy for a while."

It was somewhat true. I had felt mostly relieved when he stopped calling, but also a little surprised. I could see my little show of emotion helped him, though. I could see the little smile he was trying to hide. He was a good man, and if it made him feel better to think he had gotten to me, it wouldn't do any harm to let him think it.

I reached out and shook his hand. He met my hand with a firm shake of his own. I respected that about him. Unlike the rest of society, he allowed me to be me. He had never tried to force me to conform to his or society's ideas of womanhood and for that, I was grateful to him. I would maybe miss him a little. Might as well give him a parting remark to remember me by. "Oh, and do you remember a conversation we had once about driving a car?"

"Why — not exactly."

"You said a bad driver was only safe until she met another bad driver? Well, I met another bad driver, didn't I? I mean, it was careless of me to make such a wrong guess. I thought you were rather an honest, straightforward person. I thought it was your secret pride."

He looked flushed, and I knew I had said the right thing. Men never wanted things to end calmly. Why else invite me out if he didn't want to hear about how it wrecked me when he stopped calling? I liked him well enough, and I couldn't give him true passion, but I could give him this.

"I'm thirty," he said matter-of-factly. "I'm five years too old to lie to myself and call it honour."

I watched as he turned and stalked off, knowing he was half angry and half regretful but that I had given him what he wanted.

If he wanted to pretend he was the honest one here, I could let him. What he believed didn't change the truth; anyone who swore they didn't lie was a liar. Only the truly honest people are truthful enough to call themselves liars.

Daisy

Jay was dead. I couldn't believe it but there it was indisputably in black and white on the front of some Chicago newspaper. "Jay Gatsby, party king of New York City, murderer, murdered in cold blood."

I bought the paper, needing to read it but not able to in public. I needed to know, but didn't want to see. I made it home in a trance before pulling out the paper. I skimmed it and was shocked to find that Myrtle's husband George had murdered Jay and then killed himself. The paper was saying that Myrtle and Jay had been having an affair and that Jay ran her over to keep her quiet and then George killed Jay to avenge her.

It was too much to take in, and I was struggling to breathe through my tears. I wasn't sure if I was crying for him or myself, though. It was sad, clearly. He had been murdered to avenge someone who wasn't even dead, but I couldn't fight the feeling of relief that I wouldn't have to be around him again. That made me cry harder. I knew he wasn't a good man. What he did to me wasn't right, but I felt despicable for not being sad about his passing.

It didn't matter that he forced me into being intimate with him or that he would have killed me for leaving him if I had given him the chance; I still felt like the villain for not mourning him.

When I had cried all the tears I had left, I picked myself up off the floor and decided to write Jordan a letter. I was halfway through the letter before realizing that while it was addressed to her; it was more of a journal entry. I was talking to myself, not to her, and likely wouldn't have given it to her to read even if she had been here. It read:

My Dearest Jordan,

I just read that Jay is dead and I can't believe it. I know he was the worst sort of man for how he hurt me and would have ended my life if he had the chance, but knowing he's gone and I don't feel sorry is killing me. He forced himself on me when I was young. He took advantage of me when I was too young to know better. He was old enough he knew what he was doing, and he manipulated me, and then he left me. He broke my heart when he left, and I thought I would never feel happy again.

He paved the way for Tom to slither his way right into my life and play the hero. I fell for him as easily as I did because Jay made me feel worthless when he left. Tom was able to sweep in and act like the knight in shining armor when the only person he was helping was himself. I had been so desperate to get away from the town gossips and out of my parents' home that I was willing to believe the best in him. He was nice for long enough that when he changed, it broke me again.

I convinced myself I was the problem and bent over backward trying to fix things. I tried to do whatever I could to mend the trust he had said I broke, but whatever I did wasn't good enough for him. When he started to put his hands on me, I was convinced I deserved it. I know how crazy that sounds, but I kept thinking if I was just a better wife, a more caring person, kinder to him, he would stop hurting me. He didn't. I was wrong, but I was never the problem.

There was something broken in him long before I came along, and it wasn't my responsibility to fix it. I tried, but you can't fix someone who doesn't want to change, and he didn't see anything wrong with the way he was. He told me time and time again that I forced his hand. It wasn't true. He chose violence and when he didn't, I took its absence for kindness.

I don't know if I ever loved either of those men, but I can say for certain they never loved me. You don't hurt and berate the person you love. You showed me that, love. You showed me that love can be gentle while still being strong. You showed me that love doesn't have to be painful. It doesn't have to hurt. It can lift you up.

When Jay came back, I thought he would help me. I thought he might want to out of the kindness of his heart because he had cared about me, but I was wrong. He hadn't ever actually cared about me, just about himself and how I could benefit him, and when he came back, it was no different.

He had always wanted something from me. Back when I was young, he wanted my body. Now that he was back, he wanted me to be his. He was continually pushing me for things I wasn't ready to give him. When he came back into my life, it was worse. I know now that he's gone, but I still see him when I close my eyes. I still feel like he's in front of me, pushing me to go further, pressing his lips to mine while I'm trying to pull away. I see his manic look before he almost crashed the car, killing us both. He would have done it. If I had been honest with him that I didn't want him the same way he wanted me, he would have ended both of our lives.

I know it's only been a few days, but I still wake up in moments of terror thinking I'm back there, that I'm in a car about to crash. I bolt upright in bed and have to remind myself where I am and that I'm safe. I have to remind myself that he isn't with me anymore. It might be selfish to say, but if it will help me to sleep better at night, I'm glad he's gone. I'm glad I won't have to worry about him showing up again and trying to hurt me. I have enough stress in my life with Tom being around that I'm glad Jay's gone. Tom has his faults, but he never tried to end my life.

I feel guilty saying it, but Jay Gatsby wasn't a good person and I'm glad he's dead. Glad might be an overstatement, but I'm certainly not mourning him. His life was no great loss.

I stopped there, knowing this was never going to see the light of day, but still enjoying the feeling of catharsis it gave me. Maybe there was something to writing down your feelings. It didn't make them go away per se, but it gave me a chance to explore and process them more carefully than I normally did.

I took to writing out my feelings much more often since I found it helped me to feel less helpless. I took care to hide the book, but Tom was surprisingly leaving me alone now, so I doubt he would have noticed it, anyway. It seemed with Jay and Myrtle both dead, things were mostly back to normal for him.

I wondered if he was entertaining himself elsewhere, but hardly cared.

Jordan caught up with us in Chicago just a few weeks after we had left New York. Neither of us knew what the plan was, but having her with me was enough for now.

She spent the nights with me since I woke up often with nightmares. Her first night here, Tom had insisted it wasn't proper for us to share a room, but quickly relented when I woke up screaming from a nightmare.

He learned after that night that having her there calmed me and he stopped complaining.

It didn't surprise me that he was supportive of anyone besides himself dealing with me, but I couldn't be upset about it.

The nights started to get a little easier with Jordan there to brush back my hair and hold me through the worst nightmares, bringing me back to myself.

I couldn't have gotten through those early days without her.

CHAPTER SIXTY-SEVEN
Daisy

Things started to get easier as time went on. Jordan didn't leave my side, so Tom was on his best behavior and we spent far more time with Pammy without his interference. The nanny even started being kind to me.

"Darling, how would you like to go for a picnic today?" I asked Pammy one brisk fall morning.

She grinned her little gap-toothed smile and asked, "What's a picnic?"

I giggled at that and motioned for Jordan to come forward with the basket. Of course, it was full mostly of Pammy's favorite snacks, hardly anything that could be considered real food, but I was just happy to be spending time with her.

The nanny had been kinder too now that Pammy was getting older and let us take her on our own. Jordan had found a beautiful spot under some maple trees in a park. It was just shy of chilly, making it the perfect day with a light shawl. We wrapped Pammy up until she giggled that she was too warm, and then we ushered her outside.

Pammy ate a bite of everything from the basket and then abandoned the rest to me and Jordan. She ran around the park looking at the fallen autumn leaves and watching the squirrels. Jordan had her arm wrapped around my waist in a way she normally didn't risk in public, and it was perfect.

I would have given anything to have whisked Jordan and Pammy away right then and there, to have more moments like that. Unfortunately, with Jay out of the picture now, it was going to be a while before we could make that a reality, but I was coming to terms with that. If we had more days like today, I was sure I could continue to deal with the bad ones.

Tom's moods ebbed and flowed. I never really knew what I was getting from him. He continued to start pointless arguments, but at least he kept his hands to himself now. I could handle him hurting me if it was only with his words. It was an improvement, after all.

Jordan didn't agree.

"I hate seeing him treat you like that," she told me after a particularly rough dinner. "I hate that he feels like he can talk to you like that and that you won't let me say anything to him."

I knew it was killing her to not step in, but it would just make things worse if she did. "I know how hard it is for you. I'm so sorry, but I appreciate so much that you're holding back."

"I can't stand this for much longer. I'll get you both out of here, I promise. My girls are too good for this."

Even though it was probably the hundredth time she'd said it, it still made my heart melt every time hearing her refer to me and Pammy as her girls.

"I know you will," I told her, and I believed she would eventually, but I had lost hope it would be soon.

We were interrupted by a knock on the door. When I opened it, the staff handed me a letter before turning and reclosing the door. I looked down at it and saw it was addressed to "Miss Jordan Baker" and handed it off to her.

She looked down at it curiously as I watched on over her shoulder. She hardly ever got mail. "Maybe it's our long-lost friend," she said, examining it.

I knew without her having to say it that she meant Myrtle. We didn't dare speak her name where Tom might hear, but I knew that was who she was talking about. I knew it worried Jordan that we hadn't heard from her yet, but I wasn't too worried yet. It had hardly been long at all, and if I had been in her position, even with her husband dead, I might have wanted to have stayed lost a little longer.

After all, Tom was still out there. Maybe she was worried about him finding out she was still around.

The return address was for a legal firm, so it was possible, but unlikely it was her. There was a chance it was related to the inquest that was likely to still be going on for the murders of Myrtle, Jay, and the death of George, but I had hoped Jordan had stayed removed enough that she wouldn't be called on to appear in court on the matter.

"What do you think it's about?" I asked wearily.

"I'm not sure," she said carefully, "but there's only one way to find out." She tore into the letter, freeing the paper inside, and quickly unfolded it.

I hadn't gotten past the introduction when I heard her gasp.

"What?" I asked nervously, skimming the letter, but nothing immediately stood out to me as alarming since I wasn't well versed in legal jargon.

"It's my aunt," she said, still scanning the paper.

"What about her?" Jordan hadn't mentioned her since leaving the city and I couldn't imagine what she would be having a lawyer write to Jordan about.

"She's dead."

"Oh my god," I said under my breath before wrapping my arms around her waist and pulling her back into my chest. "Are you okay?" I asked softly.

I knew they weren't close per se, but she had been spending a lot more time with her when we lived in the city.

"I'm fine. I just can't believe she's gone."

"I know what you mean. Death always feels like a surprise."

"No, I can't believe she's *finally* gone. I thought she was going to live to be a hundred. They say evil never dies, and I can't believe they were wrong."

A harsh laugh came out of me that I choked back. "Jordan! You shouldn't say that!"

She turned to me with a smile. "Why not? She was a shrewd, unlikeable woman and her death doesn't change that."

I blinked a moment, surprised. She wasn't wrong, of course, but those sorts of things weren't things you were supposed to say. "Well then, I'm not sorry?"

"That's the spirit," she said with a grin. "Congratulate me."

"Absolutely not!" I said, appalled. "A woman just died. I'm not going to congratulate you for that."

She barked out a laugh and said, "No! No, not for that. That's not all the letter says."

"What else does it say?" I asked curiously.

She was quiet for a moment.

"What does it say?" I asked again.

She still didn't say anything, but I felt her start to shake in my arms. I turned her around to face me and was startled to see tears were falling down her face over a tentative smile. "What's wrong?" I asked, wiping away one of the tears with the pad of my thumb.

She shook her head and tried to smile wider, but she was still crying. "Nothing, absolutely nothing."

"You're crying. It's not nothing," I insisted.

"I just can't believe it."

I knew grief did crazy things to people, but I didn't know what to make of her reaction.

"Can't believe what?"

"We're free."

I paused. "What do you mean?"

She pushed the letter to my chest and said through a choked sound of a sob, "She left me everything."

I gasped, understanding slowly catching up to me. She couldn't be serious, but I hoped she was. "Everything?"

She nodded vigorously. "Everything."

"We're free?"

"More than that, we're the wealthiest women in the country, or I am, and I'll share everything with you the moment you're legally divorced."

Divorce. I turned away and took a moment to breathe. It was surreal. Divorce was a word I had never let myself think. I worried if I hoped too much and too often for it that I would jinx it, but now it was an actual possibility.

"I don't know what to say," I said, tears streaming down my face. I turned around and saw Jordan was on a knee in front of me and the tears fell harder. "Jord, what are you-" I choked out, but she interrupted me.

"Daisy Fay, I love you more than life itself. You're my guiding light and my home. You're my best friend and I can't picture my life without you in it. Wherever you are is where I want to be. Will you do me the honor of making me the happiest woman in the world by letting me pay for your divorce?"

I choked out a laugh at that, with tears still streaming down my face. "I didn't really think that's where you were going with that, but yes. A million times yes, to this and anything else you might ask in the future."

She grinned at me. "I love you."

"And I love you."

I couldn't believe it. The next couple of days were a whirlwind of activity. On top of the news about Jordan's aunt, we also received word from Myrtle that she was set up a little ways outside the city and had just been to see her sister. Apparently, her sister had been drinking, and it took a good deal of convincing from Myrtle to get her sister to believe she wasn't a ghost.

Myrtle thanked us a million times in the letter and said she hoped I was well on my way to getting out myself. She also made sure to say she was more than willing to return the favor and testify against Tom if we needed her to. It was perfect timing since Jordan had been having issues with hiring on a lawyer. Apparently, no amount of money was high enough to hire a lawyer onto a groundbreaking case they thought they would lose.

Myrtle changed their minds. The next lawyer Jordan and I went to, one of the best in the country, didn't turn me away. He was hesitant, but when she showed him Myrtle's letter and explained Myrtle's involvement and offered him a year's salary, he was on board. Myrtle was able and willing to testify to Tom's abuse and adultery. Jordan and I had helped her because it was the right thing to do and would have helped her regardless, but the full circle moment of her being able to help me out of a similar situation wasn't lost on me.

Daisy

The lawyer drafted a legal notice for me to give Tom saying I was taking Pammy and would see him in court.

I wasn't sure I would have the nerve to do it, but the wheels were already in motion and he was bound to find out eventually. Jordan and I made plans to move back to New York into her aunt's old apartment she now owned. I had loved the city and now that Jay wasn't around, there was no more reason to avoid it. Besides, the apartment was more than big enough for the three of us girls.

I was packing up some of Pammy's things with Jordan when Tom came in. Pammy and her nanny were in the other room, readying her for the journey.

Tom surveyed the room. There were outfits scattered everywhere as we decided what she would and wouldn't need in New York. In short, the usual carnage of my packing. "Are we going somewhere?" he asked with a raised eyebrow.

I hesitated for a moment and looked at Jordan for a beat. I wasn't sure if it was the right time. I wasn't sure if we were ready. She gave me a small nod. I took a deep breath. She was right.

I turned back to Tom and said, "Actually we're not," I said, gesturing between me and Tom, "but we," I motioned to me, Jordan, and Pammy in the other room, "are."

He looked taken aback. "And just where do you think you're going? I didn't agree to a girls' trip."

When I didn't say anything, he continued, "I know I've been allowing you more freedom lately. I figured you learned your lesson in New York, but apparently I've been being too kind." He took a step closer to me. "Maybe you need a reminder of who's in charge." Jordan stepped in between us and I was grateful for that, but I could handle him.

I stepped around her and said, "Actually, things are going to be changing."

I went and grabbed the legal notice from my handbag and turned back to him. "You might act like you own me, but you don't. I'm my own person and I refuse to allow you to continue to mistreat me and our daughter."

He blinked in surprise and looked down at my outstretched hand. He took the paper automatically and unfolded it. I watched as he scanned it and his eyes widened. "You can't be serious."

"I am." I'd never been more serious about anything.

"You can't be!" he exclaimed. "You're not leaving me."

"I am," I repeated.

"You can't do this to me. What about everything we've been through?"

What a joke. More like everything he put me through. I had lost count of how many times he had cheated on me, never mind the times he had lied to and manipulated me. "What about trust?"

"You know I never wanted to hurt you."

I might have believed that a few years ago, but now there had been too much damage done. I wasn't just leaving for Jordan. My heart had been out of the marriage long before she had come along. If she hadn't been there to love and support me, I might not have had the courage to leave, but I had wanted to for a long time. "Intentions don't excuse actions."

"You can't do this."

"I can and I am."

"This is madness. I'm really just trying to protect you. If you go through with this, they'll lock you up and throw away the key. Daisy, I know I've made mistakes, but I do love you."

He might have, but that wasn't enough. "Not enough not to hurt me."

"You're really going to do this?"

"I am. I'm not okay with living the lie we've been living. I loved you once, but you broke my heart and my trust again and again until I wasn't able to salvage my feelings. You beat the love out of me a long time ago."

"So we'll live separately. I'll put you up in a nice townhouse in the city. You won't have to see me often, but you can't leave."

Again, that would've sounded good to me a couple of years ago, but now that I had a way out, now that freedom was so close I could taste it, I knew I could never settle for anything less.

"I'm sorry. I really am, but that's not good enough. I'm divorcing you."

"But you can't. McCormicks don't divorce."

Again with the McCormick bullshit. I couldn't care less what his family did or didn't do. That had nothing to do with me. Besides, he might've been a McCormick by blood but it wasn't even his name.

"It's a good thing you're not a McCormick then."

He narrowed his eyes and took a step toward me.

Jordan stepped in front of me again and said, "I wouldn't do that if I were you, *Buchanan*." She looked at me and added, "In fact, if I were you, I would think awfully closely about how you let us leave. You wouldn't want the court to have more to hold against you."

He glared at Jordan and looked past her at me. "This is really how it's going to be?"

I nodded. He made his bed and I would revel in watching him lie in it.

"This is insane. You won't get away with this. You won't get a cent. I'll make sure of it."

"I don't need your money."

He blinked at that, surprised. "How the hell did you afford the lawyer, anyway? You don't own anything."

His eyes narrowed. "Was it that bootlegger, Gatsby?"

I didn't care enough to correct him. He swore up and down before saying, "You'll regret this," and stalking out of the room.

We would see about that, but I certainly didn't regret anything right then, or later when Jordan and I walked out of there with one of little Pammy's hands in each of ours, and I highly doubted I would regret it later.

I hadn't seen Tom since walking out on him in Chicago and I was nervous to have to face him in court, especially since we hadn't seen Myrtle yet. We had sent her the address and the money to get here from the city, not that she needed the money anymore. Jay had done right by me in setting her up for life like I had wanted. He had his faults, but I was glad he had been able to do that for her.

I had been an anxious mess all morning. My lawyer was trying not to show he was sweating, but as the time ticked closer and Myrtle wasn't there, we all got more nervous. He assured me she wasn't the entirety of our case, just that things would go smoother if she were here.

She was coming. I might not know her that well, but she assured me she would be here, and I trusted that.

At least I did until we only had ten minutes left before we had to appear in court. Jordan, the lawyer, and I were all watching the clock now. I swore the second hand sped up as we watched, but still no Myrtle.

Nine minutes left.

Tick, tick, tick.

Eight.

Tick, tick, tick.

Seven.

Tick, tick, tick.

BANG! The door slammed open, and we all jumped in our seats and turned to the door to see a disheveled, out of breath Myrtle. I jumped out of my chair and rushed over, wrapping her in a hug. "You made it!"

She was breathing loudly, but hugged me back tightly for a moment before stepping back. "Did you doubt it?" she asked with a grin.

Maybe a little, I thought, but I said, "Of course not!"

"I did," Jordan said from behind us. Myrtle laughed loudly at that.

"I said I'd be here. Got a little lost and turned around on the way, but I'm here with-" she looked at the clock, "five minutes to spare. That's plenty of time!"

I laughed at that, just relieved she was here. Jordan stepped up and took her turn hugging Myrtle. When she pulled back, she started trying to smooth down Myrtle's wild curls. After a minute, they looked a little less like she had just woken up, which I considered a win. Jordan looked at them again and said, "That'll have to do."

The lawyer no longer looked flustered, but gestured for Myrtle to sit down and said, "Ms. Wilson-"

"Myrtle please," she interrupted.

I saw frustration flash over his face before he relented, "Myrtle, as our key witness, it's important you stay in here until we call you. We want the court to see Mr. Buchanan's genuine reaction to seeing you. Can you do that?"

She grinned. "Easy as pie. You just knock when you need me, honey."

He looked at me. "Are you ready, Ms. Fay?"

I didn't feel ready to face Tom but I wasn't sure I would ever feel ready. I wanted this behind me, though. I was ready to finally be free. I was ready to never have to see Tom again and ready to become Ms. Fay again. Ms. Fay wouldn't shy away from Tom, and I wouldn't either.

"I am," I said, and followed the lawyer out to my future, with Jordan following closely behind.

The lawyer had prepared me well for court. The beginning was slow, and the judge was highly skeptical of me, but slowly I could see we were starting to win him over. Tom had put up a good front at the beginning, but the longer the day dragged on, the more frustrated he became. Tom was now being borderline disrespectful to the judge, and I could tell from how the judge was treating him now that it was helping our case.

"Mind your manners, Mr. Buchanan. There are ladies here." The judge warned him for the third time in the last hour after he said something I didn't hear but knew must have been inappropriate.

"My wife is hardly a lady."

It was hardly the worst thing he had said about me, but most of the courtroom gasped. "Mr. Buchanan, decorum!" the judge yelled out. "Ms. Fay hasn't been insulting you and I expect you to give her the same level of respect she has been giving you."

"She's Mrs. Buchanan," he said with a sneer. My lawyer had, at my urging, requested the court refer to me as Ms. Fay. It was what I had been going by since I had left Tom, and it's what I preferred. My lawyer had considered it for a moment before agreeing it would help our case to make the court see me as my own person and not just Mrs. Buchanan. "Has her alleging I used to abuse and cheat on her not been her disrespecting me?"

"Objection," my lawyer said quickly.

The judge turned to him. "On what grounds?"

"The truth can't be disrespectful." My lawyer turned to Tom and said, "If you don't like the truth, perhaps you should have been a better man."

"Objection!" Tom's lawyer shouted. "They haven't proved a thing. They're just insulting my client."

My lawyer smiled at that and turned back to the judge. "Your honor, I'd like to call a witness."

My lawyer crossed the courtroom and knocked on the door to the conference room we had been waiting in before swinging the door open.

I looked over at Tom to see him looking unbothered and watched as my lawyer stepped out of the way so Tom could see Myrtle behind him.

"Your honor, this is-"

"Myrtle? But how? You're dead!" Tom burst out.

The court gasped as one before the judge demanded quiet.

"The one and only," she said with a wink, walking to the witness stand and taking a seat. "I'm not dead, but I'm about to make you wish I was."

I couldn't believe the judge was still dragging this out. Myrtle had more than proved that Tom was an adulterer and an abuser, but the judge was still hesitating.

After far too long of the lawyers going back and forth, the judge called for silence, "I haven't struggled with a case this much in a long time," he said. My heart dropped. This couldn't be happening. We had more than enough proof that Tom wasn't a good man. What more did he want?

"You have more than proven that there are grounds for divorce here, and if that's what you want, I'll allow it." He paused and Daisy started to smile a little. I tried to give her a reassuring grin, but only managed a grimace. I didn't like his silence. "But when it comes to the matter of the child, I can't in good conscience say she should stay with her mother. It won't be right to make your husband pay for your lifestyle for you if you're divorced, and as a divorced woman, you wouldn't have the financial means to take care of her. I can grant you the divorce, but your child would have to stay with Mr. Buchanan."

Anger rose in me and before I thought better of it, I said, "Wait. She does have the financial means to take for her."

The entire court looked at me. The judge didn't look pleased but asked, "Do you have additional evidence?"

"I do," I said, grabbing my purse and standing up.

He nodded, and I walked over to the judge's bench.

"I have documentation showing that half of the entirety of my inheritance will be transferred to Ms. Fay the moment she is legally divorced."

He looked at me dubiously. "And half of that would be?"

I pulled out the verification of funds the lawyer had asked for and a check. I passed the paper over to him and was incredibly satisfied to see his eyes widen in shock. "If you'll allow me to borrow a pen, I'll make out the check to Ms. Fay right here and now."

Daisy's lawyer stepped up with a pen and I looked at the judge. "Would that be sufficient?"

He cleared his throat and handed back the paper. "Yes, Ms.-" he hesitated.

"Baker."

"Baker," he continued, "with that check to Ms. Fay, I can grant the divorce and full custody of their child to Ms. Fay."

"You can't be serious!" Tom yelled out.

The judge narrowed his eyes at Tom. "I've had just about enough out of you. Court's adjourned. I expect not to see you harassing your ex-wife in my courtroom."

Tom sneered at me and Daisy, who had run over to me. "You'll regret this," he said to her.

I hugged her tightly and kissed the top of her head. I was so proud of her, and I was sure neither of us would regret what was without a doubt the best decision of Daisy's life.

Epilogue

Two Years Later

-Daisy-

I had been up for an hour already writing in my journal, when I looked at the clock and noticed the morning was getting away from me. I quietly slipped over to the bedroom and creaked the door open. Jordan was sprawled out on our bed with her arm under Pammy's head. Pammy was cuddled into her and my heart melted seeing my two girls like that.

I had never doubted that Pammy loved her Auntie Jordan, but I had worried at first that it might be hard for her to adjust to the idea of Jordan being around instead of Tom, but she adjusted quickly. It helped that her old nanny came to visit often. She had quickly become like part of the family. Anyone that loved Pammy as much as she did was alright with me, but she solidified our friendship when she finally apologized for believing Tom. I didn't blame her, but it was nice to hear anyway.

Pammy was ecstatic about it being just us girls. She would often talk about how much happier she was with Auntie Jordan and her momma than she was when we lived with her father. She told me she was happy

I was happier and spent more time with her now. I even heard her confiding in Jordan that, "Momma cries less now."

That broke me. I had to hide in the bathroom for a little while to regain my composure. I was incredibly grateful she was happy now, but hearing that she saw and understood so much more about what when on between me and her father than I thought had broken me. I hoped he was miserable.

I blinked away the thought. I was with my girls now I wouldn't change that for the world. I sighed. They looked so peaceful asleep, and I hated to wake them, but we had a full day ahead of us.

We had a place a little ways outside of the city in New York, but Pammy loved to go into the city. Like her mother, she loved Central Park and the hustle and bustle of the city. Today, we were having a picnic in Central Park and were going to take a horse-drawn carriage ride around the park. Pammy had been really into horses lately and I was sure she was going to love it.

Central Park was every bit as beautiful as always. The juxtaposition of the tall city skyscrapers surrounding the trees and sprawling park was enough to leave me in awe. Central Park was the one place in the city that you could go and be guaranteed to escape the noise and chaos of the city. It was the best of both worlds.

After our picnic, Pammy asked to go to a little bookstore a couple of blocks away. It was a favorite of hers and we loved that she loved reading, so we took her whenever she asked.

Jordan and I let her browse the children's stories and took a look around ourselves while keeping an eye on her. I was lucky she was so incredibly well-behaved and rarely needed to be closely watched. I was looking at a romance story that looked interesting when I heard Jordan say, "What the-" She cut herself off before she said anything inappropriate where Pammy could hear thankfully, but her tone had me whipping around.

"What is it?" I asked.

She held up a book for me to see. I looked at it and froze when I saw the title 'The Great Gatsby'. I hadn't heard that name in a long time. It didn't occur to me until reading the name just how long it had been since I had last thought about him. I was proud of myself for that. He didn't haunt me the way he used to anymore.

"It has to be a common name, right?"

Jordan shook her head slowly. "I haven't heard the name before or since."

"What are the odds it's a coincidence?"

She flipped over the back of the book, and I watched her face pale. "Not good. Look." She handed me the book, and I saw what she meant. It was written by a Nicholas Carraway. Nick.

"What the-" I blurted out.

"Exactly!" she said.

"Have you talked to him?" I asked.

"No, you'd know if I had. You haven't, have you?"

"I haven't heard from him since he sent over Jay's journals a few months after Jay died."

I still didn't really know why he did it. Jordan had thought that maybe he was trying to make me feel guilty. She thought he hoped we would read them and regret having played a part in Jay's death. I didn't feel guilty, though. I didn't kill Jay or have a part in causing his death, but I wasn't sorry he was dead.

I was surprised by the amount he had written though. He journaled a lot. We debated whether to read them, but in the end curiosity got the best of the both of us when a paper slipped out with a poem on it. The poem read:

"Daisy Fay,

The one that got away,

Has settled across the bay.

But she might as well be an ocean away.

Does she look at that same bay,

everyday,

in the same way,

and cry out to her dear beloved Jay?

I hope that wind carries my love to her,

And that during those quiet, lonely days,

She can hear me say,

"My darling Daisy Fay,

The one that got away,

And settled across the bay,

Now that I've found you again,

I know that come what may,

Like my love,

You'll be here to stay."

I had looked at Jordan, who met my eye, and we both had immediately burst into giggles.

"We're terrible-" I said, through giggles.

She laughed harder at that, shaking her head, "No, he's terrible and so is his poetry."

She wasn't wrong.

"Should we put it away?"

"After that? Absolutely not, I have to know if there's more where that came from."

Most of the journals were about me. He went on and on about his love for me, but it was clear he had an unhealthy obsession and, even more clear that he hardly knew anything about me. He was in love with the idea of me, and if I had loved him it would have been a tragedy, since I never would have held up to his idea of me.

"What are the odds we aren't in the story?" I asked her cautiously.

She quickly flipped through the book and said, "Not good. I saw your name more than a few times and mine at least a couple."

"Damn," I said under my breath.

"Exactly."

"So, we're buying it, right?"

"We're buying two and starting them the moment we get home. What could have possessed him to write about us in the first place?"

"He did always seem to idolize Jay. I'm sure it hit him hard when Jay died."

We got Pammy a couple of books and left for home, not wanting to delay it any longer. I needed to know what he had said about us. Thankfully, the book was short, so we would hopefully be able to read through it quickly enough to know how bad the damage was.

Jordan, who read faster than I did, put Pammy to bed, as I settled onto the couch with the book. I was determined to try to stay awake long enough to make it through the book.

I was only a few pages in when Jordan came and settled in next to me. We stayed like that for a few hours. As I tore through the book, I became more and more angry. To hear Nick tell it, Jay was some sort of saint. I couldn't stand the way he painted me as a villain. I was glad Tom at least earned the same treatment, but Jay was apparently faultless.

Jordan's aggravated huffs and quick pages flips told me she agreed with me. When I got to the end, I closed the book and tossed it down. I still couldn't believe what I had just read. To hear Nick tell it, I had stomped all over Jay's heart and was responsible for his death. He had written that I was driving the car that hit Myrtle. It was technically true, but Jay was in the car, too. I understood why Nick would think I was to blame for Myrtle's death since he didn't know she was still alive, but it was beyond frustrating that Jay had been in that car too, but Nick didn't blame him.

Jay Gatsby was the perfect golden boy party king of New York City and I was the floozy who flounced in and out of his life on a whim and lured him to his death.

Jordan threw her book down. "What the hell!"

"I can't believe he did that to us."

"I can't believe I ever thought he was a good man. The nerve on him. He actually says he's one of the few honest people he's met. What a joke." She jumped up and started to pace. "I can't believe he would do that. It would be bad enough if the story was accurate, but that's not at all what happened. To hear him tell it, you were half in love with Tom and with Gatsby and I was playing Nick like a fiddle."

"Well-" I cut in.

She chuckled. "I suppose that part's true, but still, the rest of it is a whole lot of lies."

"Do you think he knows?" I asked.

"Knows what? About Myrtle?"

I shook my head. I highly doubted Myrtle being alive would've escaped making it into his book if he had known. "Do you think he's admitted to himself how he felt about Jay?"

"I highly doubt it."

"I knew he idolized him, but I don't think I knew how deeply his feelings ran until reading this. Nick loved Jay."

She nodded. "I had my suspicions, but I was never really sure." She said thoughtfully before adding, "But his grief doesn't excuse his actions. He came for us. He published an entire book about how terrible of a person you are and that can't be forgiven."

I felt the same way about how he had talked about Jordan. She got a slightly better treatment in his story than I did thankfully, but he still wasn't kind.

"You know," I said slowly, "there might be something we can do."

Her eyes shot to mine. "Like what?"

"Well, he told his story. We could tell ours."

She considered a moment and said, "I'm not much of a writer."

I thought for a moment. Maybe she wasn't, but I was. I had been journaling every day for the last couple of years. I wasn't sure I fancied myself a good writer, but I had certainly been practicing. "What if I write out my story and you can chime in every once in a while with your own thoughts?"

She paused for a moment, saying, "That's not a bad idea." She snapped her fingers and said, "Wait I have an idea!"

She ran out of the room and I heard her riffling around in the sitting room. "They've got to be here somewhere."

I was about to get up and offer to help when she came careening back into the room with Jay's journals in her arms. "You can use these, too!"

That was brilliant. That way it wouldn't just be my word against Nick's, but mine, and Jordan's, and a bit of Jay's. Nick wasn't going to be happy, but he hadn't cared about my happiness when he published that. I missed the friendship we had formed, but it was more apparent than ever that our friendship had died when Jay did.

"I think that just might work." I went to my desk and grabbed a fresh journal and a pen, "and I know just how to start it." And I started to write.

'The first thing you have to understand is that Nick Carraway is the worst sort of liar, for he lies not only to everyone around him but, above all, to himself. When talking of his own virtues, he declared he is one of the few honest people that he has ever known. If I know one thing to be true, it is this; if a person tells you they don't lie, they're lying.

You may think you know everything about me, Daisy Buchanan, the unworthy object of Jay Gatsby's love who stole his heart and abandoned him the moment the relationship was inconvenient. I have quite the reputation, but that's not me. Well, it is me, in a sense. I am Daisy, but that's not my story.

In his story, I'm quite the villain, but this story isn't his, it's mine. My story is a story of forbidden love, a story of a girl struggling to find her place in the world, discover who she is, and understand the desires of her heart.

In order for you to really understand what led to the fateful events of the summer of 1922, we have to go further back. I won't talk of my childhood or upbringing. I suspect no one besides myself would care. I know my audience and I know you've only opened this book to hear about him, so I won't delay. I will jump straight to the action, the day I met Jay.

I was only eighteen when the army stole everything that mattered from me. In retrospect, I suppose the army wasn't to blame for everything that happened. Some of the choices were my own, and some were made by a certain lieutenant, but back then, I chose to blame the army.

It was the fall of 1917 when the lieutenant swept into town and took Louisville by storm. A month later, he was stolen away by the army, after having taken everything I had to give and more...'

THE END

So, what did you think of the Beautiful Fools Duet?

I would love to hear any and all of your thoughts! If you would be so kind as to leave any review it would be greatly appreciated. Any review, good or bad, long or short, is always welcome.

For updates on what's coming next, you can find me:

Visit my website: Thelibraryofsarahzane.com

Tiktok: @libraryofsarahzane

Instagram: @libraryofsarahzane

Facebook: Author Sarah Zane

About the Author

Sarah Zane is an author of happy endings for traumatized queers.

As a bisexual, it should be shocking to no one that she has more than one genre she loves and writes. She writes across genres but guarantees that a Sarah Zane book will always be queer and always have a happy ending eventually. She has a particular fondness for writing sapphic pairings since they tend to be underrepresented in books.

She lives in New England with her 2 black cats named Gatsby and Mr. Darcy. When she isn't writing, she can be usually be found taking forest walks, visiting castles, planning exotic trips she can't afford, or cuddled up with one of her cats crying over fictional characters or yelling at them about how badly they need therapy.

For more from Sarah Zane, check out...

Off Script: A Book Ball Fantasy Adventure
A fantasy adventure story about Sadie, a fantasy author whose first convention goes haywire when her characters literally jump off the page.

Cosplay and Confrontation
A sapphic rivals-to-lovers cosplayers romcom that takes place at the same fantasy convention in Off Script.

Under Lock and Key
A sapphic cozy fantasy retelling of Bluebeard about a blue-haired temptress innkeeper and the mysterious woman who wanders into her inn and falls for her charms.

Becoming A Bi-con
A spicy sapphic popstar romcom with fake dating about two ex best friends who have to set aside their past problems in order to work together for both of their careers.

Coming Soon...

The Siren's Song

A sapphic romantasy about a runaway nun turned pirate and her long lost love turned siren.